# Readers love
# PIPER DOONE

## *Playing Hard to Forget*

"Bravo, Ms. Doone. I look forward to more from you, and recommend this book."

—Love Bytes

"Even though this is a full-length novel, this is really easy to read and the plot moves along at a rapid and steady pace."

—MM Good Book Reviews

"This is a story of love conquering all…"

—Prism Book Alliance

## *Something to Die For*

"This was a very interesting story… the storyline kept me turning the pages till it was over, and it was something new and fresh to read."

—It's About The Book

"…this is a completely different story to anything I've ever read before, and I'm happily surprised with how much feeling and story Piper Doone managed to fit into such a short story."

—The Novel Approach

By PIPER DOONE

Forced Impressions
Playing Hard to Forget
Something to Die For

Published by DREAMSPINNER PRESS
www.dreamspinnerpress.com

# FORCED
# IMPRESSIONS

## PIPER DOONE

Published by
DREAMSPINNER PRESS

5032 Capital Circle SW, Suite 2, PMB# 279, Tallahassee, FL 32305-7886 USA
www.dreamspinnerpress.com

Forced Impressions
© 2016 Piper Doone.

Cover Art
© 2016 Aaron Anderson.
aaronbydesign55@gmail.com
Cover content is for illustrative purposes only and any person depicted on the cover is a model.

ISBN: 978-1-63476-763-7
Digital ISBN: 978-1-63476-764-4
Library of Congress Control Number: 2015914747
Published January 2016
v. 1.0

Printed in the United States of America
⊗

This paper meets the requirements of
ANSI/NISO Z39.48-1992 (Permanence of Paper).

As always… JPL. You got out of my dreams and got into my car, and I thank God every day that you did.

And to Beenee and all the border runs we are too lazy to make. Someday, lady. Someday.

To Watabiyatchi Spencer, who made me promise to make her a character and not kill her off.

To Sam, who is about that 305 life enough to help me remember the swear words in Miami Spanish.

To Mary D-T, who inspired me once with Tweety Treat.

To R. Cooper, who makes me a better person just by existing in this universe. She is the reason there are snowflakes.

To my 10th grade Honors English teacher, who told me I would never be a writer because I was too weird.

To my college sophomore Survey of Literary Humor professor, who told me I *would* be a writer *because* I was too weird.

To my senior year of college Creative Writing professor, who made us interpret Violent Femmes lyrics and write poetry about IKEA. I hated your class, and I'm glad I forgot everything you said the moment I graduated.

And to me, because I've never had a book dedicated to me and it probably won't happen otherwise. I love you, me. You're the reason I get up in the mornings. That and the alarm clock.

# Acknowledgments

MY DARLING STA,

When you were two and I was six, you tried to eat Granny's Bible and also my favorite book, *The Penguin Who Hated the Cold*.

I hope that you won't eat this book. Or will at least learn to season the pages better.

# Chapter 1

BEYOND THE neon lights and traffic jams full of tourists in rented minivans on their way to ride rides and spend money until there was nothing left, lay a seedy, trashy, and dark side of Orlando. Too many minimum-wage jobs created a deep need for its residents to supplement in less than legal ways, turning to drugs, prostitution, and theft to make up for what twelve hours of smiling and pushing buttons didn't.

Officer Jonah Landers—no, *Detective* Jonah Landers now, after the promotion, thank you—was about to experience this underworld firsthand. This wasn't like busting johns as a beat cop. Jonah was going undercover for the first time with his new squad, something he had been waiting for since the possibility of promotion came up. This was his chance to prove himself. He wasn't going to be hassling johns. He was going to *be* a john.

Jonah was twenty-eight and, with his light blond hair, pale blue eyes, and body that was... okay, not perfect, but at least toned from spending long *minutes* in the gym, hardly looked like the kind of man who would need to pay for the pleasure of someone's company, in his humble opinion. But he wasn't about to turn down the opportunity just to placate his ego. The job was easy enough: go to the club, The Flat Tire, a dance club downtown, and look like he needed a friend. They'd dressed him in a sleazy but expensive suit and slicked his hair back at the station. If he looked money enough, the girls should come running. All they needed was proof there was a prostitution ring running in the back of the club. Easy in, easy out. So they kept telling him.

"Bust these up all the time, Landers. Ain't nothing big. Good one to cut your teeth on, though, and I'll be here to talk you through it." A gruff voice from the front seat of the hopelessly conspicuous unmarked police sedan Jonah sat in interrupted his thoughts. The department had partnered Jonah with Detective Peter Holland, a rough and tumble guy of about forty, but no one seemed to know for sure. All anyone seemed to know was that he transferred in about five years before from California, and he had Army Ranger training, but that could be an educated guess from the regulation haircut, deep tan, and even deeper scars that littered his skin just as much as it could have been fact. Not a good way to start a partnership, but Jonah had been ready to be a detective since graduating from the police academy, and he was willing to make anything work. Even secrets between partners. Especially since Jonah had a few secrets of his own.

"Just remember: get in there. Act lonely. Order expensive drinks. Get their attention and get back there. Don't drop cover for nothing, okay? Not even when they're cuffing you." Peter's eyes sparkled with amusement at that last part. Playing the perp meant playing the perp all the way. Uniforms would cuff him and put him in a cell with the real criminals to keep up the appearance. Sometimes that extra bit of information to seal a case came in those hours after a bust.

"I got it." Jonah wasn't too enthused about the arrest part of the op, but criminals not making him for a cop gave him some value on future cases. He slumped in his seat and prayed that no one would feel the need to tase him.

"Don't take off your suit jacket or we lose the feed." His jacket had been fitted with the tiniest of cameras in the lapel. Doing everything by the book and having proof of it would greatly increase their chances of a conviction.

"Yeah, I got it." They'd been over it at least a dozen times just since they got in the car.

"Don't let these girls get to you, either. The club lights may fool you into thinking they look pretty, but don't let them touch you. No telling what they got. You gonna be able to keep your hands to yourself?" Peter eyed Jonah with a smirk on his face.

Of course, the biggest secret between them was that Jonah was 100 percent not into girls. Not even when the club lighting was right. The city government didn't frown upon its employees being gay; Orlando was well-known for being a very gay friendly city. But Jonah also didn't see how his love life was anyone's business. And there was a part of him that believed assignments like this would become scarce if just one person thought it might be too difficult for Jonah to play his part because there were girls involved. Gay friendly or not, some beliefs died hard. He watched enough TV in his downtime to know that people still questioned the out gay man playing a straight man on a show.

"*Peter*. I got it. I'll be fine. I swear. Will you please stop acting like I'm going to screw this up?" Still a newbie to Peter. Jonah wondered how much longer that would last. He pushed a hand through his blond hair in a futile attempt to tame it and adjusted his tie.

Peter threw up his hands in mock surrender. His biceps were bigger around than Peter's head because he was always first in, last out at the gym where Jonah spent most of his time changing the channel on the elliptical machine's tiny TV to look for something more motivational than reruns of *Seinfeld*. "Look, this is your first time out. And, yeah, we'll be around and ready to come in as backup, and this looks to be a routine bust, but it can be nerve-racking your first time out. Hell, it's nerve-racking every time out because even a routine bust can go so, so wrong." There was more to that, and Jonah knew he would never get it from Peter, so he chose to ignore it. The rumor was that Peter moved across country after almost losing his entire squad in a drug bust gone wrong, and Jonah couldn't imagine how bad that must have been to spook a giant beast of a man like Peter that badly.

"I'll be careful." Jonah made one last plea with his hair, which was threatening to break the will of the super-strength styling gel they'd had to use to beat his curls into submission, and straightened his suit jacket. They were at the drop-off point just around the corner from the club. After a quick confirmation to the tech team monitoring his tiny camera and mic that everything was working, he was out the door.

The music was loud. He could hear it tumble out the front door of the club from a few blocks away and in downtown Orlando with all the raucous nightlife that was saying something. It was shit music, trashy music, thumping beats that no one could actually like, but still pretended they did. The club was an old converted auto care center that had gone under in the recession. The club owners had kept the industrial glass-and-brick aesthetic when they had renovated the space, and it did a decent business not relying on shtick like the businesses around the theme parks tried with much failure. To the people who frequented the club's legal front, the music was good, the dancing good, the drinks better, and the chances of getting laid were amazing. Too bad it was probably going to go under after the bust. Sure, some other club would spring up in its place, but the legal part of the club would leave a sizeable hole in the Orlando nightlife landscape.

The crowd seemed a good mix of seasoned locals and bleary-eyed tourists who had somehow found their way beyond the siren call of the theme parks. Jonah was always surprised to see that tourists knew there was an entire bustling city apart from the roller coasters, animals, and singing robotic children.

Top-shelf whiskey in hand, Jonah settled at the bar and scanned the crowd as he took a sip and hoped it would push down the knot in his stomach. For all the reassuring he did to Peter, he was a nervous wreck. He didn't have to fake loneliness for the hookers. Even in a room with 500 other people and an entire team backing him up both inside the club and out, Jonah felt terribly alone right then. But this was his first big test and even though every member of his squad had dozens of these under their belt and could do a bust like this in their sleep, the glass still shook slightly in Jonah's hand when a busty brunette with dark skin sauntered up to him, all miniskirt and cheap heels.

"Hey." She smiled shyly and played with her long dark hair, and he suddenly felt the need to cover her up with his jacket and give her a lecture about places like these and guys like he was pretending to be. "You look lost. Where are you from, handsome?"

Jonah swallowed. This was it. "Kenosha. Uh… Wisconsin." He pushed up his sleeves nervously. It was only *mostly* for show. He was nervous as hell.

She sat down next to him and motioned for the bartender to bring her a drink. "And what brings you to the City Beautiful? Work? Pleasure? Bit of both?" She was touching his arm lightly, rubbing circles with her fingers. Her nails were pink. A princess pink, like his little sister used to wear when she was going through that ultra girly phase around ten. She looked almost as out of place as Jonah felt.

Just like they'd rehearsed over and over. "Work. Well, for me anyway. My wife and kids are at the parks enjoying the rides. Told her my meetings ran over so I could—"

"Enjoy a few rides of your own?" She sipped on the wine the bartender had set in front of her and crossed her legs—what seemed to be seductively—toward him. There was a filmy layer of light blue fabric that draped on the skirt when she moved, and if it weren't for the tight layer underneath, he could add public indecency to the list of crimes she was about to be charged with. The matching colored crop top wasn't leaving anything to the imagination either. Jonah wondered what her major was.

He made a point to look down toward her legs for show. "Something like that, yeah. Wasn't crazy about them coming, but she insisted. I like a little more freedom when I travel, but look where we are, right? Of course they wanted to come."

She smiled. "So what do you like? Slow rides? Or thrill rides?" Only in Orlando could this terrible double entendre happen. He wanted so badly to roll his eyes at how terrible her pick-up lines were. Did this actually work on straight guys?

Jonah raised an eyebrow and leaned in toward her. Her perfume was just as innocent as her pink nails. Flowery and sugary. "I like a little of both." Seemed like the right thing to say.

"I know a place in back where I can make that happen for you." She meant it to be sexy with her huge brown eyes opened wide, Jonah was sure of that, and were she his type, it might be. But Jonah made a big show of squirming uncomfortably on the barstool like he was about to come in his trousers anyway.

He smiled his sleaziest smile at her. "Do you?" He felt bad that in a few minutes she would be in cuffs. She looked like the kind of girl who was just trying to pay off student loans.

She grabbed his hand and tugged at him until he stood. "Come on. Let's go. You can go up and down these hills all you want." She ran her free hand over her ample chest and suddenly he didn't feel so bad for her after a line like that.

"What's your name, sweetheart?" Jonah hoped it would be something that was real about her. If only so backup knew what to call her when they were arresting her.

She turned back and winked at him. "Jasmine." This fucking city. What a riot.

"You're doing great, Detective. Get back there and get us some video of the place. Give us something we can use in court." Peter's tinny voice came through his earpiece.

Jasmine—the outfit finally made sense. She probably bought it in the adult Halloween unlicensed costume section under "Sexy Sultan's Palace Princess" or something—took him to a cordoned off area with two burly guards at the entrance. Where the rest of the club was modern and almost sterile with its white painted brick walls and industrial lighting, the back area looked exactly like what it was: an expensive sex den. Private areas were marked off with silky hanging fabrics, and there was a smoky haze in the air. The sounds of sex echoed through the room. Jonah made a pointed effort to walk as slowly as he could to the empty area Jasmine was pulling him toward. He wanted to gather as much information on video as he could. There was little to no expectation of privacy once people were back there, and Jonah saw more flesh in the thirty seconds he had been there than he had in the last decade.

Jasmine guided him to a soft oversized red sofa and pushed him down into it. She started unbuttoning her shirt, and Jonah knew it wouldn't go much further without price negotiations, which was exactly what he needed her to get to end this whole thing.

"For $100 I give you a nice, slow dance. For $500 I give you the ride of your life. What do you say?" She smiled again and danced a little like it was a preview of what was to come. Thank God. Finally.

He faked an eager and dirty smile. He already needed a shower to cleanse himself of this. "All the way, sweetheart. I don't have a limit." It was all going to be over soon, and it was going so well.

He heard Peter relay orders to the backup team and knew they were close enough that he wouldn't have to see much more of her show before they stormed in.

Jonah shifted his weight to give the illusion that he was going to reach for his wallet. His hand tried to instinctively drift to his jacket's inner pocket where his badge lay hidden inside before he realized what he was doing and quickly diverted it. The orders were coming fast through his earpiece. Backup was making its way through the crowd. Once they took care of the bodyguards, she would be in cuffs and he could drop this terrible act.

"I like your style, mister." She winked, and it just made him feel bad all over again for her.

Heavy footsteps interrupted his thoughts, and Jonah looked up to see a man of about forty standing five feet behind Jasmine, staring at Jonah like he wanted to kill him. Dark haired, Hispanic… and a little too intense for Jonah's liking.

That was… unexpected. *Stay cool. Play it off. Don't break cover.* "Do ya mind here, buddy? Little busy." Admitting he was starting to sweat was admitting defeat.

Jasmine's head whipped around, and she turned back to Jonah and giggled. "He's a... new policy. That's Christian. Back here he's God. You gotta show him you can afford me before I do you. The owner was tired of getting stiffed and screwed. That's your job." She giggled suggestively, and Jonah wanted groan and walk out. How did straight guys do this? "So Christian has been here a week and, trust me, farm boy, *everyone* is happier."

There had been no mention of this in the briefing. Or the thirty re-briefings that came after that just to make sure Jonah knew everything, including how the girls took the payments. This was the kind of turn Peter warned him about. How could they have missed this? *New policy.*

This was also a problem, as Jonah had about a buck thirty-nine in his wallet. Backup needed to hurry up.

*Stay cool. Stay cool.* "Yeah, sure. No problem. What do you prefer, man? Cash or plastic?"

Christian groaned like Jonah was the biggest idiot on the planet. "I really hope you're fucking around with me right now, or your face is going to meet the bottom of my boot real quick. Cash only. Pay up. $500. I'm not in the habit of letting people pay after they pump. And I'll tell you this much: if you've made it all the way in here and you don't have the cash, you'll be leaving here without some teeth." Definitely Cuban. His accent was unmistakable. Not uncommon in Florida, but less so in Orlando than in Tampa or Miami. His dark features and black leather jacket made it difficult to make out more details in case something went wrong and Jonah had to describe him later. He was about five foot ten, maybe a little less, with about two weeks' worth of a beard, but "short, dark, and Cuban" wasn't going to make for a good BOLO if he escaped.

There was too much commotion going on in his ear to try to signal that he was in trouble. *Don't break cover for nothin'.* Peter's words ran through his head. Where the hell *was* everyone?

Jonah threw up his hands in surrender. "Okay, man. I'm just here to have a good time, all right? Five hundred cash. It's in my wallet." He slowly reached for his gun and badge out of inexperience and fear and stupidity, but a loud noise threw everything into disarray.

"Police! Nobody move!" The team had finally stormed their way in. There were screams and shouts among the chaos of cops yelling for everyone to be still. Jasmine screamed, and Jonah jumped up to grab

Christian, but a uniform had made his way into view with a sleazy, balding guy in his late fifties in his grip. Must be the pimp.

Christian turned to the cop and the man and stormed them both, screaming, "You sold me out? You fucking sold me out? I'll fucking kill you, asshole! I'll fucking kill you!" Christian rushed toward the man despite the cop holding him. Even with several inches on both the men, there was no way the officer could handle the two of them, especially if Christian was going to try to kill the older guy like he certainly looked like he was.

Jonah took the distraction and rushed toward Christian to take him down, pushing Jasmine out of harm's way as he went, but Christian must not have been as distracted as he seemed. He turned toward Jonah just as he reached into his pocket for his badge again, trying to identify himself against orders, and something was coming at him hard and fast, right toward his face.

Jonah didn't have time to react, even though everything seemed to be going in slow motion. Christian's left fist hurtled toward him and within a split second it dominated his field of vision until a sharp whack to his face sent him crashing to the floor.

# Chapter 2

THE NEXT ten minutes were a blur. Everything seemed to be happening at once. Jonah struggled to stand, but the pain was incredible, and it made him dizzy. There was more yelling, and he looked up to see Christian finally in cuffs before realizing that blood was pouring down his face. The metallic tang made Jonah cringe as he absentmindedly licked his lips and looked around for something to soak it up.

A fuzzy, blurry uniformed cop helped Jonah up and got him outside into the fresh air. She sat him on the curb and called for an ambulance despite Jonah's halfhearted protests that he was fine.

One by one people started filing out of the club in handcuffs, including a crying Jasmine and Christian, who laser focused on Jonah as he walked out with a deadly scowl. The guy was a full three inches shorter than Jonah's six foot one inch frame and about thirty pounds lighter than Jonah, but he was a ball of rage that was, admittedly, terrifying. Minutes later the ambulance showed, and there was a flurry of movement as two paramedics rushed over to Jonah.

The flashing lights of the squad cars made his head hurt, and the paramedic made it worse by shining his penlight right into Jonah's eyes.

He tried to bat the paramedic away and blinked a few times, trying to bring everything into focus. "What happened?"

"You got sucker punched. Guy has some power too. I heard the hit." Peter had joined them and looked like he was wavering between concern, regret, and just the tiniest hint of amusement.

What a great first undercover operation. Jonah gingerly touched the knot that had formed on his face. At least the bleeding had stopped. Mostly.

The paramedic cracked a cold compress and handed it to him. "Yeah. You're gonna be okay, though. You didn't get knocked out, right? Looks like he didn't get you that badly. Gonna look like hell for a while. Keep this on it, and it may take care of the worst of it."

Jonah had so been hoping for a paramedic a little more professional and compassionate to his plight. He obviously wasn't going to be all right. He was going to look like he fought and lost to a combine harvester for the next month, and he was sure, despite the paramedic's insistence otherwise, that his nose was broken and would require plastic surgery. His brother had broken his nose in a freakish lacrosse accident when he was twelve, and it never quite looked the same. Jonah looked like his own crime scene with a banged-up face and a bloody suit. He hoped the department had a good dry cleaning service, because the stains weren't coming out with Tide no matter how long it soaked.

Jonah pressed the pack to his face and winced when it touched his sensitive skin. "Yeah, speaking of, who in the hell was that?"

Peter shrugged. "Don't know. He's not talking yet. He might change his mind at the station, if we're lucky." Peter turned to the paramedic. "He's okay, right? That's what you said?"

The paramedic shoved some more gauze up Jonah's nose, an entirely unpleasant experience that made him want to ensure both the paramedic and Peter knew exactly what he was going through firsthand. "I wouldn't make him run a marathon or nothing, but he doesn't have a concussion. He should probably take it easy for the next few days. That face is going to be sore for a while. And the bruising is going to be epic."

Peter sucked his teeth and looked back toward Jonah. "Yeah, while we're on the subject of going to the station… I hate to do this, newbie, but—" He said it in a way that indicated he didn't hate it at all.

Jonah tried to roll his eyes in annoyance, but *fuck* that hurt. "Are you serious? Still? How long do I have to play this out?" Face smashed and he still had to play the perp, and the gauze up his nostril made him sound like he had a nasty sinus infection when he talked.

"Till it looks good, newbie. You knew the deal. Don't think I didn't hear that you tried to break cover to get that guy. I'm almost glad he knocked you down. He actually saved you from a major screwup. You think you can handle undercover work if you break character at the first sign of trouble? You're not ready, Landers."

Jonah scoffed. "I made a judgment call."

Peter sighed. "Yeah, well, it was a shit one. Get up." Peter pulled Jonah to standing and slapped the cuffs on him.

Peter at least had the humanity to uncuff him in the squad car so Jonah could reapply the ice pack, but he also didn't say a word to him the entire ride.

Jonah was stuck in the tiny cell for hours, watching his colleagues walk freely back and forth to get to things like a vending machine and a private bathroom. That part he could probably have handled just fine. That Christian was in the cell with him was the part that made it unbearable. It was humiliating enough to have been sucker punched in the first place, but to share a cell with the guy who did it, and who kept looking over at Jonah like he had the plague, was the worst. Jonah tried not to look at him. Mostly he didn't want Christian to see just how much pain he was in and how much damage one punch had inflicted. Maybe a little because the guy was just a bit scary. Neither explanation left him with much dignity.

No one was saying anything, either. It was a complete waste of time for Jonah to be stuck there. It was only after the sleazy older guy Christian had gone after in the first place came to join them in the cell that Peter grabbed Christian for his turn in the interrogation room.

"Hey. Hey! What about me? My wife's gonna wonder where I am, you know." There was no reason for Jonah to be there, and he was more than a little annoyed.

Peter smirked as he dragged a belligerent Christian by the cuffs. "Relax, Prince Charming. You'll get your chance to spill too."

The ice pack was only slightly below room temperature at that point, but Jonah wanted to believe it still had some magic left in it. Some Advil wouldn't have hurt either.

It was about twenty minutes later that Peter came back to the holding cell. His demeanor was different. Cocky Peter had given way to serious Peter and that was probably not a good sign.

"You." He pointed at Jonah. "Your turn."

Peter unlocked the cell, and Jonah quickly followed Peter down the hall into the purposely uncomfortable and dank interrogation room. They weren't alone in there, either. His eyes fell immediately on some members of his squad and a scowling Captain Jeffrey Malone. He never expected to be alone when there would be debriefing to do, but what he really didn't expect was to see Christian standing in a shadow in the corner of the room, uncuffed and arms crossed.

With a badge clipped to his belt.

All the air in Jonah's lungs escaped much like Jonah wanted to escape from the room. "Holy shit. You're a cop." It wasn't a question and he didn't have the energy to be outraged.

Christian rolled his eyes. In the light Jonah could finally see they were green. Not that getting a description mattered anymore. "I could say the same about you, kid." The accent wasn't fake. That was a start to something real about him.

Jonah turned to the rest of the room in confusion. "Can someone please tell me what the hell is going on?" Was this some sort of elaborate hazing ritual? First undercover operation and he gets punched out by a mystery cop? Nothing was adding up. Maybe he wasn't ready for this whole thing, because there was an angry voice deep down inside him that told him he should be able to piece this together faster.

Malone, with a sigh that made him seem much older than sixty-odd years, spread his arms wide in mock graciousness. "Detective Jonah Landers… meet *Detective* Rafael Santos of the Miami-Dade Police Department. He was on loan to the state to investigate, well—"

"To investigate something a hell of a lot bigger than this two-bit prostitution ring, I can tell you that much." Christian—no, *Rafael*—was pacing back and forth, clearly agitated. "Not that it matters now anyway because I just lost months of undercover work in there tonight. Now I gotta lose even more wasting my time here so I won't break cover. Do you Mickey Mouse cops even know how badly you screwed my case?"

Captain Malone, three years from retiring with full pension and getting grayer by the day, never took kindly to an insult to his department or his city. "You can put that blame right back on yourself, Detective. Not one man here knew you were undercover or even knew there was another agency working this. We are Orlando cops investigating Orlando crime, and the moment you stepped into *my* jurisdiction was the moment you should have made your presence known to me."

This set Rafael off. "I don't answer to you. I answer to the state of Florida. You got a problem with how I did things? You take it up with them. I had a job to do, and I've been deep for over six months, and now there's no telling when I'm going to get to come up. This isn't about college girls trying to make a buck to pay for college classes. It runs so much deeper than that. The state's looking at the bigger picture here—drugs, sex slavery, human trafficking. You have no idea what's going on in your little town."

Malone pursed his lips. "Oh, you better believe I'm taking it up to Tallahassee. I don't care what's going on here. You don't make a move here without informing me of it. I may not be in charge of you, but I am damn sure in charge of this city. My men could have killed you tonight."

Rafael raised his eyebrow and looked straight at Jonah, still nursing his bruised face. "Yeah. Okay."

Was he... was Rafael *chuckling*?

"No offense, *Captain* Malone, but I hope you got better than this kid over here."

Jonah knew his face was red along with what must be the purple-black of bruises. He looked away from Rafael, not wanting to get into a pissing contest at that moment.

"Ah, look on the bright side. You took that punch like a pro. If I had made you for a cop I might have thought twice about it, but I didn't think there was a chance in hell you were carrying a shield." Rafael wasn't complimenting his acting skills as much as he was insulting his cop skills, and they both knew it. Jonah never truly *hated* anyone in his life, but this guy was itching to be the first.

Jonah finally managed to just about blink both his sore eyes properly and refused to acknowledge Rafael. The night was not supposed to be ending up like this. He should be three or four beers deep by now, celebrating his first successful undercover operation with his squad. He didn't even know if his face would allow him to drink a beer or anything else until the swelling went down. Or that he could even smell the yeasty, hoppy goodness of a beer again. The thought sent Jonah reeling. What if this guy had damaged his sense of smell? What if he couldn't make it as a cop and his only option was to train to be a high-end food taster or sommelier or scratch-and-sniff-sticker maker and he couldn't do it because he had no sense of smell left? Jonah didn't drink wine or think they even made scratch-and-sniff stickers anymore, but that wasn't the point. He *needed* his sense of smell and what if one punch had killed it forever? The panic rose and ebbed in about three seconds as he realized he was being ridiculous. The payout from the state from a "loss of smell" lawsuit would probably cover more than what he would make in a lifetime as a sommelier. Okay, *now* he was really being ridiculous.

Rafael groaned. "Ah, kid. Look. I'm sorry, all right? I thought you were a perp trying to make a getaway."

Jonah finally felt compelled to speak. At least this part he could defend. "I thought you were going to do something stupid. I thought—"

"Yeah. You haven't been at this long, have you?"

*Great. Here comes another round of Kick the Newbie.* "First one." *Probably last one.*

Rafael's face softened a bit—the first sign there might be a human underneath the bravado. "Don't take it so hard, newbie. You may have helped me save my cover by taking that punch."

*Okay, maybe not.*

Jonah was a good person. He tried to live a good life. He'd never murdered anyone or spat in a rude customer's food at his first job making pizza. He saved every turtle lost in the street from getting run over. He didn't illegally download music... much. But he obviously had done something truly evil at some point to deserve this.

"Yeah, because that will make the pain—and this black eye—go away faster, won't it?" The irony that *now* he looked like the kind of man who would need to pay for sex, at least for the next month, was not lost on Jonah.

"Look. The man I was going after has a lot of information he has refused to give up. You've got him in custody now, and he thinks *I* think he sold me out. It's not going to matter that he didn't as long as he thinks I'm going to come after him for it. You offer him protection from me and he'll sing, and maybe I can salvage some of this. It's the least you can do." Like anyone in Orlando was willing to do this guy a favor. He hadn't even said please.

Jonah turned to Malone and sighed. "Look, Captain, can I just go back in the cell now?" Sitting in the cell would be a lot more dignifying than letting Rafael insult him some more.

Malone sighed. "No, Detective Landers. You're going to fill out your paperwork on this and go home. Detective Santos is insisting he go back in the cell to save his undercover status, and I'll be honest here, I don't want him having any access to my unarmed men."

"Oh, come on! It was an honest mistake!" Rafael threw himself into the nearest chair and slumped down in it. Did they not teach humility or remorse in Miami?

Malone ignored Rafael. "Oh, and Detective Landers, be sure to mention how much of a surprise Detective Santos's presence was, all right? Underline it in Sharpie. Highlight it. I want everyone who reads this to know just how this went down."

Rafael threw up his hands. "Oh *God*. Do I need to remind you that you have twenty-three suspects in custody right now? All you wanted were the hookers and johns and *you got 'em*. You didn't know anything about how deep this ran. That was my job. You charge your little guys in this and let the big fish go so I can do my damned job. Getting them back out there is the only way I can track this to the top. Now, put me back in the cell and let me finish what I started!"

Malone waved his hand dismissively and shook his head. "Holland, you heard what the detective said. Cuff 'em."

Peter was up and across the room in a split second. It was probably all the Crossfit that had turned his calves into makeshift rocket launchers or whatever fitness miracle they were claiming these days. "Gladly, Captain." He made a bigger show than necessary of cuffing Rafael and shoving him roughly to the door. "Let's go, *Detective*."

Rafael looked back at Jonah with a smirk on his face. "See you around, kid. Sorry about the face. I hope I don't get the opportunity to mess it up again. If you get me."

No one spoke again until the door clicked closed. Malone looked to the ceiling and blew out a breath. Even though Jonah was still new, he had already learned that meant a tirade of legendary proportions was about to erupt from his captain and all anyone could do was wait for it to happen, hold on tightly, and be prepared.

An hour and curses upon every police precinct in the state, with a special attack on Tallahassee and a lengthy aside about breaking cover and when it was appropriate (never) later, Jonah finally felt comfortable enough to sneak out and finish his paperwork at his desk, carefully avoiding the holding cell area.

Overall, the night was a profound success. If he counted still being alive and still having a job a success, that is. Jonah crawled into bed three hours later and tried to forget the whole thing ever happened.

# Chapter 3

*Two Years Later*

THE HEAT of a Florida winter was a special kind of heat. It was mocking and cruel, a smug boast of its victory over the cold that tried to invade it like the millions of snowbird seniors did every year. February was always the worst, with one sweet day of temperatures in the low 60s before shooting back up into the 80s the next day. Nature was a tease that way, even if Jonah did live for that day every year.

But this year was different. Everything was different.

His suitcase lay on his unmade bed, a bittersweet reminder of what was to come and what he was leaving behind. It had been just a month since Jonah knocked on Captain Malone's office door to give him the news.

*"I've put in for a transfer, Captain. Out of this city this time. Maybe out of Orange County." Jonah set the paperwork down on Captain Malone's desk.*

*Malone didn't look at them. "Are you sure this is what you want?"*

*One year away from pension and the time to bullshit around things was long past by that point. Malone wasn't dumb, either. No matter how hard Jonah tried to hide it, they all knew something was different and wrong.*

*Jonah sighed. "No, but a change in scenery would do me good. Besides, you're gone in a year, Peter got promoted... it's time." It was a lie and they both knew it. It had taken him a long time to accept it, but Orlando was not meant for Jonah, and Jonah was not meant for Orlando. Like an ill-fated relationship, they did not mesh the way he'd hoped. Probably the way Malone had hoped too. The city that had welcomed Jonah once with open arms when he was fresh out of the academy had turned its back on him and his career since his promotion to detective. The precinct turned Jonah down for every advancement opportunity that came across his desk after that, almost like headquarters had regretted even the first promotion. He'd attempted a lateral transfer, but the powers that be flatly denied that request too. He just wasn't good enough.*

*Jonah was stagnating, and it was just as much his fault, fulfilling his own prophecy the more jaded he got about staying in Orlando, as it was his surroundings. The same types of cases over and over again like a giant game of whack-a-mole. Jonah was bored, unable to professionally grow, and it was killing his career. Staying in Orlando would never help him become the cop he wanted to be... the cop he needed to be.*

*But Malone was too generous and loyal to the squad and the men and women on it to force Jonah out, especially since there had been a Peter-shaped hole in the squad that took a long time to fill. It was time Jonah forced his own way out, or he'd be stuck as a lowly detective for the rest of his career. He loved Orlando. It was his home. But he needed to step out of his comfort zone.*

*Malone finally looked up. "You've become a good detective, Landers. You could be a great detective in the right place." Malone smiled wistfully and invited Jonah to sit. It reminded Jonah of the times Malone had to break the news to him that headquarters had denied his request for something better. Again. "You're a bit rough, still. Maybe a little personally and emotionally involved sometimes. But a damn fine detective. Any precinct would be lucky to have you. You need a rec or anything?"*

*"It would help. If you're offering, that is." A compliment was not what Jonah had expected, but it was welcome. It was no secret that Peter's replacement was a bit resentful at being paired with Jonah and his relative lack of experience, and they weren't working out. Jonah suspected it was a symptom of the bigger disease only moving on could cure.*

*"Yeah, I can do that. Where are you looking?"*

*Jonah shrugged. "There are few openings north and a few more down south. Not really looking for a small town, though. I'd like Fort Lauderdale or Miami, maybe. Tampa if those fall through. I just don't want to take a step backward, you know?"*

*Malone nodded. "I know, Detective. It's a different world down there, though. Different kind of crime and definitely different kind of victim. Lot more money down there, and the money is local rather than from tourists."*

*"That's what I want. Murder, extortion, massive drug busts. Just something other than tourist crimes. You think I can hack it?" He needed the anonymity of a large city. He didn't want to end up in Ocala or*

*Sarasota or Lakeland where everybody knew everybody else and their private business.*

*"Landers, when you first came to me you were this wide-eyed puppy who just wanted to get out there, solve the crime, and get the bad guy. It's been two and a half years now, and you're still a wide-eyed puppy who wants to solve the crime and get the bad guy... just better at getting the bad guy now. Your enthusiasm for the job is both a weakness and a great strength, and you need to learn how to balance it better. It will make up for what you lack in experience for now until you get in deep and everything becomes second nature, but right now it's holding you back, and you know it. You just keep that sense of right and wrong and you'll be fine. South Florida would toughen you up pretty quickly. A lot more so than staying here would. I tell you what. I've played golf with a guy on the county commission for Miami-Dade a few times in some youth charity tournaments. Let me give him a call and see what I can do, all right?"*

*Jonah was floored by the generous offer and thanked him profusely before Malone issued Jonah a mock annoyed "Now get outta here. I've got work to do." Jonah was going to miss the old man.*

It wasn't a total lie. Jonah was thirty and ready for something more than investigating tourism related crimes in Orlando. It was fun at first, busting dads from Ohio who ventured a little far outside of the tourist corridor and ended up in the arms of a prostitute off Orange Blossom Trail, or recovering thousands of dollars of stuff from disgruntled maids at three-star hotels, but that wasn't what Jonah wanted out of his career. He wanted to investigate *real* crimes. Jonah Landers was meant for something better.

Okay, that wasn't entirely it. There was a guy. There was always a guy, wasn't there? Except this guy worked in the parks and recreation department for Orange County and was also cheating on Jonah with a whale trainer at one of the theme parks. Jonah had tried to play it off like it was no big deal, but he really liked Chris. They had dated for over a year and a half, and Jonah had mistakenly thought Chris might have been the one. To say he was heartbroken didn't begin to cover it, but in a moment of clarity Jonah had realized that not only was he meant for a better career, he was meant for a better man. And cheap, flashy, transient Orlando was not the kind of place to find either.

Getting out of Orlando and making a new start in a new city was the best thing, Jonah decided. He didn't care that people—well, Chris—might get the idea he was running away. He saw it as running toward something: a new job in a new place with better opportunities and no jerk ex-boyfriends to bump into at city hall and employee picnics. It was a win-win.

It was also only sort of a lie when Jonah said he wasn't looking at small towns. He really didn't want to go to the middle of the state and investigate who took a herd of cows or where there was a meth lab hiding, but despite Malone's surprise compliment and offer to help, Jonah didn't think he had a chance in hell outside those tiny towns.

Which made the call from Miami that much more of a pleasant surprise.

Things moved surprisingly fast after that, meeting with the captain there, interviewing, and ultimately getting the offer.

Jonah could barely afford a studio apartment in a not-so-great part of Sweetwater, a neighboring suburb, but he'd take a cheap, poorly decorated, thin-walled studio apartment in Sweetwater over his nicer one bedroom in Orlando any day—even if it was only slighter bigger than a cheap hotel room and the carpet was worn and stained. Okay, and he could hear the *telenovela* blaring from the TV two apartments over, and the landlord warned him that the wall-mounted air-conditioning only worked about half the time, and even less in the summer. Also, there was a slight gap underneath his door that was large enough for any manner of bugs and lizards and possibly a snake to get through. But still. It was his first step to a new life in a better place. It had to be. There was no going back.

He took the few belongings and pieces of furniture he had collected over the years and threw them into the tiny trailer he'd rented (he made sure to leave everything of Chris's, including their photos together). It was a lonely, boring drive from Orlando to Miami, full of cow fields and garish, tropically pink houses along the turnpike. He'd thrown together a playlist for the ride and made it to "Love Is a Battlefield" before giving up and turning to some bland alternative rock station he picked up outside West Palm Beach.

The closer he got, the more the colors of Miami started to replace the homogenized, boxy residences, and Jonah started to feel energized by his surroundings. Even the graffiti was brighter in Miami, he noted with amusement as he sat under a saturated overpass in traffic. He'd been to Miami on college road trips before and had been mesmerized by the sights and sounds and even smells of the city, but as he unpacked his trailer to the beat of a radio in someone's window blasting a horn-tinged Latin melody, suddenly Miami became a real place and not just a destination for good mojitos and more palm trees per capita than should be legally allowed. He had two days left before he had to start work, and it was a perfect amount of time to explore and get familiar with his new home.

It took him less than a half a day to move his stuff in and get everything situated, and he vowed that with this new job, he would make an effort to live a little less like a transient college student. Chris had lived with three other guys the entire time they dated, and there was never a need to impress him. Chris had been happy just to have a place to go to that didn't smell like four guys.

Of course if smell had really bothered him, then he wouldn't have run off with the whale trainer, but that was in the past, and the past was not going to affect his future here. That was his other vow.

By the end of the first night—after letting his senses guide him through beautiful neighborhoods alive with colorful murals that honored the city's cultural history, and people dancing on the sidewalks to music blaring from little walk-up cafés serving fragrant *ropa vieja*—Jonah had found his new favorite bakery. It was a Cuban place on his way to the police station that served *pastelitos*: Cuban pastries, so delicious he could have cried. He'd also found his new grocery store—or, well, the closest location of the chain grocery store he usually shopped back in Orlando. Some things didn't *have* to change, after all. Even if the grocery store inexplicably had valet parking and was full of cars more expensive than some people's houses. Jonah had to laugh to himself. *Miami*. His new home.

By the end of the second day, he'd found the fastest way to a good beach that he was probably never going to see again in daylight thanks to his curse of easily sunburned skin, some restaurants he wanted to try when he started getting paid again, and some decent-looking bars. As his head hit the pillow, early that night so he would be rested and ready for his first day, Jonah, trying to ignore the sounds of the couple next door having loud, obnoxious sex, couldn't help but think that everything was finally going right for him.

# Chapter 4

JONAH WOKE up to the ringing of his phone's alarm. This was it. The first day of his new life in Miami. Today he would meet the men and women of his new squad and start solving real crime in a big city. No more small-time pickpockets at tourist traps. No more suicides in cheap hotel rooms—or at least the hotel rooms would be expensive. No more credit card scams by people pretending to sell discount theme park tickets outside convenience stores. And maybe a chance at becoming a better cop.

Jonah couldn't think of a better way to start his first day as a Miami detective than to go to his brand-new favorite bakery, Ramon's. He'd always had a weakness for Cuban food, and it was just his luck that Miami had the best Cuban food off the island. He figured he had just enough time to grab breakfast on the way out and be in his new captain's office with time to spare.

Right on time Jonah settled in line at Ramon's with less than a minute until 7:30 a.m. Droves of hungover investment bankers and high-end real estate agents were stumbling in, desperate to wake up long enough to make enough money to fund the next weekend's parties.

There were three people in front of him: a woman with a run going up the back of her stockings, balancing a thick stack of folders in her arm and chatting away on her phone like she was the only person in the building, and two dark-suited men engaged in a heated conversation about portfolios or stock options or something that sounded both ridiculously important and ridiculously boring at the same time.

The woman had an obnoxiously large order and refused to get off her phone while she relayed pastry after pastry request to Ramon and his wife, who maneuvered around each other like they were performing a beautifully choreographed routine, ignoring the impatient woman's sense of entitlement. They were perfectly in sync and even as they balanced hot coffee and delicate pastries, they never bumped into each other or spilled anything. Jonah hoped to have that kind of relationship someday.

Jonah rocked back and forth on his heels a few times out of anxiety and maybe a little boredom. He only stopped after he grazed the man behind him, which elicited a gruff throat-clearing from him. Jonah turned to find an attractive Hispanic man in his early forties staring up at him, with dark hair, graying just a little at the temples, and intelligent, but impatient, green eyes. He mumbled an apology and turned back around, wondering how everyone in Miami seemed to look like models and movie stars. Next to everyone, Jonah looked like an awkward six-foot-one twelve-year-old on his way to the first day of Bible school.

The two suits, thankfully, seemed to be in a hurry and ordered quickly. Jonah could almost taste the sticky sweet guava pulp by this point.

The mantra of "go go go" running through his head was interrupted by his phone beeping at him that he needed to get on the road now or risk being late.

Jonah was not going to be late on his first day. But he was also not leaving without food.

*Finally.* No one was left between him and his delicious breakfast. He ordered a guava pastry and a café Cubano and went to the end of the counter to wait for them.

The woman at the front counter—Ramon's daughter, Jonah guessed—who was about twenty-five and clearly put on the front lines to attract more male customers with her low-cut shirt and long dark hair, handed him his pastry to tide him over until the coffee came.

He moved to the end of the counter and bounced along to the music while he waited.

"*Lo siento.* I'm sorry, senor. *No más.* We just sold the last one." Ramon was talking to the attractive, impatient man.

The man sounded a little more than agitated. "Just sold out? To who?"

Jonah turned just in time to see Ramon pointing right at him. Jonah had sticky pink pulp on his lips and a flake of pastry hanging off his chin, a sugary, unintentional boast of his prize. The man looked right at Jonah with murder in his eyes, and all Jonah could think to do was smile sheepishly and wave.

His coffee couldn't come soon enough.

Jonah finished off his ill-gotten pastry in his car as soon as he sat down, but he made the coffee last, sipping at red lights and letting the caffeine and illegal amounts of sugar gradually shock his system into high gear instead of letting it hit him all at once as he listened to a playlist of cheesy uplifting songs he had made especially for the occasion (he swore his phone had silently judged him for putting the theme song to *Laverne & Shirley* on there).

There was a charm to his new station that his old one lacked. Where Orlando had bland, cookie cutter buildings, virtually indistinguishable from its neighbors, Miami had seen fit to give its police stations buildings that fit its rich culture and the neighborhoods they served. The station, right in the heart of south Miami, covered an area from Little Havana down to Coconut Grove and came by its tropical Caribbean influences honestly. It was a beautiful place to be booked and thrown in jail, for sure, with its terra cotta tile floors that gave way to blue Spanish tilework up the walls. Far from the stuffy and artificially lit station he'd left behind, the South Miami station invited as much natural light as it could hold. If it weren't for the cops and criminals and holding cells, it could be an intimate restaurant.

He'd driven around the day before to see some of the other stations in the district and was amazed at the painstaking attempts to enhance the landscape around them. They'd paid tribute to the famous Miami art deco movement in one station, with glass brick and graceful curved lines that popped with blues and greens, and even threw a nod to Miami Vice with another: an all-white building with pinky coral accents by one of the beaches—much better than the plain stucco stations of Orlando that could have just as easily been a post office or the electric company.

Jonah parked his car in the lot and watched the light sea breeze rock the date palms that lined the front flower beds and took a deep breath before ascending the steps. This was it. His new life was waiting for him inside the building and all he had to do now was go inside and meet it.

Captain Ileana Luis, somewhere in her early fifties, if the sensible pantsuits were any indication, was everything Jonah, or any cop worth his or her salt, would ever want in a boss. Word was she was fair and strict and followed the rules to the letter of the law. She tolerated no nonsense and demanded no less than perfection from the cops she oversaw.

She had mentioned in the interview that her precinct had the lowest turnover rate in South Florida, and she was proud of that, but it also made them pretty long in the tooth in some ways. She was all too happy when Jonah's information came across her desk, she'd told him. Fresh blood.

Newer ideas. They'd lost their oldest detective to retirement the previous month, and she did not like being a man down during snowbird season when affluent seniors from up north were most vulnerable to the dirty scammers and thieves Miami also seemed to attract around the same time. That Jonah was relatively inexperienced wasn't a concern for her, she had assured him. She had just the detective to partner Jonah with to get him where he needed to be.

Jonah had immediately liked Captain Luis and was eager to meet his new partner if he or she was anything like her. If Jonah had learned anything in his short time as a detective, it was that he needed people like Luis to balance him out, emotionally. The hardness he needed just wasn't quite there yet. He still held out some small hope that humanity didn't suck as much as everyone around him tried to convince him it did. He wondered if that was part of what had always held him back.

Jonah announced himself to the hopelessly outdated goth-looking woman of about twenty-three, who wore all black and took great pains to make sure Jonah noticed that he interrupted her obviously personal phone call when he got there. He managed to avoid her death glare and wait patiently in the lobby for Luis to call him back to her office until boredom quickly got the better of him. He tried once or twice to coax a little information about his new squad out of the receptionist, but all he managed to get was a cryptic and annoyed, "Just don't piss off your new partner and you'll be fine." She shrugged. "Mostly."

She went back to texting the dark lords of the underworld or whoever it was, leaving Jonah to wonder about that, but before he got too far into his thoughts, the desk phone rang.

"Captain?" The receptionist looked up at Jonah and pursed her lips that were a definite nonregulation black. "Got it. I'll send him in." She hung up the phone and pushed the security button to open the door behind him. "Go on in. Your destiny awaits." She had obviously meant that sarcastically, but she was right.

Jonah tossed his empty coffee cup in the bin by the front door, straightened his jacket, and held his head high as he walked toward her office. This was going to be amazing; he just knew it.

# Chapter 5

THE BLINDS to Luis's office were drawn closed, and he heard a male voice along with hers behind them. It must be his new partner.

Jonah knocked once on the door and nervously pushed it open.

"Ah, here he is now," Captain Luis said to the mystery man in her office. Her hair was tied back in a low ponytail, and she had donned another sensible pantsuit. Jonah liked consistency in a boss. "Detective Rafael Santos, I'd like you to meet your new partner, Detective Jonah Landers from the Orlando PD."

Jonah breathed in sharply with trepidation rising from the pit of his stomach and walked all the way in.

What he saw made him stumble a bit. Standing across the desk from his new boss with a familiar look of murderous intent on his face was none other than the man from whom he had stolen the last guava pastry from not forty-five minutes before.

So much for first impressions.

Jonah shook his head and quickly regained his composure. He could play it off. He'd buy him one tomorrow. It would be fine. It surely wasn't a sign that this was doomed from the beginning, right?

Jonah enthusiastically grabbed Detective Santos's hand and shook it. "Nice to meet you, Detective. Sorry about breakfast, okay? Probably not the best way to start off things, right? How about I make it up to you tomorrow?" He laughed awkwardly.

Rafael pursed his lips a little and softened a bit into the handshake, but as soon as the moment came, it was gone. Rafael's piercing green eyes had gone wide, and he pulled back abruptly.

"*You.*" Rafael backed up some more and shook his head. "*You!*"

Jonah shrugged because he didn't know what else to do. "Me? I'm sorry, I'm a little—"

"*Detective* Santos, can you please explain what you're going on about?" Luis already seemed agitated, and Jonah wouldn't have minded an explanation himself.

"I can't work with him. I don't need a partner. Send him to Palm Beach so the rich old ladies there can eat him up. But I won't work with him." Rafael plopped himself in a chair defiantly while all Jonah could do was stare in confusion. Was it really *that* bad?

Luis gritted her teeth. "I don't recall this being your choice, Santos. Not that it's going to make a difference to me, but do you want to explain your refusal?"

Rafael looked straight at Jonah. "Sure. Two years ago. Orlando. Some trashy nightclub downtown. I was undercover for the state. This guy and his *crack* squad set me back nine months after blowing in and screwing my case while they hunted for small-time hookers!"

Jonah blinked and it hit him. He'd shaved the beard off and traded the leather jacket for a more sensible suit and tie, but there he was.

Rafael Santos.

Of course.

How could he forget?

Aside from Rafael being connected to a night Jonah had tried hard to forget, that was. *Rafael Santos*, that cocky detective who stormed in and thought he was a god running his secret little case and not telling anyone in Orlando and then—

"You punched me in the face! I had a black eye for a month! You almost broke my nose! You weren't even supposed to be there! And you're really still blaming us for setting you back?" The awful memories of his first undercover op came rushing back to Jonah.

So much for second impressions, he guessed.

Rafael pointed an angry finger at Jonah. "You're damn right I punched you in the face! Who in the hell taught you to rush a suspect like that? What if I had pulled my gun on you?" Rafael turned to Luis. "He's too green! He's only had his shield for, what, two years? Maybe three?"

"Detectives! That is *enough*!" Luis banged on her desk with her fist and the noise startled both of them into silence. She reminded Jonah of his mother, if his mother were a five-foot-ten, black-haired Puerto Rican instead of a five-foot-one rotund Norwegian. "I don't care what happened two years ago and I don't care who punched who and I certainly don't care about your petty argument. Santos, you need a partner. Landers, you need a job. If you both would like to keep *this* job, I suggest you find a way to work past your differences and start seeing eye to eye. Santos, you're my best detective and also my most seasoned detective. If anyone can take Detective Landers under his wing and get him where he needs to be, it's you. And, being that you are the most seasoned detective, you could use some fresh ideas. We are dealing with new types of crime all the time, and we need to be on our toes. Landers brings some much needed modern ways with him. Hence, you are partners. Are we clear?"

Rafael groaned. "Yes, Captain."

"Yes, Captain," followed Jonah.

"*Good.*" Luis sat back down and refused to make eye contact with either of them. "I'm sure with some time you two will get on like a house afire, like my *abuela* used to say. Santos, where are you on that stolen car case?"

"I was just—"

"Perfect! Take Jonah along. Get him acquainted with our fair city." She opened a random file that was on top of a large stack, presumably to indicate the conversation was over.

Rafael blinked rapidly a few times and turned to Jonah with an incredibly fake smile plastered to his face.

Jonah tugged his shirtsleeves higher and lolled his head around a few times like he was warming up for something. There was no point arguing, and he really didn't want to have to look for a new department. He also didn't feel he should have to. This was Santos's problem.

Rafael mock graciously held the door open for Jonah and gestured grandly for him to go out first. "Ready to roll?"

*Yeah, right off a cliff probably.*

Rafael exited the captain's office wordlessly behind a jittery Jonah.

Yep. That had not gone well at all.

# Chapter 6

THAT FIRST day was awful. Obviously. The second day wasn't much better. The first whole week was pretty bad too. And, even if Jonah used complicated math and a high-paid spin doctor, he couldn't have salvaged their first month either. Rafael was quiet, intense, and focused. He kept a lot close to his chest, and Jonah wasn't about to have another mysterious partner like he'd had with Peter. He'd asked around the station a few times, but he never got more facts than what amounted to a staff bio on a webpage: born and raised in Miami to Cuban immigrants, never married, a bit of a foodie, and very ambitious.

Jonah was, according to Rafael, the living embodiment of a sugar high. Jonah talked too much. He gave his opinion when Rafael didn't want his opinion. And his opinion was wrong, anyway. He jumped the gun. He had too many of his own ideas on how to do things, and it wasn't "how things were done in Miami." His taste in music sucked. He didn't hold his weapon correctly.

"What do you mean I don't hold my gun right?" Jonah let his head roll skyward as Rafael doled out another round of insults.

"You look like a bad '80s cop show. Have you even fired a gun? Like, ever?"

"Yes of course I have!" *Not really.* Well, to get certified. And to keep his certification. And target practice. Jonah found himself wishing he'd spent more of his free time at Robertson's Range, the place all local cops learned to shoot and could practice in their off-hours back in Orlando, instead of wasting his time on Chris.

"Mmm-hmm." Rafael halfheartedly raised an eyebrow and went back to ignoring him, as was the usual after he was done telling Jonah everything he was doing wrong that day.

That had earned Jonah a day at the range, one of his days off, actually, proving to Rafael that he was competent with a firearm. It wasn't as nice as Robertson's, not as state of the art, and it was even farther south than Miami, ensuring that, even in the dead of winter, the sunscreen he'd invested in would fail spectacularly.

Jonah lost a suspect during a foot chase through a rundown section of town (in his defense the guy grew up in the neighborhood and knew the twists and turns better). He *accidentally* insulted the wife of a county commissioner when she accused the gardener of stealing (he wasn't and she was treating him like a leper even after they found all the items safe and sound in a safe she had forgotten about. Jonah didn't care how rich or powerful someone was, they still had an obligation to treat others like human beings). He actually did stop to help old ladies cross the streets despite Rafael's taunting that he could arrange that on a permanent basis. He put a plant on his desk to give it some personality ("You know that isn't really bamboo, right? And it's not actually lucky?" Rafael seemed to delight in being a killjoy, but Jonah wasn't going to let something that small bother him. He bought two more by the end of the week just to see the reaction on Rafael's face). He missed teeny tiny details in case reports. And the best insult of all: Jonah was trying too hard.

But the two of them, at least professionally, were on *fire*—arrest after arrest on top of arrest. And even though Rafael frequently reminded Jonah about how much he couldn't stand him, there were moments where, after an arrest, or when Jonah bounced in and couldn't stop himself from excitedly yammering on about an idea he had on a case, Rafael's face softened like he was starting to warm up to him.

Sometimes Jonah could catch the faint hint of a smile cross Rafael's lips. But as soon as Rafael noticed Jonah sizing up his reactions, the moment was over. Jonah took it as a sign that he could win Rafael over. Someday. Maybe. There was no way Rafael could deny that the differences in their personalities made them a good match. And, in his own gruff way, Rafael was teaching Jonah a lot and sometimes even looked like he was enjoying himself when Jonah put forth tremendous effort just to see if he could wring a begrudged compliment out of Rafael.

By the end of the second month, Rafael had seemed to finally accept that Jonah wasn't going anywhere and laid off the worst of the newbie ribbing and the forced groans every time Jonah slid into the passenger seat on the way to a case. Rafael still wouldn't let Jonah take the lead, though.

Or drive the car.

"I've lived here my entire life and you just got here, kid. One wrong turn and you're driving the wrong way on the Dolphin Expressway and we're both dead. I'm not dying with you in the driver's seat. Don't want to get teased in the afterlife."

Jonah sighed and stared at the passing palm trees. "Rafael, the car has GPS." Jonah fiddled with the radio, which drove Rafael crazy. He eventually settled on the most annoying '80s pop song he could find.

"I'm the only GPS this car needs, Landers. When you can tell me three different routes to overtake a fleeing suspect, then maybe I'll let you drive. Until then, sit there and tell me all about our vic and why she thinks the mailman stole forty grand in diamonds from her supposedly unbreakable safe." Rafael turned the radio back to the Spanish pop station it had been on before Jonah changed it.

Jonah sighed but grabbed the case file from in between the seats. He wondered if it was actually a slight improvement in their relationship that Rafael was only insulting Jonah's lack of Miami surface streets knowledge, or if he was just getting used to Rafael and had stopped noticing as much.

# Chapter 7

WHAT WAS stopping Jonah's self-esteem from taking a hit was that everyone else in the station embraced him rather quickly. The rest of his squad were a dream: professional and helpful and always ready with a private commiseration at Rafael's disapprovals of Jonah.

Jenny Garcia and Brad Edgewood, two other members of his new squad, were partners and had been for many years. They seemed to have a sort of psychic bond with each other that made them a deadly combination, even though their personalities could not have been any more different. Off the clock they were close friends too, something Jonah found he was actually a little jealous of, and frequently invited Jonah and the rest of the station for beers after work. Where Rafael was supposed to work on Jonah's professional development, Garcia, a recent divorcee living up the newly single life, had appointed herself to take care of the social end.

"You look like a lost and lonely puppy, Landers, and I can't stand it. Have you met anyone since you got here?" On the clock Garcia dressed a lot like Luis, only slightly more fashionable than sensible. Off the clock the skirts got a lot shorter, the shirts a lot tighter, and the heels became deadly weapons. Jonah had decided he liked her a lot.

Jonah shrugged. "Haven't really had the time, I guess. And I just got out of a really messy relationship that ended terribly, so I'm not really looking for anything serious right now."

Garcia pursed her lips and raised an eyebrow. "Honey, no one said anything about finding your soulmate, okay? You need to have some fun. This is Miami, *papi*. Whatcha like? Tall, dark, and available? Or maybe a nice older guy who will take you to Art Basel and then to a fancy café in Coral Gables, hmm?"

Jonah did a double take. "Guy?" He hadn't told anyone.

"*Sí*. I mean, you *are* gay, right?" Garcia looked at him like he was a four-year-old who just lied about stealing from the cookie jar.

"Well, umm… I—yeah. I am. But—" How did she know?

Garcia smirked. "Please. I'm a detective. I'm a damned good detective. And a mom. No one can hide anything from me." She must have seen the look on his face, because her expression changed to something almost protective. "*Pero* like, don't worry, okay? Literally no one around here cares. We don't live in the past here in Miami. We got 'em gay, straight, bisexual, you name it."

Jonah nodded, because what else could he do?

Garcia patted him on the shoulder. An odd gesture for someone so deadly and downright scary out on the street. "Don't worry so much, *mijo*. I swear, all anyone cares about is if you do your job well. I haven't seen a man or woman kicked out or kicked off for being anything other than a screwup in all my years here. I mean, look at Grace." Grace was the wannabe goth receptionist he'd encountered on his first day. "She's a bit rude, right? Skirts the dress code with all that black? She's a romance novelist, and I don't mean those sweet ones with the Scottish Highlanders on the cover. She's pretty hardcore—lots of graphic sex, werewolves, reapers, murder, torture, you name it. Nothing really work friendly at all. But she can filter out the victims from the locos who come in thinking the moon is following them and want it arrested like you wouldn't believe. She single-handedly saves this station hundreds of hours a year that we used to waste dealing with false reports. So, no one cares if she lets her freak flag fly. We all have freak flags here, okay?"

Jonah felt a little better and even more so when Garcia conceded that it wasn't her tale to tell to the rest of the station. He liked her even more.

But as he drove to Coconut Grove, a bustling, ritzy, well-shaded neighborhood in south Miami that no one on the force would ever be able to afford to live in unless they bought the smallest house with their combined incomes, and the tapas place Garcia swore was so good he would see the face of God in the sticky guava-glazed ribs, he realized she was right. He was lonely.

As much as it pained him to think it, he even kind of missed Chris. At least, the Chris he had thought he had known.

Sure, going to new bars and restaurants was fun, but he was still going back to his tiny, poorly insulated apartment alone. He supposed Garcia was well meaning in trying to help him find someone, but so far the Miami social scene was looking to be a dud. The Venn diagram of guys Jonah liked and guys Jonah was finding at the bars and the gym he joined did not overlap at all.

And it was then Jonah realized Garcia was right again. He needed some fun—mindless, stupid, noncommittal fun.

Or maybe a boyfriend.

Or a boyfriend-like guy. Boyfriend Lite.

Or just a fun guy to hang with. Maybe exclusively.

The tiny place, decorated like an artist's loft with terrible modern art—all for sale starting at the low price of only $300 for a two-by-two-inch canvas rendering of someone's cat—adorning the exposed brick walls and hidden between trendy boutiques selling one-of-a-kind designer clothes and soap that cost $50 a bar, was packed for a Wednesday night, but Garcia had commandeered a large table by the bar. Everyone was in an unusually good mood, but they had every right to be. Their arrests were up, their closed cases were up, and Captain Luis hadn't yelled or threatened anyone in two weeks. It was cause for a celebration.

Even Rafael surprised everyone by showing up.

Jonah hadn't even noticed at first, having been deep in conversation with Brad and trying to get to know him a bit better. Sandy haired and six foot three, Brad was a family man: wife, two kids, grilling on the weekends, huge Dolphins and Heat fan despite being from New York originally. He was also a bit of a sci-fi geek. He had as little in common with Jonah as he did with Garcia, but, as nice as Brad was, Jonah had little interest in pursuing a meaningful friendship with him like he wanted with Garcia. He was a good cop, but he was also a bit boring.

Brad had leaned into Jonah when Rafael walked in and didn't immediately run for the hills when he saw the crowd. "I don't know what you're doing to him, man, but this is the first time Rafael has come out to one of these in at least five years."

Jonah didn't know how to respond to that. He had no bearing on Rafael's social life, even if he *had* asked twice if Rafael was coming, just in the name of peacemaking in a social setting.

He felt almost relaxed for the first time in a very long time. Everyone was laughing, drinking, talking, and he had to admit that Garcia was right again: the ribs were amazing. He even sent a drink over to Rafael as a sort of apology for being… well, for being Jonah.

Jonah was on his second mezcal-tinged cocktail when Garcia stumbled over to him with a guy around Jonah's age who he had seen around the station but hadn't yet had interaction with. He wasn't dressed like a cop, either off or on duty, with his loose jeans and what looked like a truly vintage Siouxsie and the Banshees shirt. Which was *awesome*. Jonah had a secret soft spot for '80s music, and it used to drive electronic dance music-loving Chris up a wall.

"Landers, you aren't saving that seat next to you, are you?" She smiled and pushed the guy forward.

*Subtle, Garcia.* He should have known this was her plan all along. He was stuck now, but the guy was cute, with long, straight dark hair, even darker eyes, and skin to match. He looked Native American, if Jonah had to guess. In this part of Florida, Seminole or Miccosukee, maybe.

He actually appreciated that Garcia cared enough to go out of her way to try to set him up and also take the extra step of finding someone so attractive, because there was no point pretending it was something different than Garcia playing matchmaker. Jonah shook his head a little and smiled as he offered his hand.

"Hi. I'm Jonah."

The man caught the look and grinned back as they shook hands. "A.J. Just transferred in?" He had the tiniest hint of an old Florida drawl, that little twang of the South that refused to die out completely no matter how many people came down from New York and New Jersey.

"Yeah, from Orlando." Jonah pulled out the chair a bit to invite A.J. to sit, and Garcia nodded her head and fist pumped the air as she backed away. *Really subtle.*

"I'm tech. You'll probably see me more when you do some heavy ops, undercover and things like that. How are you liking it here so far?" The low light coming from the candle centerpieces on the table lit up A.J.'s dark features. It was a gorgeous combination.

Maybe it was the booze talking, but Jonah couldn't stop himself from replying, "I think I like it more now," with a silly grin on his face.

Gorgeous or not, A.J. was intelligent and easy to talk to. Jonah made a mental note to bake Garcia a pie in thanks. And another mental note to learn how to bake a pie. And a third to just go to the store and buy a nice pie because notes one and two just weren't going to happen. Especially if there was a chance that A.J. could be filling some of his spare time.

The crowd had thinned out a bit by 10:00 p.m., and Jonah and A.J. were finishing a shared order of chocolate chip cookie dough flautas, which had sounded disgusting when A.J. first suggested them, but had quickly become Jonah's favorite thing on the wholly amazing menu. A few coworkers were left and had all since migrated to the bar, leaving Jonah and A.J. alone at the once jam-packed table to talk and learn about each other.

The flautas were messy, dripping with chocolate sauce, and a drop was clinging to A.J.'s chin. It was as cute as it was distracting.

Jonah pointed to his own chin. "You've got a little…."

A.J. raised his eyebrows in embarrassment, but quickly swiped it away with a finger that he immediately and, to be honest, obscenely sucked clean.

"Did I get it?" A.J. stuck out his tongue and licked his lower lip like he was making sure there wasn't more. Jonah tried very hard not to think about it.

It still took a second for Jonah to focus long enough to answer him, and A.J. grinned as he leaned in close to Jonah.

"Listen, I don't really care to have the entire station privy to my private life. Well, beyond Garcia, who is going to know whether anyone tells her or not. But I really want to kiss you right now and I think doing it right here in front of half the station is going to ruin the moment, so can we get out of here?"

Jonah did some rough calculations on the last time he'd been kissed and just how much he wanted to be kissed and came up with an answer that sounded a lot like "God, yes" in his head, and he could only pray he didn't actually say that as A.J. stood and reached out to help Jonah stand.

His legs felt like jelly, and it was probably more from the anticipation than it was from the mezcal, considering how long before then he'd cut himself off. He stretched before attempting a step, twisting his torso to work out the kinks from sitting so long. Out of the corner of his eye, he saw Rafael looking strangely at Jonah, and he turned all the way to make sure he was actually seeing it.

Rafael was nursing a drink while someone from Vice was trying to get his attention, but Rafael seemed focused on Jonah, and he wondered if it was normal to still be thinking "what did I do wrong now" this far into their partnership.

Jonah gave Rafael a half wave and turned to A.J. "Yeah, let's get out of here. Too many eyes right now, I think."

A.J. laughed and pulled Jonah along. "I couldn't agree more."

Jonah felt like a teenager, getting in a car for the express purpose of making out, even if A.J.'s was a hell of a lot nicer than Jonah's beat-up sedan and super roomy with soft leather seats.

A.J. laughed as he cracked the windows so they wouldn't die of heat stroke. "Feel like you're in high school again?"

"Something like that." Jonah reached up and played with an arrowhead dangling from the rearview mirror. Why was he so nervous?

"Well, I don't want to scare you off by asking you to come back to my place so soon, but I do want a little privacy right now." There was the tiniest hint of a sea breeze coming into the car, and it felt like heaven in the completely unwarranted heat of early March.

"And I'm sure we don't want to give Garcia the satisfaction just yet. Probably best to make her wait until she can't take it anymore and explodes as payback for being so obvious." The arrowhead swung back and forth between Jonah's fingers.

"I'm Seminole," said A.J. suddenly.

"Okay?" Jonah wasn't sure where this was going.

"In case you were wondering about the arrowhead. I'm Seminole. A proud Seminole. I like to get that out of the way pretty early because some people learn I'm Native American and automatically assume I fit every bullshit stereotype. I've heard every casino and alcoholic joke out there." A.J. paused and cringed. "Not that you would make a joke like— God, sorry! That was rude. Sore subject, the details of which I won't bore you with on the first date."

Jonah grabbed A.J.'s hand. "No, it's okay! I was born and raised in Florida. I've heard the stereotypes and slurs you've most likely encountered before. You don't have to worry about that with me." As much as the cop in Jonah wanted to know more about the story behind that, he wasn't ever going to press the issue if it made A.J. uncomfortable. As diverse and progressive as Florida could be at times, Native appropriation was still a hot button issue, and Jonah's first real encounter with it had been in high school, when the students had successfully petitioned to change their old traditional mascot, which was, to modern eyes, extremely inappropriate and offensive to Native Americans, to the not at all offensive Loggerhead Turtles, a name that was heavily sponsored by environmental groups. Jonah guessed it had been a win all around, except for the small pocket of racists who picketed the meeting when they had announced the change and then took their children out of the school in protest.

Besides, being a semicloseted gay man made Jonah all too aware of how cruel the world could be to minorities.

A.J. nodded in response and looked relieved. "Good. Okay, now that the uncomfortable part is out of the way...."

He wasted no more time and leaned in to kiss Jonah softly, letting Jonah control how far it went. A.J.'s lips were soft, and there were the last hints of chocolate on them. It felt so good to be touched and intimate with someone, even if it was just a kiss. That was probably the best sign that it had, indeed, been far too long.

A.J. deepened the kiss and reached up to touch Jonah's face, moaning a little into his mouth when Jonah shivered under A.J.'s touch.

Jonah let himself melt into A.J., matching his movements and rhythm as they kissed. It felt so, so good and losing control seemed like a good option when A.J. broke the kiss and started moving down Jonah's neck, leaving a wet trail that gave him goose bumps when the air hit it.

"This good?" A.J. whispered it against Jonah's skin, and he could feel A.J.'s hot breath as he spoke. Now he really did feel like a teenager, because when was the last time something as innocent as this made him feel so dirty?

But just as A.J. felt he needed to get something out before they went any further, Jonah needed to address the elephant in the room concerning his relationship hang-ups.

"Yeah, it's good, but...." Jonah pulled back a bit. "Listen. I just got out of a really messy relationship that ended pretty badly. I'm not looking to jump right into something serious. I like you, and I think I could like you more as we go on, but right now—"

"Right now are you okay with kissing me?" A.J. pursed his lips.

"Yeah?"

"Are you okay with just kissing me right now and seeing where this goes with no pressure?" There was no way he could be this perfect.

"Well, yeah."

A.J. shrugged. "I can respect that. Look, I get messy breakups. I do. And I get that they can really fuck you up. I'm not out to scare you off, because I think you're cute as hell and easy to get along with."

Jonah smiled, a bit confused by A.J.'s forthrightness, but it was a welcome change. "Okay, then. I'm going to… uh… go now, because I have to be up in about three and a half minutes to go to work."

Jonah leaned back in and kissed A.J. before moving to open the car door. "I had a really nice time tonight. I would like to do it again. I mean that."

"Yeah, me too. How about I check in with you next week to see if you're free and we can grab a drink or something after work? Without Garcia, of course."

Jonah opened the door and slid out so he could go around to A.J.'s window. "I'd like that."

One last kiss and Jonah stood up straight to walk to his own car a few rows over. He would never admit out loud that he had a little more bounce in his step as he walked, though.

It didn't last long. Rafael was making his way to his own car at the same time, and the moment he locked eyes on Jonah, the weird look he'd been giving him at the bar came back with a vengeance.

"Didn't you leave a long time ago? What were you doing out here?" He sounded more annoyed than usual.

Maybe it was some newfound confidence because someone had expressed an interest in him. Or maybe it was something else, but Jonah could not find a shit to give about Rafael's opinion of him and how he spent his time.

"It's a free country. I wasn't aware I had to run every minute of my social life by you."

Without another word Jonah turned and walked to his car.

For the first time in a long time, even with his neighbors fighting loudly in Creole and the flashing neon of the landscape that his cheap blinds refused to block, Jonah fell asleep with a smile on his face.

# Chapter 8

HE WAS slightly—okay, maybe more than slightly—hungover the next day. He'd stopped drinking well before he was actually drunk and probably would never have blown above the legal limit at any point, but damn did that mezcal do a number on him. He prayed the criminals in Miami would all decide at once to take the day off so he could sit and pretend to do paperwork, but there was as much chance of that happening as there was of the Advil he inhaled doing a damn bit of good.

The best he could hope for, realistically, was to at least look like he wasn't suffering. He skipped his now normal pastry and coffee from Ramon's for something cheap and disgusting at a drive-thru because getting out of the car more than necessary was just cruel, and he slid into his desk chair with barely a minute to spare.

He really *did* have a ton of paperwork to get through, stemming from a trio of back-to-back arrests that dovetailed into one another. The forms might as well have been written in Russian, for all he could make out in the tiny text. He leaned in closer to try to get a better look, and as though he had been waiting for the opportune moment, Rafael came up behind him and clapped a hand on his back roughly, making his already screaming head rattle.

"What's *up*, partner? What a *glorious* day to be here first thing in the morning! We're going to get *so much* accomplished today. Let's go for a ride. There's crime to solve and perps to chase on foot and bright sunshine to bask in." The sarcasm was as thick as the sludge at the bottom of his fast food coffee cup, and Jonah vowed to never drink mezcal again.

"Can I help you, Rafael? Or are you just being an ass for the sake of being an ass? I have work to do." He turned back to his stack of papers and pointedly ignored Rafael.

"Not today, partner. Not today. Captain wants us to follow up on that store robbery." Rafael threw the case file down on top of Jonah's other files and it landed with a *thwack* that echoed in his head.

Jonah sighed and massaged his aching temple with the heel of his hand. At least the store that was robbed sold decent coffee even if didn't sell gasoline. Jonah had grown up in the suburbs of Tampa and even Orlando, with its big city dreams, was still a glorified suburb. If there was a convenience store, it sold gas. That was the law of the land. Fill up, get a slushie, grab some chips, and go. One and done. The idea of a convenience store that was just a store was, well, inconvenient, and with his headache, it annoyed him even more.

"Fine. Let's go." Jonah stood and grabbed his jacket from the back of his chair.

It only occurred to him that going with Rafael meant going back out into that damned sunshine when he pushed the door open and was hit with a ray reflecting off a nearby car. He heard Rafael chuckle to himself as Jonah raised his hands to shield his eyes like a vampire.

Rafael threw on dark sunglasses and banged on the hood of the car as he went to unlock the door.

"Let's roll, *partner*." There was no mistaking the huge shit-eating grin on Rafael's face. He was enjoying this thoroughly. So much for all the progress Jonah had thought they had made.

Rafael sang along annoyingly to the songs on the too-loud radio for the first five minutes or so, every now and then glancing at Jonah to, Jonah guessed, ensure he was still being tortured by all of it.

The expressway was backed up for miles. In Orlando the traffic jams were 90 percent tourists and 10 percent construction. Jonah had gotten the idea in his head that radio stations would save so much money by recording the traffic report one day and replaying it every morning into infinity because the problems were the same problems in the same places every day. In Miami, though, it was just as likely to be two alligators fighting in the middle of one highway as it was a ten-car pileup on another. Most days probably both at the same time.

"So, you and Choya, eh?" Rafael had finally stopped singing, but Jonah had tuned that out minutes before, and the sudden question caught him off guard.

"Choya?"

Rafael shook his head. "Jeez, you sleep with a guy and don't even know his last name. I don't know why I expected anything different."

Jonah straightened up, a little—no, a *lot*—annoyed by the implication, and also the intrusion into his personal life when Rafael wouldn't even spill the beans on the tiniest part of his life outside the station. But first a mental note to remember that name because he and A.J. hadn't actually gotten around to discussing that detail, which was *so* not the point.

"You mean A.J.? I didn't—you know, I don't know how this is *any* of your business, Santos."

"If *this*," Rafael said, pointing to Jonah, "is what happens when you're with him, then it damn sure *is* my business. You're no good like this, and you know it."

"Not that I owe you anything, but I would be like *this*," Jonah said, pointing to himself in a mocking imitation of Rafael's previous remark, "whether A.J. and I were together last night or not. He had nothing to do with how I am today. I underestimated the strength of my drinks. I won't make the mistake again. Lesson learned. Can we move on now?"

Jonah definitely did not care what Rafael Santos thought of him, and he surely wasn't thinking of ways to redeem himself, no sir. That was for people who gave a shit, and Jonah Landers was not one of those people, even as he actually made an effort to stay quiet and take copious notes and didn't interrupt Rafael once when he was questioning the convenience store owner—except to ask a question of his own that seemed important enough. Rafael looked annoyed at first but then seemed almost impressed with the content of the question. It was a small victory, but Jonah would take it.

It was far more than Rafael deserved when Jonah interviewed the store owner's son at Rafael's demand, and Jonah didn't even make a sarcastic jab at him about not saying please first.

By his second cup of free coffee, though, souped-up with an extra hit or two of sugar, Jonah was sure it was just the hangover and not some strange, wholly unearned loyalty making him so amenable to putting things to rights with Rafael, even though whatever was up Rafael's ass was of his own doing and no fault of Jonah's.

By his third cup, this time with a shot of caramel in it because, what the hell, coffee kind of tasted terrible even when it was good coffee, Jonah had a moment to stop and watch Rafael in his element. Rafael had a quiet intensity about him that put people instantly at ease. He was so good with witnesses and victims, nodding as they spoke and looking them straight in the eye when he promised that he wouldn't quit until they caught the perp. There was a confidence there that was both enviable and fascinating to be around.

Rafael was so sincere and sympathetic it was hard to believe that he was the same guy who sucker punched Jonah and frequently suggested he transfer to another precinct because he needed the peace and quiet. It almost made Jonah wonder which one was the real Rafael and which one was just an act.

Halfway through the fourth cup, black, like his vision was going, when Jonah's heart was starting to beat like one of Animal's, from The Muppets, drum solos, Jonah couldn't stop himself from glancing over at Rafael's ass in those tight trousers that must have been tailored by someone who knew what they were doing, and Jonah was more sure than ever that it was most definitely the hangover and all the caffeine that made that seem like a good idea. Three times.

Jonah immediately switched to water and hoped Rafael didn't notice his wandering eye. At least the frequent bathroom breaks gave him a few moments to be far enough away from Rafael that he wasn't tempted to look again.

Jonah didn't want to contemplate what thinking Rafael, who hated him with a passion normally reserved for real honest to God criminals, had a nice ass meant in the grand scheme of things. He didn't want to contemplate it all the way back to the station while he sat in uncharacteristic silence in the car with Rafael. The morning traffic, having cleared, should have made for an easy ride back, but Jonah insisted they stop for a restroom. Three times.

Thankfully he didn't have to not contemplate things for long after he got back to the station. There in the main hallway, pushing a cart of complicated looking audio equipment, was A.J. Choya in a blindingly white shirt that contrasted amazingly with his dark skin. A.J. looked up just in time to see Jonah walk by and grinned shyly at him, but Jonah wasn't in the mood for shyness or pretty much anything else that didn't end with him releasing some of his obviously hangover-induced sexual frustration.

"Hey." Despite Jonah's own admission that he wanted to take it slowly, and despite everything working inside his body to ensure that he couldn't make a good decision right then, Jonah decided to go for it.

A.J. stopped and applied the foot brake to the cart. Jonah couldn't name one piece of equipment on there if his life depended on it. They looked expensive, though, and it really hit him then just how different Orlando and Miami were. Orlando thought they had made the big time when they bought a few Segways for beat cops in tourist areas. Miami seemed to toss around money like city hall was printing its own reserve.

A.J. nodded and grinned. "Detective. Can I help you?"

Jonah leaned in a little closer. "Yeah, I was thinking maybe that cup of coffee, but, like, not actual coffee because I think I drank all of it this morning. What are you doing tonight?"

A.J. made a big show of looking skyward and scrunching his face in mock deep thought before locking eyes with Jonah and grinning. "I'm doing absolutely nothing tonight. I'd love to grab a cup of 'not coffee' with you. There's a great place a few blocks over from here. Amazing sandwiches because I don't know about you, but by then I'm usually starving."

Jonah smiled. "So, it's a date?" And that wasn't a word he had been expecting to use so soon, but there it was and it felt nice.

A.J. nodded emphatically. "Absolutely. I'll e-mail you with the address in a few. Right now I have to get these to Vice before they start whining. They've been working this sex ring supplier for a while and they get more and more annoying the closer they get to a breakthrough."

"Oh—oh, yeah, great. See you there, then." Jonah prayed he didn't sound as desperate and awkward as he thought he did as he walked back to his desk.

"Where were you?" Rafael didn't bother to look up from his notes.

"Using A.J.'s last name, thanks" is all Jonah would say, just because he knew it would get under Rafael's skin to think he facilitated any part of getting Jonah and A.J. together. Rafael stopped scribbling on the page for a second but quickly went back to it, if a bit more aggressively than before.

Jonah still didn't see what the big deal was unless Rafael was just as against Jonah finding some happiness as he was about being Rafael's partner.

Jonah sat down in a huff across from Rafael and began translating his chicken scratch handwriting into something everyone else could read as well. For a long time neither of them spoke.

"You did well out there today." There was no pretense or setup for the surprise comment from Rafael almost fifteen minutes of silence later, and Jonah let the words hang in the air for a while. There seemed to be no rhyme or reason to Rafael's mood swings regarding him.

Jonah bit his lip and scratched the back of his neck. "Thanks?"

"No, I mean it. You asked a lot of good questions. I almost think you've been paying attention to me. You're actually getting better." Rafael still hadn't looked up.

"Detective Santos, are you paying me a compliment?" Rafael was an annoyingly frustrating man sometimes.

Rafael snorted. "No. Just observing that my teachings aren't going to waste, that's all."

Jonah rubbed the bridge of his nose and fought back a grin. It was totally a compliment in its own weird way, but he let Rafael hang some more before thanking him because the compliment-to-ribbing ratio was not so good he still couldn't be a little shit to Rafael at opportune times.

"Don't get cocky." It was Rafael's usual response after Jonah thanked him for a compliment, and Jonah started to suspect that he had said it so many times recently that it was becoming an involuntary response. Maybe Jonah *was* getting better.

Jonah let his mouth win the battle, and he broke out into a grin. This was shaping up to be a good day after all.

# Chapter 9

JONAH WOULD never admit out loud there was a little more spring to his step for the rest of the day (beyond what the caffeine overload was doing for him), but more than that, he would never even consider admitting to himself that it was just as much from the fact that he had a real date later as it was from Rafael's surprise approval.

It took a long time after the clusterfuck at The Flat Tire for him to get back on track. It was a bad blow to have everything go so wrong his first time out. Jonah Landers was nothing if not the kind of man who would bust his ass to get back in everyone's good graces after almost screwing things up on his end and giving himself away as a cop. It was a hard road and an uphill battle to get put on even the mildly good cases after that, but if Jonah could come back from that, he could win over Rafael Santos too. Even if everything he'd had to do in Orlando was pretty much Rafael's fault anyway.

With the early setting sun, the day was finally cooling down as Jonah met A.J. by the front door of the little run-down coffee shop promptly at 6:30 p.m. Someone had taken the time to decorate the place with yellowed crocheted lace curtains and plastic gingham table coverings about forty years before and never again made the effort to refresh them. It was homey in a way that put Jonah at ease despite his still rapidly beating heart. Once they were seated, A.J. ordered something with chocolate and caramel in it, and it didn't take a detective to notice that A.J. had quite the sweet tooth. Jonah made do with more water and a Cuban sandwich. The caffeine hadn't *quite* worked its way out of his system yet.

"So, tell me about Orlando. I can't imagine anything but hotel crimes and theme park characters getting arrested for things theme park characters shouldn't be doing." A.J. was so easy to talk to and was genuinely interested in his stupid stories.

Jonah cocked his head. "Well, you're not too far off, actually. Add in tourists who pretend to be lost when we catch them with hookers and a lot of local crime thanks to low wages in the area and you pretty much have it."

"Seems… exciting." A.J. puffed his cheeks and blew out a breath. "Whatever made you want to come to boring old Miami?"

Jonah debated telling A.J. the truth, but it seemed a bit early to bring up the past. "I needed a change. There are only so many times you can respond to the same types of calls, day in and day out. It was either Miami or some small town where I'd be investigating who let the prize cow loose. It was a tough decision, I tell you."

A.J. smiled from behind his chocolate sugar water flavored with a bit of coffee. "What was his name?"

"Sorry?"

"What was the name of the real reason you left? Didn't you tell me you just got out of a messy relationship?" A.J.'s expression was playful, but it was a bit unnerving how even a tech guy he barely knew could see right through him like a seasoned detective.

Jonah sighed and shrugged. There was no need to lie if he was as bad at it as everyone made him out to be. "Chris. Long story short, he wasn't the guy I thought he was, and I wasn't the whale trainer he wanted me to be."

A.J. cringed. "Ooh, left for a whale trainer. That's harsh. Doesn't he know that captive whales are a huge faux pas this year?"

"I guess he didn't get the memo. Or the memo that says maybe don't sneak into my apartment to do it because the both of you live like frat bros well into your late twenties." He hadn't talked about the details with anyone, and it felt good to cleanse out that wound, but he wondered if A.J. was the right person to be pouring his heart out to about his previous relationship.

"Oh, man. I hope a whale eats both of them. You deserve better than that." A.J. smiled a bit wistfully. It was a cute look on him.

"Got me here, didn't it?" The last thing Jonah wanted was anyone thinking he sat at home planning revenge or pining for the one that got away, because truthfully he hadn't thought of Chris much at all since he started in Miami. Even less so since he'd met A.J.

"Maybe I'll send him a thank-you card. But, like, a mean one." A.J. raised his almost empty cup. "To the future, right? To new cities and new experiences, and new people in our lives who respect the world around them and don't try to contain it for their own pleasure."

"I can drink to that." Jonah raised his own glass of water and clinked it to A.J.'s. "So how did you end up on MDPD? What made you decide to work in law enforcement? Where are you from?"

A.J. clasped his hands together. "Well, I had the typical childhood, hunting for food in the wild, scalping the white man, riding buffalo, predicting the weather by how the eagle flew, you know, all that."

Jonah blinked hard and stared at A.J. for a second before A.J. laughed. "I'm joking! Sorry! Actually, I grew up in Coral Springs, and I went to MIT. My parents raised me in the traditions, with all the stories and tales, and I participated in some of the heritage festivals and events, but you'd probably be more likely to find me hunting down good sushi rather than a bear or buffalo. Actually, we don't have buffalo here, now that I think about it, so scratch that. Anyway, I joined MDPD the year I graduated, and I've been here ever since."

"Do you still practice any of it?" Jonah was genuinely curious.

"Some. It's important to me to not let the traditions die. I mean, it's tough enough being a racial minority that has a very bad past when it comes to acceptance. But add being gay, a sexual minority, to that and I feel dually obligated to celebrate who I am and also break the stereotypes."

Jonah was impressed. "That's really awesome, A.J. I like that you haven't compromised who you are to get here. It's admirable. And obviously it hasn't harmed your career any."

A.J. nodded. "Yeah, Miami is great like that. The whole station is pretty diverse and that's a big part of what drew me to Miami. I, too, had a decision to make about coming here or going to work as a small-time tech in a small town. Some of those places scared me."

Jonah nodded. "Tell me about it."

A.J. smiled. "Actually, I'd rather you tell me the story behind you and Rafael. What's up with you two?"

Jonah raised an eyebrow. "Me and Rafael what? The guy hates me." It hit him as soon as he said it that he only addressed how Rafael felt about him and not how he felt about Rafael. It suddenly occurred to Jonah that he didn't hate Rafael as much as Rafael despised him.

"Jonah, I've been here a long time, and I've never seen Rafael get all riled up like he does with you. He was pissy with his last partner, but they were more like an old married couple that never should have stayed married that long. George, that was his name, was a pretty shit cop. Lazy as hell. Terrible with a victim and even worse with a perp. And thought he knew everything, even when it got people hurt. From what I've seen, you're doing a decent job. What's the deal, do you think?"

Jonah didn't want to bring up that horrible night in Orlando. Ever. Especially not on a date. "He thinks I'm too inexperienced. Loud. Talkative. Too eager. I look like I 'learned how to be a cop from watching TV.' I could keep going."

A.J. shook his head. "And even putting those all together is less offensive than anything George ever did, and those two were partners for a decade. No, there's something else. You certainly know how to push his buttons, don't you? Maybe he's just jealous of your good looks."

"Doubtful, but thanks. Everyone here is like a movie star with perfect hair and perfect tans and perfect clothes, and meanwhile I blend in with the sand when I go to the beach. Orlando is not glamorous or sexy."

Jonah had never gotten out to the beach much before he moved to Miami, maybe only heading over to Cocoa Beach a few times with friends, so he had never had occasion to curse his parents and every generation back for only procreating with northern Europeans to ensure he would never tan. The moment he took off his shirt to reveal pasty white skin in a sea of glowing gorgeous bodies on an ill-advised morning on South Beach when he first moved in, he knew his days of not going to the beach were just hitting their stride.

"Well, not since you left." A.J's brown eyes were sparkling.

Ah, hell, who needed the sun anyway. He smiled shyly at A.J. and took a huge bite of his sandwich.

They ended up kissing again in A.J.'s car after they walked back to the station together. It was more organic this time, now that they knew each other a little better. It wasn't the mind-blowing fairy tale kissing he'd been secretly hoping for, but there were so many changes and so many new parts to his life—and, yeah, he was still a little wary after Chris—he didn't dwell too much on that as A.J. kissed that really nice spot under his ear.

"Mmmm… could do this all night." A.J.'s breath was warm on his skin, and it was making Jonah feel like just kissing all night wouldn't be enough. It was late, and Jonah was wavering between needing to go to sleep and needing to see how far A.J. was going to take things. All of him knew he was sexually frustrated and should probably just go home and take care of things himself before he really messed things up with

A.J. He seemed like a really nice guy and a guy who liked to take things slowly. Maybe after Chris that was what he needed for a bit.

Besides, first real date was too early to start *the talk* when it obviously wasn't a possibility yet, so Jonah resigned himself to getting worked up with A.J., then going home to jerk off later. It really was the only solution.

He found a small hickey on his neck as he was undressing that night, and he really felt like a teenager again, being so keyed up and now marked from making out in a car. He shook his head and smiled because what else could he do? It was actually kind of cute if he stopped to think about it.

That is, until Rafael saw it peeking out from his shirt collar the next day. Jonah got the impression that it was either unprofessional or childish or both, judging from Rafael's reaction.

"Who hurt you, Rafael? Who stole your fun from you?" Jonah smiled sympathetically. That was definitely childish and unprofessional, but Rafael had already put that out into the world.

Rafael's face grew darker, and he stuck Jonah with the bulk of the day's paperwork. It was almost worth it. He still wasn't sure why Rafael felt Jonah had to run his social life by him, and he wasn't entirely sure why he made an effort to show off the hickey by wearing a low-collared shirt. He also wasn't quite sure why he was a little giddy at Rafael's reaction.

# Chapter 10

HE PLANNED a second date with A.J. by the end of the week. They ended up on South Beach, but at sunset so Jonah didn't feel so self-conscious and also so he didn't have to embarrass himself with multiple, generous applications of sunscreen. The water was still a bit chilly and the winter jellyfish and Portuguese Man O' War migrations floated along the coastline, but they managed to find a nice warm spot in the sand and watched the moon rise out of the ocean as the cruise ships sailed by.

"How did you know I needed to just relax like this?" Jonah could have fallen asleep right there if it weren't for the garish neon lights and cacophony coming from the bars, restaurants, and clubs behind them. They both knew they would have to head up to at least Palm Beach, two counties away, to find a decent beach that wasn't reserved for the ultrarich or their nightlife. "I figured you would want to go to a club or some wild place Garcia swears has the best house music or margaritas or something. How does she do that?"

A.J. laughed. "Garcia missed her calling as a social director for a cruise ship or something. Maybe a travel agent. She's got the hookups all over the city. She knows literally everyone, and even if she's taken someone away in handcuffs, she can still manage free drinks at their place for life. But that's beside the point. You looked a little tense earlier. Not the best state of mind for bright lights and lots of noise. You don't strike me as that kind of guy anyway, even if the mood is right."

Well, he wasn't wrong. Jonah hated the club scene. And also, he *had* been tense. For lots of reasons that may or may not have rhymed with "Bafael," that he wasn't ready to admit to himself, much less a guy who seemed to want nothing more than to have a good time with him. "Yeah… thanks. For this. I didn't know how much I needed to just sit and do nothing for a while, and this is the perfect place for it."

"Not for nothing, but you know, I do know a bit about nature and our connection to it. Kind of part of who I am and all." A.J. grinned in the blue, pink, green, and yellow tinged semidarkness and leaned over to kiss Jonah.

Stretched out on makeshift recliners made of wet sand molded into shape and an old blanket A.J. kept in his trunk, it was easier to get closer when they kissed and, under cover of darkness, Jonah felt comfortable getting a bit handsy, testing A.J.'s reaction to him without worrying *too* much about a public indecency charge. He ran his hands across A.J.'s back, feeling smooth, warm skin under his loose shirt and up to the back of his head, tangling his fingers in his, frankly glorious, hair. A.J. let out a little noise that made Jonah feel just a bit dirty, and A.J. kissed him a little harder while he let his own hands roam.

They kissed for a long time, pausing only for breath and the opportunity to kiss farther down each other's bodies. Jonah unbuttoned a few of A.J.'s buttons to get access to his chest, and A.J. signaled his approval by whimpering slightly when Jonah's lips slid across his collarbone and down his rib cage.

This was definitely what he had needed after everything that had happened in the last few months. He had uprooted his whole life because of a breakup, been partnered with a man who hated him, was far from perfect at his new job, and heard about every little mistake he made. He knew he was really too green and soft to even do his job correctly, but for the time being, he was in the arms of a gorgeous man who seemed to want nothing more than to put his lips all over him and make him feel good.

A.J.'s hand roamed farther and farther south until it rested gingerly on the waistband of his jeans. It was probably not the best idea to start something they definitely could not finish there on the beach. It was probably also not a good idea to take A.J.'s hand and push it just a little farther down, but all of a sudden it was the best idea when A.J. palmed his erection and Jonah couldn't stop the groan that escaped his lips.

A.J.'s nimble fingers slid downward a little more before pushing in and sliding back up to the tip. Jonah let his head fall back and enjoy the sensation and yeah, this was definitely what he needed. Jonah maneuvered his own arm between them to touch A.J.'s cock through his loose fitting pants, but A.J. stopped him and pulled his own hand away from Jonah.

The beach was mostly empty by that point, and the few who remained were preoccupied with their own late-night-beach activities. A.J. sat up and straddled Jonah's lower half. A.J. stretched out on top of him until they lined up perfectly so they could kiss and grind on each other. The heat and friction felt nice as Jonah thrust up against A.J., his dick twitching at the very real possibility of getting off in a public place.

He wondered just how cold the ocean was if he needed to destroy any evidence were he to come in his jeans, but before he could lose his erection by thinking of going waist deep in the freezing cold Atlantic, another boner-killing distraction beat him to it.

Jonah's phone began blaring with the loudest, most startling ringtone his phone had. It was the one he reserved for numbers associated with the station. And calling after hours could mean only one thing.

He didn't want to break the spell with A.J., but he had to answer the call. "H-hello?"

"Landers, you sound like you're running a marathon. And I saw your physical performance scores, so I know that's not possible. Where are you?" Rafael. Of course.

"Good to talk to you too, *partner*." Jonah had taken to calling him partner with implied emphasis for as long as it would take Rafael to call him partner back and mean it. He chose to ignore the immature dig on his physical performance since A.J. didn't seem to have any complaints about it. "How can I help you?"

"Double homicide. Where are you?" repeated Rafael, this time sounding a little more annoyed.

"South Beach. I'll leave now." A.J. was still on top of Jonah, and he gave a sour look that Jonah could just barely make out in the dark. He rolled off nonetheless.

"Shit. It's going to take you forever to get off the island. Meet me there. I'll text you the address." Rafael ended the call before Jonah had the chance to respond.

A.J. had stood to brush the sand from his clothes, and he reached down to help Jonah up. "Duty calls?"

Jonah sighed because he didn't want it to end, but he *really* wanted to work a double homicide. Or even a single homicide. Any homicide, really. "Duty calls. Can we pick this up later?"

A.J. pulled him in for a kiss and squeezed his ass. "You bet. Come on, I'll walk you to your car."

The beach may have been abandoned, but South Beach was jam-packed, and it took him twice as long to get back to Miami than it had getting out there, but at least it gave him extra time to compose himself after getting so worked up with A.J. Once across the bridge he programmed the address into his GPS and saw it was in the neighborhood of Flagami, the farthest away it could be while remaining in their jurisdiction. It was going to take him another hour in traffic to get there. Rafael was going to kill him, even though there was no reason for Jonah to stick close on his day off.

# Chapter 11

THE SCENE was gruesome when he finally came upon it. Dozens of police cars surrounded the area, a low-income suburb filled with duplex apartments badly in need of repairs and cosmetic fixes. The flashing lights momentarily blinded him as he crossed under the police line, pushing his way through a throng of reporters for the local news. The investigation was in full swing, and Jonah found Rafael in the apartment next to where the neighbors had found the bodies, interviewing the little old lady who lived in the next apartment about what she had heard, if anything. Jonah tried to slip in unnoticed, but Rafael caught his eye and shot him a dirty look, never missing a beat with the witness.

Jonah waited patiently for Rafael to finish before asking about the details of the case and what he could do. Jonah hated going in blind more than anything. He felt useless and pointless. He watched Rafael coax answers out of the neighbor, who seemed a little reluctant to give up information out of something that felt, to Jonah, a lot like fear. Rafael picked up on it too, promising full police protection if she talked and was maybe willing to look at a lineup later on. Jonah gleaned a little bit of information from Rafael's questions and her answers, and it became clear the main suspect was a jealous, jilted lover of some sort.

"What took you so long?" The interview was over, and Rafael had turned off the charm. Or turned on the mean. Jonah still wasn't sure which one it was.

"Sorry! Traffic. I'm here now. What can I do?" Why was Rafael trying to make him feel dumb for not being five minutes away like Rafael obviously was? It was his day off.

Rafael explained the case and who the victims were. Carissa Spencer, female, twenty-six, part-time college student and manicurist. Lived in Pembroke Pines, north of Miami. Roberto Gutiérrez, male, thirty-three, fitness instructor. Lived in the apartment. Female was engaged but not to the other victim. They were having an affair and the theory was that the fiancé, Michael, also, presumably, of Pembroke Pines, last name unknown, age unknown, occupation unknown, current location unknown, found out, stormed down to Miami to catch them in the act, and murdered both of them in the heat of passion. Pretty typical, but also pretty sad.

"The girl's best friend just got here. Find out what she knew about our vics' relationship. If she knew at all. Find out about her family and where they are."

The best friend, April, was crying hysterically and demanding to see the body just to be sure it was her. She was young. Too young to be losing a longtime best friend, and Jonah channeled Rafael as best he could to calm her down and get her talking. He was still surprised when the technique worked, and she started spilling on the affair and how evil the vic's fiancé was. There was abuse, physical and mental, maybe sexual, but Carissa had begged everyone to leave it alone. Roberto was, by all accounts, a decent guy, and Carissa had secretly talked of leaving Michael—April helpfully supplied Jonah with his last name, Howison—when it was safe for her to do so. Carissa and Roberto met once a week or so, and Carissa claimed she was in class or out with friends to explain her absences. Michael apparently had grown suspicious. And April revealed, Michael spent a lot of time at a particular adult entertainment club in Fort Lauderdale, right up US 1, and if he was playing dumb about the whole thing to avoid suspicion on himself, they would probably find him there.

Jonah took copious notes and thanked her for her statement, telling her that they weren't going to quit until they found who did this and arrest him. It was what Rafael would say. He encouraged her to go home and get some rest because there really was nothing she could do there at the scene. He handed her his card, told her to call if she remembered anything else that might be important, and walked her to her car to ensure that she left.

He rejoined Rafael, who was finishing up the tragic, unwanted task of talking to Roberto's parents, who had arrived while Jonah was taking April's statement. They were in their midseventies and beside themselves with grief. It was heartbreaking to watch, and even though Rafael was talking to them in Spanish, it didn't take fluency to understand the conversation.

Rafael sent uniforms to get them home safely before they had to move Roberto's body. No parent needed to see that. Jonah gingerly engaged Rafael about the possible whereabouts of the fiancé, Michael, and Rafael took a moment to dig the palm of his hand into his forehead, squeezing his eyes shut before speaking.

"Never gets any easier, kid. Never. And if it does, you're in the wrong line of work. If you take away nothing else I'm trying to teach you, take that. It should be as difficult to tell a parent their child is dead the hundredth time you have to do it as it was the first time. Keep in your mind always the looks on their faces, the cries of grief, the pain as the mothers claw at you, hit you because they can't process properly that you just told them their child has been murdered."

Jonah locked eyes with Rafael and saw a sadness on his face that was a stark departure from anything he had seen from him so far. "Got it, Rafael." And he meant it too.

Rafael nodded. "Good. Good. I'll send some uniforms to check out this club and let's see if we can't get this guy in interrogation to make him sing before dawn."

# Chapter 12

THREE HOURS later Michael Howison burst into the station a blubbering, slobby mess, yelling at everyone and everything, and making a melodramatic case for not having previously known about the condition of his fiancée. He was escorted by the officers who had driven north to find him, and apparently his tirade had started the moment they found him getting a lap dance, which they had interrupted to give him the bad news.

Forensics hadn't returned any results on prints or DNA yet, so they had to hope for a confession if they wanted him behind bars that night. Rafael ordered him into an interrogation room and put Michael on ice, placating him with sodas and snacks (future trash ripe for the taking once his fingerprints were on them) for a while until he calmed himself down enough to talk.

Rafael requested to interrogate Michael alone. Jonah thought there was no way Luis would go for that, but she had happily obliged like it wasn't an unusual request, and Jonah wondered why he needed to stick around at all. Soon after, though, Rafael asked him to wait in the observation room on the other side of the interrogation room and watch. Jonah begrudgingly did as he was told but only because he'd stashed a bag of chips in there a week before, taped to the underside of a file drawer in an empty cabinet where no one would find it, and he was starving.

Of course Michael denied everything and claimed he was at the club all night, but with a wide window of opportunity and a short drive to and from Fort Lauderdale, Rafael was relentless in trying to get that confession from Michael. He put on a great show when Rafael asked him about Carissa's affair, claiming he knew nothing of it and bursting into tears. Jonah was starting to believe the guy, but Rafael never let up, and if Jonah had learned one thing in his short time in Miami, it was to trust Rafael's gut.

Jonah sat on the other side of the two-way mirror and watched Rafael work his magic on the guy. After a few minutes, Jonah realized why he was watching and not doing. Rafael was working this guy over, and it was intimate and private and fascinating to observe but not something anyone else should have been a part of. Jonah hoped to be able to be on that level someday. He found himself speechless at the way Rafael twisted and turned his words until Michael was so confused he didn't know what he was saying anymore. Rafael was a regular silver-tongued devil, using his words like a trickster to get Michael to talk. Jonah could have watched it all day. Michael hadn't even realized he was a suspect yet thanks to Rafael, and as such, he hadn't lawyered up. Rafael morphed from sympathetic friend, to angry cop upset there were no witnesses, and then to guilt-stricken over not having more information on Carissa's killer. Watching him almost explained the dizzying back and forth between Rafael hating Jonah and praising him, and it just made Jonah more confused as to who the real Rafael was. If he were an actor, he'd win all the awards.

Garcia and Luis joined Jonah with Chinese takeout in their hands like Rafael was both the evening's entertainment and also not as big a deal as Jonah felt he was. He almost wanted to defend Rafael or be offended in his place, but he pushed that feeling deep down as Garcia tossed him a fortune cookie and he cracked it open, thankful for the small amount of sugar to help keep him awake.

*Someone from your past will be a big part of your future.*

He'd have taken more stock in the fortune if all six of the lucky lottery numbers weren't twenty-three and the Chinese phrase to learn wasn't "dung beetle." He absentmindedly crammed the strip of paper into his wallet, where it fell into a deep recess in the sadly empty spot where cash should have been.

Jonah popped both halves of the cookie in his mouth and went back to watching Rafael in his element. Garcia leaned over and nudged him with her elbow. "You ever watched the master at work?"

Jonah didn't look away from the scene on the other side. "No," he breathed.

"Great, isn't it? He only brings this out when we really need it. It's a risky move, what he's doing, but it absolutely works on these drama queen suspects. They crave the attention and Rafael turns on the charm and, boom, confession time. I don't know if it's pheromones or those good looks or hypnotism or what, but when he turns it on, he turns it *on*. Oh, wait, I think this is it! I've got $20 on a confession before 3 a.m." Garcia grabbed Jonah's arm in anticipation.

Michael looked uncomfortable in his chair as Rafael had been pacing back and forth, mumbling and occasionally stopping to talk loudly near Michael's ear. Michael had looked close to breaking for nearly ten minutes, but something must have given in him enough for Garcia to take notice and shush everyone.

"Oh my *God*! She was cheating on me with some *yoga instructor*. What the hell would you do, huh? Just let her get away with that?"

Garcia passed an egg roll to Jonah without taking her eyes off the proceedings. "Here we go, *papi*."

Rafael kneeled down by Michael's side, a look of sympathy and innocence washing over his face. "Of course you had to take care of it. How could she do that to you?"

Michael's head fell to the surface of the cold metal table with a bang. "I didn't mean to kill her, man. I just wanted to scare her. And he got in the way. I couldn't let her go after that. Going to the cops? She'd ruin everything for us if she told."

Jonah's eyes went wide, the cold egg roll in his hand forgotten. He couldn't believe it. Just like that, Rafael had a confession. No lawyer. No drawn-out case. No forensics. Just Rafael talking a confession out of him. It was the most amazing thing he'd ever seen. Garcia fist pumped the air, and Luis sighed in relief. Jonah could only sit in awe and try not to look like he was a starstruck teenager meeting her favorite boy band.

Even in the horrid fluorescent lighting, Jonah could see the flush that colored Rafael's cheeks as he turned to the mirror and gave a smug thumbs-up before he reached in and grabbed his cuffs to formally arrest Michael.

Jonah wouldn't say he went home and jerked off while he replayed that scene in his head later on, but only because he was too busy jerking off while he replayed that scene in his head to waste energy on talking.

# Chapter 13

JONAH ONLY contemplated whether or not that whole thing should have been hot briefly in the shower the next day, but thinking about it just made him incredibly hard, and he stopped worrying about it so he could jerk off again. For the record, the record he kept for making quick excuses for things he didn't want to think about, it was getting cut short with *A.J.* on the beach that had made him so horny for everything he saw. Because Rafael Santos doing his job and arresting a murderer wasn't hot.

Not at all.

Not a little bit.

Well, maybe a little bit.

Damn it.

A.J. called later that afternoon to slyly ask when they could try their date again without interruption, and Jonah was so spent he couldn't imagine it being physically possible to get another erection that day. He still wasn't ready to admit a problem, though. At least not a Rafael-shaped one.

Jonah did meet up with A.J. the next evening, when Jonah had had enough of not thinking about things. A.J. wanted to show him around some parts of Miami-Dade that weren't the beach or on Garcia's never-ending list of great places. They ended up at the Coral Castle, a tourist attraction that served as sort of a Stonehenge for South Florida and was, Jonah had to admit, pretty cool considering how much his time in Orlando had dulled him toward tourist attractions. He and Chris had done them all over the span of a month just for fun one rainy summer. Observation towers, pirate-themed dinner shows, and a whole museum dedicated to US presidents that was hokey but secretly awesome… they had done them all. The Coral Castle was hauntingly beautiful, with massive coral stone carvings strewn about the grounds.

A.J. delighted in telling the tragic, romantic, and mysterious history of the castle and how no one knew how one man moved all the coral stones to build it. A.J. told the tale of the architect's broken heart and how he built the castle as tribute to his lost love, who left him right before their wedding. He was a great storyteller, and Jonah temporarily forgot about everything that wasn't actually bothering him, because *nothing* was bothering him. Damn it.

Jonah tried very hard to make sure he was thinking of A.J. when they kissed that night. And again on the next date to Vizcaya, where they strolled the garden grounds of the beautiful former-estate-turned-museum that, despite looking like an old Italian villa, seemed right at home in Miami. And the one after that, to the zoo, where it poured for three quarters of the day and they only managed to see a flamingo and an iguana running loose on the grounds before they were unceremoniously kicked out due to extreme lightning in the area. But on the next one, a lazy day at Everglades National Park, where they watched in utter fascination and terror as a large snake devoured a small gator, Rafael didn't cross his mind. Jonah could finally admit he'd had a little brain hiccup but was back on track—especially since things had started to even out with Rafael, or at least he'd learned what pushed Rafael's buttons and did so only when he knew he could duck fast enough. Work in general was going well, and he'd settled nicely into an almost predictable and comfortable routine.

# Chapter 14

THE RAINY season had begun in Florida, and no matter how violently the wind shook, how loudly the thunder clapped, or how much extra time he had to spend at the station after his shift was over because the roads were flooded, the fallen palm fronds blocked the surface streets, the electricity was out, and there were no working traffic lights for miles, Jonah always loved this time of year. The storms never lasted long, and they were a reminder that nothing that terrible lasted forever. Jonah could have just about set his watch by the first thunderclap, always around 3:00 p.m., and as much as he loved how the storms cooled everything off, if even for a few minutes until the sun came out and left everything a tropical humid mess, he was still damned glad he wasn't a traffic cop anymore, having to direct traffic around the obstacles the storm caused.

It was pouring longer and harder than usual on what had started as an increasingly normal day for Jonah. The unusual rain was something the weather people on TV always chalked up to a "tropical wave," which was somewhere between summer storm and something more to worry about, like a hurricane.

But a hurricane *was* about to hit the police station. A nasty, destructive beast of a hurricane named Tamatoa Teiki.

As much as Orlando had been full of people paid to dress up and play characters, Miami was full of *real* characters. And they made a lot more than a dollar above minimum wage. It wasn't unusual for Jonah to walk into the station some days having to dodge fully costumed flamenco dancers arrested at the Calle Ocho Festival, the annual street event in Little Havana (it was the first time he had seen Rafael in casual clothes; Rafael had been a reluctant witness to the epic fight between two of the dancers and was not happy to have been pulled from away from the festival on his day off), or an entire ballet dance troupe made up of middle-aged drag queens (apparently a semiannual occurrence, so much so that they received a standing ovation from everyone with a view of the holding cells as they danced a scene from *Swan Lake* to pass the time). And there was that one time an assault backstage at the benefit concert for kids with ADHD in lower income areas around Miami-Dade starring various acts from the 1980s, appropriately—or, inappropriately, some said—called '80s-HD, sent a dazzling array of New Wave, Pop, and Synth acts from Jonah's childhood to the station to give reports until it looked like MTV in 1986 had exploded all over it.

It had been hard enough to contain his feelings on being around so many celebrities—even if they *were* has-beens—but once the first '80s quip slipped out (upon discovering the vic had been pushed down a flight of stairs, Jonah blurted out, "But did he fall *head over heels* down them?"), it was difficult to stop them from coming (Did anyone hear him *shout*? Is the perp *wanted dead or alive?).* He'd faced quite the verbal beatdown from Rafael after that, even if it was Jonah who had eventually put everything together, figured out who the perp was—a jealous groupie, naturally (some stereotypes died hard, even after thirty years)—and then gotten the entire station free tickets to the show. Edgewood politely declined for family reasons, Garcia went because it was a party even though her '90s Miami upbringing afforded her an appreciation of mostly songs with "whoop," "whump" and "tootsie roll" in the lyrics, and A.J. wore an old Bauhaus shirt and The Smiths pins, but it was Rafael whom Jonah caught singing along to all the songs with the tiniest hint of a smile on his face.

The next afternoon Jonah had gotten back from some follow-ups with Garcia to find a steaming hot takeout container on his desk filled with *tamal con lechon,* a shredded pork tamale with onions and extra lime, and a minty and tart *limonada* just like he liked it from the Cuban food truck that parked around the corner. Jonah wasn't going to come right out and say it was Rafael in some sort of uncharacteristic display of thanks, but there had been an identical container in Rafael's trash can later that day. He knew acknowledging it would mess things up somehow, but he had made a point to be on his best behavior for a few days after that.

Ballet-dancing drag queens and '80s pop stars, however, had nothing on the 400-pound be-suited Samoan man who was sitting in one of the interview rooms when the entire squad was called in early from lunch that rainy day in June.

Owner of a Polynesian airline that netted almost a billion in the last year, reality TV show star, and heir to some serious South Pacific vacation resorts known for harboring A-list celebrities and their myriad scandals the gossip columns loved to go on and on about, Tamatoa Teiki was a billionaire and, if owning several rare tropical birds worth up to twenty thousand dollars each was any indication, spent his money like one.

His whole collection, one which he never traveled without, had gone missing, along with some jewelry and other random assorted items that only the supremely rich seemed to think they always needed to travel with. This was not only a Big Deal to Tamatoa Teiki (Jonah could hear the capital letters when Mr. Teiki explained just how much of a Big Deal it was in dollars), it was also a Big Deal for the city of Miami.

The total worth hovered around three quarters of a million dollars, and Teiki's first phone call had been to his lawyer to discuss his options on suing everyone in the hotel from the valet on up. He hinted strongly that he wouldn't stop there if his possessions weren't recovered in a reasonable amount of time. Miami's airport was also a major hub for the airline and brought a lot of people and money into South Florida. Teiki further hinted that if he didn't feel safe there, he couldn't possibly tell his customers otherwise. There was a deal in place with the city that kept the airport as a major hub for the airline through the next five years. The rumors were that the airport and the city were making bank from the deal, but Teiki, under pressure from his board, had signed off on the deal even though he was never happy with it or Miami in the first place. An unsolved crime against him in the city was not going to sway his opinion favorably.

Luis, probably under similar pressure from the city, did not hesitate putting the entire squad on the case with a strong suggestion to get a running start before the press caught wind of anything.

Rafael, especially, was terrible at hiding his utter disdain for Teiki's entitled attitude and the city's willingness to roll over and demand the station drop everything for him. It wasn't the first time a well-connected person had had the city on its knees like that, according to Edgewood as he angrily texted his wife to cancel their anniversary dinner. Jonah had seen it happen in Orlando too, with celebrities who demanded special treatment, but never to this degree.

Rafael slammed a cup of coffee back and shoved a pastry in the empty cup as he threw on his jacket. "I'm a highly decorated detective in the eighth largest metropolitan area in the entire country, and I'm looking for fucking birds. My parents did not risk their lives to come to this country so I could chase after birds. My *abuela* did not sacrifice everything she worked so hard for in Cuba to come to the country with them to help raise my brothers and me while they worked long hours at the restaurant for me to be chasing after fucking *birds*."

What followed was a long string of Spanish that sounded vulgar and insulting, judging by the tone. Jonah was slowly learning the dialect, and could make out a few words here and there, but Rafael was swearing at light speed as he stomped to the car. Jonah didn't realize until later that Rafael had let loose the first bit of personal history he'd ever heard directly from him. Suddenly the foodie thing made sense if his parents ran a restaurant. And the hard work ethic if his parents had escaped Cuba for a better life. Jonah could only imagine the high expectations of a first-generation Cuban after what their parents must have gone through. He didn't know how to use the information for his own benefit right then, but he stored it in his mental file on Rafael.

# Chapter 15

THE VISTA De Los Trópicos Hotel, a beachfront resort hotel on A1A that charged more for one day of parking a car than an entire month of Jonah's rent, earned every one of its five stars before the guests even got to their suites. Nestled in lush tropical landscaping that obscured it from view of the common folks and guarded by gilded gates and well-paid security guards, it was not a hotel for vacationing families from Minnesota looking for some fun outside the theme parks. It was serious luxury that was apparent from the moment the large, eight-level fountain adorned with an intricately carved statue of a woman atop it came into view as Rafael and Jonah drove up the main road to the entrance.

"Grand" didn't even begin to describe the place. "Opulent" didn't come close. However, "swarming with cops and reporters" was a good start, and security was having a hard time keeping them at bay. So much for the low profile until they got a handle on the situation. Garcia had grumbled that Teiki's people had probably called TMZ to get the ball rolling and put more of a squeeze on the city to get things done faster.

The security was tight, probably even tighter than before the incident thanks to curious onlookers and nosy reporters itching for an angle. It was clear the hotel security team was not allowing media inside the hotel itself, but getting past the mob of bottom-feeding paparazzi proved to be a difficult task. Rafael didn't have height to his advantage, but anger was on his side as he pushed past the cameras with Jonah, Garcia, and Edgewood following.

Jonah allowed himself one brief moment to admire the view once he was inside. Orlando had its fair share of hotels he'd investigated a lot of crimes in and around, and some of them were really nice, but the Vista had an entrance fountain that was larger than his entire apartment, with water falling into smaller pools that emptied into rock-lined channels that traveled around the entire lobby. There was tropical foliage, and a soft but persistent scent of tropical flowers flowing through the room. Jonah knew he would never be able to afford even one night on a detective's salary.

"Admire later, Landers. Let's get this over with." Rafael tugged on Jonah's sleeve and pulled him forward a few inches, knocking Jonah off balance slightly. Jonah only mostly obeyed the order as he caught up to the squad.

The next four hours were a flurry of interviews, security footage, and taking statements, most of which were completely useless but at least the shaggy carpet was soft under their feet, almost as if it were backed by a layer of that expensive memory foam Jonah swore he was going to buy someday for his own bed. It almost made standing around that long bearable, and suddenly he never wanted to stay in a Holiday Inn ever again.

Jonah watched the tension grow in Rafael as time dragged on, saw how his shoulders got tight and drew up into his neck before his entire upper back started to hunch over a little. The process was taking its toll on the entire squad, but Jonah could only seem to focus on its effect on Rafael.

Jonah actually felt sorry for the guy, and it seemed like maybe he was losing his mind when the sudden thought of helping Rafael ease the tension with a shoulder massage floated around his obviously very tired brain. Jonah wondered if Rafael would be a moaner as the stress left his body under Jonah's large, strong hands, but that line of thinking had to stop before thoughts of using his hands on Rafael got, well, out of hand. Jonah had been doing so well lately.

*This is a "Dirty Thoughts about Rafael Santos" free zone. It has been twenty-three—no, make that zero days since the last incident.*

There was a small headquarters set up in a Polynesian-themed conference room, and all four detectives collectively decided on a 7:00 p.m. dinner break to go over what they had gotten so far. The room was scented with the same pervasive tropical flower scent as the lobby, the dark wood walls were hand-carved tiki patterns with bamboo accents, and it had a view of the poolside cabanas that were not only bigger than his apartment, but also cost upward of a grand to rent for just the day— and that was on top of renting a suite to sleep in once the cabana rental time was over. Jonah felt like he was in the lair of a 1960s Hawaiian-themed action movie's villain. It was difficult for him not to point out how cool that was.

Over what no one could deny was amazing food from the hotel's kitchen, they came to the grim conclusion that they didn't have much to go on thanks to unreliable, unobservant staff trained to mind their own business, especially with guests who rent out the entire top floor, and Teiki's own security, who seemed more scared of Teiki and saving their jobs than of lying to a cop.

A.J. joined them about twenty minutes later, and he looked as frustrated as the rest of them.

He pulled out a chair next to Jonah and grabbed an assortment of vaguely Polynesian appetizers, rolling his dark eyes into the back of his head in pleasure at the first bite. "I'd heard rumors, but I never believed. This is better than all the reviews I've ever read of their food. I could die right here, and I would have no regrets." He looked pointedly at Jonah and wiggled his eyebrows suggestively. "Or maybe just one or two."

Before Jonah could process that A.J. had maybe possibly just put sex on the table, Edgewood interrupted his thoughts.

"Got anything?" He really wanted to go home to his wife, and he had no qualms letting everyone know it. It was a big anniversary, and he had apparently missed the last big one and the birth of their first child as well. And his wife's grandmother's funeral. Maybe a few birthdays too....

"Not a damned thing. It's almost like they don't even want to find the guys who did it." A.J. shook his head while a bit of pineapple juice ran down his chin, and Jonah had a fleeting thought of licking it away. All of a sudden it was very confusing to have A.J. and Rafael in the same room.

Between bites, A.J. gave his account of the day up until then, and it was no better than anyone else's. The security footage was as unreliable and untrustworthy as everyone they had interviewed, which meant someone had either gotten to everything and everyone before the police had gotten there, or they had stumbled into the largest web of incompetence anyone had ever seen.

Rafael looked even more tense and agitated now that A.J. had joined them, and Jonah still could not understand why Rafael was so against Jonah trying to find a little bit of happiness. Was Rafael so jaded he wanted everyone to be as lonely as he was? Or just Jonah? He did his best to ignore the daggers shooting out Rafael's eyes and started sketching out a rough timeline based on the small bit of wholly inaccurate information they had to work with. It wasn't going to accomplish much, but it at least distracted Rafael from whatever was up his ass.

Around 11:00 p.m. they all mutually decided there was no more they could do that day. Forensics had quite a job to do, and uniforms could handle the rest of the sweep of the hotel until they all got a proper night's sleep.

Edgewood had bolted around 8:00 p.m. when the rest of the squad took pity on him and his wife waiting at home, furious that they had lost the reservations Garcia had gotten them at the last minute that morning, thinking they wouldn't go too late. Garcia, never a big complainer, whined that her kids were calling the babysitter "Mom" now. Workaholic Rafael looked like he hadn't slept in days and just wanted to pass out on the nearest surface instead of continuing to work. It was probably the worst time for a new and demanding case to pop up.

# Chapter 16

THERE WERE still throngs of reporters hanging around the front doors, and they were hungry for a statement of any kind since Teiki wasn't talking unless it was to insult the hotel, the police department, or Miami itself, and even then it was through his personal spokesperson.

And it was then that the case took a turn for the worse. And, as usual, Jonah seemed to be at the center of it. In hindsight, always in hindsight with Jonah, he didn't mean to say it. The words just tumbled out like they always did, but this time it wasn't making childish '80s music jokes or taunting Rafael. With all the camera flashes and reporters screaming at them as they walked out, Jonah was disoriented and a little dizzy from the chaos. Rafael pushed through the crowd with an assertive "No comment. No comment at this time. The investigation is ongoing" and Garcia, A.J., and Jonah following closely, under strict orders to keep their heads low and as covered as possible, drafting in Rafael's annoyance at the reporters to make it through.

The reporters and bloggers were yelling out questions and trying to goad any of them into throwing out a bone. Jonah suddenly felt way too claustrophobic and needed to get out of there. He instinctively reached for Rafael's jacket like it was a lifeline to freedom. He hadn't meant to, but the lights were too bright and the people were too loud and he was too tired to process the cacophony. The paparazzi were new to Jonah, even if he knew he would have to face them someday coming to Miami.

Rafael turned around, looking somehow even more annoyed, but his face quickly changed when he locked eyes with Jonah. The anger and annoyance turned to something more determined and almost protective, and Rafael didn't push Jonah's hand off his jacket or walk faster to avoid him like Jonah was prepared for.

Rafael led Jonah a safe distance away from the mob, behind a patch of banana trees, before giving him the once-over. Jonah fully expected some sort of insult thrown his way. He'd probably deserve it. But Rafael still had the weirdly concerned look on his face. "You okay?"

"What? Yeah. Fine. Just—" *Not embarrassing at all. Let's have an anxiety attack in front of every major news outlet and your partner and see what that will do for your career.*

"First time in one of those?" Rafael was still eyeing him like Jonah was going to pass out or something. It was strangely comforting. "Don't worry. They take a little getting used to. Just don't give them anything to go on and assume they are everywhere with all this going on. You'll be fine."

Jonah took a deep breath and cocked his head to the side. "You're not going to yell at me?"

Rafael's eyes went wide. "And make you feel worse than you do right now? I'm not a complete monster, kid. Besides, I saw the look in your eyes. Looked a lot like me the first time, I would imagine. It gets easier."

Jonah nodded and realized he felt a lot better than he had a minute before.

"Thanks." There was no sarcasm or hidden meaning. The word rolled off his tongue and it felt strange coming out, like finally having an intimate human moment with Rafael would suddenly change everything. It was a silly thought, of course. He and Rafael should have been this decent to each other from the start. They were *partners*.

Garcia and A.J. untangled themselves from the mess a little slower, and Jonah guessed he had some color back in his cheeks when they finally arrived because no one gave him a second look. He didn't want to have to explain himself again to the mother hen and his maybe sort of boyfriend, anyway.

"God, they're miserable bastards. All of them. I bet by this time tomorrow there will be a telethon for these birds sponsored by *TMZ*." Garcia seemed to have as much disdain for the paparazzi as Rafael did.

In hindsight Jonah should have waited until they were back in the safety of the station, where no nosy reporters were allowed, but his endorphins were going crazy inside in his body thanks to the exhaustion and chaos—and maybe just a little of Rafael showing a human side. "Yeah, I can see it now: Teiki-en Away. Or just Teiki-en with a bunch of bad Liam Neeson jokes. Or, oh wait, I've got it! Tahiti Tweety!"

Garcia giggled a bit but held up a hand to quiet Jonah. "The Tahiti Tweety Telethon. Better not say that too loud, or it's going to be the headline tomorrow. These vultures are ruthless that way."

Rafael shushed them all with a look and shooed them toward the valet entrance.

Jonah was expecting a quiet ride back to the station, but Rafael was still agitated and needed to cool off. Jonah had noticed a pattern to moods like this that ended with him unusually talkative. True to form, Rafael made an unexpected turn down a small street in Little Havana. For being so late at night, the street was still alive. The light from the storefronts and streetlights lit up the people hanging out in front of the bodegas and cafés, playing chess or eating a late-night snack. They all seemed relaxed and happy. Jonah had no idea why they were there, though.

Rafael pulled into a parallel parking spot and shifted into park. He was quiet for a long time before Jonah felt a little uncomfortable in the silence. He looked at Rafael, who was staring at a small clapboard-sided house shaded by a large ancient banyan tree and surrounded by overgrown vegetation, thanks to neglect.

Rafael sighed and turned to Jonah with a look that Jonah could only describe as serene intensity, and he knew that description didn't even make sense, but there was no other way of putting it.

"Raf—ummm… what are we—?"

"I was born here," Rafael said quietly. He pointed at the run-down house he'd been staring at. "Right there in that house. My older brothers were watching cartoons while my papa and *abuela* helped my mother bring me into this world. It was hard for people like my parents to get good medical care back then, so they figured it was just as good to have me at home where *Mamá* could be comfortable. She took a whole week off after I was born, and then she was right back in the restaurant my parents ran. *Abuela* would take care of us boys and bring me across the street… look, that place on the end." Rafael pointed to an immigration office at the near end of the strip. "That's where it was. She used to take me over there so *Mamá* could feed me, and then it was right back across the street so she could work. And as I got older I could share the leftover daily specials she brought home for dinner. It was heaven, growing up here, even though we never had money or a nice house. Teiki grew up with everything he ever wanted and look how miserable he is now, even sitting on a pile of cash so big he could never spend it all in his lifetime. See that mural there?"

The mural was a colorful, if slightly faded, depiction of a man and a woman at a large table, rolling out dough and filling it with what looked like shredded meat. There were smiles on their faces, and it was obvious they were in love.

"Yeah?" This was the longest string of words Rafael had ever said in his presence without insulting him, and Jonah did not want to break the spell.

"Those are my parents. Look how happy they are in it. My brother, my oldest brother, painted this when he was seventeen. It was a stupid hot summer, and we couldn't afford to go to camps or anything like that, so my brother painted this to pass the time. We, my other brother and I, wanted to help, so Papa bought us sidewalk chalk, and we sat in the shade of the building and tried to copy on the hot sidewalk what he was painting on the wall. It took him all summer. My parents loved it, and he ended up getting a full art scholarship to Ringling that year.

"I come back here sometimes when I need to think. I see my old house and my old neighborhood and my parents up there, and I remember what I came from and how far I've come since then, and it always helps. I knew I wanted to be a cop ever since I was little and sitting in this house watching the street from that window up there. That was my room. Well, it was the room I shared with my brothers. Miami was so much more dangerous back then, and there was a lot of crime through this neighborhood. Much more than we deal with now. I remember watching cops, ones that hung out at my parents' restaurant on their off-hours and looked like me, Cubans, and came from the kind of childhood I had, out there making a difference and helping to clean up Little Havana so we could even have the chance to make our chalk drawings out on the sidewalk without being scared."

Jonah nodded. He had no noble story to tell about his reasons for becoming a cop. His mother was a schoolteacher and his father was an accountant. He couldn't even blame something like a wayward brother who he had to bail out of a life of crime. David was head of IT for a huge nonprofit. Jonah just genuinely liked helping people.

He looked toward where the restaurant had been. "If you don't mind me asking, what happened to the restaurant? I mean…." He really wanted to ask where his parents were, but didn't want to be impolite.

Rafael smiled wistfully. "All good things have to end, Landers. They've moved on, my parents." Jonah was about to express sympathy, but Rafael wasn't finished. "They always loved the snowbirds who come down from the north for six months a year in the winter. Thought they were so funny with their salt-caked cars and whole winter wardrobes. So, when it was time for them to retire after some amazingly good years in the '90s and early 2000s, when Little Havana exploded, they decided to return the favor to the north and move to Connecticut for half the year and see what the big fuss was about. When it was time for them to come down for the winter, they decided they loved the area so much they were making it their permanent home. They're happy. They're living for themselves now and going on trips and getting everything they deserve. Coming here reminds me that hard work pays off, and that's why I'm such a hardass about my work, about being a good cop and my expectations for a partner."

Jonah didn't know what to say. He knew he *should* say something, because that was a weighty confession Rafael had just made, but the fact that he even made Jonah privy to any of that information was stunning him into silence.

Jonah thought hard for something to say that didn't make him sound like an idiot. "Wow. I mean... thank you, Rafael." Mission *not* accomplished.

Rafael stared at him blankly. "For what?"

"For...." Jonah waved his hand around wildly to indicate everything Rafael had pointed out. "For this. For letting me into this...." He didn't know how to finish it, and it didn't matter anyway, because he was blatantly staring at Rafael's mouth, and he couldn't stop. *You need to stop. Look at literally anything else. Maybe there's a type of palm tree over there you haven't seen yet. Why don't you turn your head and look for it?* Jonah looked up abruptly to find Rafael looking right at him.

Jonah blushed, thankful the lights weren't shining too brightly into the car, but Rafael noticed. Of course he noticed. Jonah tried to direct his attention to the mural. Maybe he could ask a question about it, distract both of them—Jonah from looking like an even bigger idiot and Rafael from noticing how much of an idiot Jonah was looking like. But Rafael didn't follow Jonah's attempt to change the subject.

He was looking at Jonah.

He was looking at Jonah's mouth.

Rafael was looking at Jonah's mouth.

Jonah froze. There was no air in the car left, even though the windows were down. He couldn't breathe. He didn't want to breathe, because one breath and it would all be over.

A million, jumbled thoughts ran through his mind and none of them made sense, but as they all started to converge into something that might be coherent, a car's horn jolted them both out of their weird trance, and just like that the moment had passed.

Rafael shifted the car out of park wordlessly and the rest of the ride back to the station was quiet. Somehow, in that ten minute detour, Jonah felt he had learned more about Miami than on any three dates with A.J. combined.

# Chapter 17

JONAH FELL into bed that night and forgot about the whole thing until he got in the next morning and a copy of the *Miami Times* was sitting on his desk with the headline "Tahiti Tweety: MDPD Is For The Birds" in two inch letters on the front page. Accompanying it were photos of Teiki's airplanes, the missing birds, and the Miami-Dade Police Department looking as clueless as possible, and a very critical story filled with quotes from Teiki, Teiki's lawyer, Teiki's celebrity friends, and Teiki's reality show producers. Jonah wondered just how much Teiki's people had paid to get that story run.

Jonah had wondered why Rafael had moved through the crowd of cameras with his head down and his jacket pulled high around his face and insisted the others do the same. At the time he'd assumed it was for the same reason Jonah couldn't bear to lift his own even if Rafael hadn't told him to keep it down—the lights flashing in his eyes every second. Looking at the photos then, he realized it was to obscure his face so no one got a decent photo of it.

Jonah threw himself down in his chair and slumped as low as he possibly could. Maybe if he just scooted down a bit more, he could disappear forever, and Rafael would never—

"I hope you're proud of yourself, Detective." Rafael rounded Jonah's desk and threw a copy of neighboring Fort Lauderdale's morning edition with a similarly mocking headline down on top of Miami's. "You had to say it out loud, didn't you?" Two steps forward, three thousand steps back. Just like that.

"Rafael, I'm sorry! What, were they hiding in the bushes?" So much for that moment of humanity.

"Didn't I tell you to assume they were everywhere? Hiding in the bushes would be the very definition of everywhere! You do realize that this is going to move our already short timeline up considerably if we want to salvage anything, including our reputations? TMZ has already picked it up, and we're being mocked around the world because we can't find some damned birds. Do you think the mayor is going to stand for this? Someday I'd like to make sergeant. I can't do that if the paparazzi have a damned nickname for us that *came from my own squad*." His accent got stronger the more upset he got, and combined with his obvious exhaustion, Rafael sounded more dangerous than he had in a long time. It wasn't as unpleasant as it should have been, though.

Jonah shoved the heel of his hand deep into his forehead and started rubbing rough circles. "I'm sorry. What more can I say? They were going to come up with their own headline anyway, and it wasn't going to be nice no matter who gave them the idea."

Rafael grunted and chugged back about half his large coffee in one go. "Yeah, but did it have to be you?" He slammed the cup down violently next to the offending papers and walked away.

Jonah sighed and opened the case file. *Better me than someone you actually like, right?* He felt almost more determined to be the one to crack the case to salvage the department's reputation with the city and his own with Rafael.

"Detec*tives*!" Luis's voice rang through the bullpen, and Jonah let his head fall back so he could look skyward and pray to the God he didn't believe in ten seconds before that he would come out of it alive and with a job.

Luis reminded Jonah even more of his mother, especially when he and his brother Dave would fight as kids and inevitably break something on the way down. That probably accounted for why he felt like he was eight standing in front of her desk with the rest of the squad looking similarly ashamed.

She didn't speak for a long time. That was also a tactic Jonah's mother used. It was unnerving and frankly a bit scary when his mother did it, and neither he nor his brother dared move or say anything in fear of setting off a chain reaction ending with the two of them grounded for an unreasonable amount of time. Grounding was probably off the table now that he was thirty and Luis wasn't his mother, which actually scared him even more.

It felt like three days before Luis drew in a deep breath and let them have it. "I don't want to know. I don't want to know why or how or who. I don't care. I don't have time to care. I've been fielding calls from every gossip column and tabloid in the country. I didn't even know who this guy was two days ago, and now I'm being sent photos of him with those disgusting fame-whore sisters. What's their name? Wait, I don't care. I also don't care about his reality show. I don't care about his fortune. I don't care what A-lister is getting married on his private island. I don't care. I want him out of my city, and I don't want *any* of you even whispering to each other when the press is around. Don't even talk to each other in your cars. Those demons can read lips. They don't deserve to know anything about this case, and I'm beginning to think that Teiki doesn't even need to know anything until we catch the perp." Jonah swore her usually brown eyes were glowing red, but the probability of his boss being a demon was most likely pretty low.

Jonah felt himself blush a bit. He couldn't even look at Rafael, but he knew he was *steaming* mad.

Luis wasn't finished. "I've got the mayor breathing down my neck on this, and I *really* would like to be able to do anything without him up my ass. I'm the youngest female captain in Miami-Dade history. I'm not going to let some spoiled heir ruin what I've worked so hard for. And each of you has a stake in this department's record, so I hope I don't have to go into detail about what it means for your future here if the four of you don't take control of this situation and fix it." Jonah decided not to rule out demon *possession* yet.

They all shook their heads. Jonah really did feel eight years old.

"From this moment no one talks to the press. Learn how to communicate telepathically if you have to, but there is no speaking around press either. I'm authorizing overtime on this, so no one sleeps until we have those stupid birds and the rest of his property back in his hands and the perp is in jail, got it?" She glared at them like she was daring them to give her a reason to reach across and strangle one or all of them.

"Got it, Captain." Jonah didn't hear any signs of annoyance from Rafael at the prospect of sixteen- or more-hour workdays. Jonah sneaked a glance over at him and, despite the compliance in his voice, Rafael looked exhausted.

By 6:30 p.m., Jonah was sure he had been thrown into some alternate universe where every hour was five hours long. Forensics was taking its dear, sweet time getting DNA back, and tech was analyzing every pixel in the security footage for possible tampering. His phone chirped quietly, and he prayed no one noticed when he went to surreptitiously check it.

*I'm gonna die. Quick dinner?*
A.J.

Jonah shot off a quick reply.

*Yeah. When?*

The response came within twenty seconds.

*NOW. I'm outside the conference room.*

Jonah smiled and put away his phone. "Dinner time. I'm calling it."

"Are you jok—"

"Rafi, come on, we've been at this all day. We can't do anything else until forensics gets back to us, and you know that it's not going to happen in the next hour." Even if A.J. weren't waiting outside to rescue him, Jonah needed a break. And some food.

Rafael sighed, and he must have been as exhausted as Jonah was to ignore the nickname. "Fine." He waved his hand noncommittally. "Whatever. Dinner. Don't go far."

Garcia and Edgewood scrambled out the door before Rafael had the chance to change his mind and call the whole thing off. Not even Garcia's jovial temperament was able to counter Rafael's bad mood, and no one could blame her or anyone else for wanting to be as far away from him as possible.

Rafael used the extra space left by everyone leaving to spread out the case files across the table and immediately buried himself in the details.

Jonah paused with his hand on the doorknob. "Whoa, Rafael. That means you too. I haven't seen you eat all day. It's not good for you."

Rafael looked up long enough to glare at Jonah. He had a bit of a five o'clock shadow. Or, rather, 5:00 the next day shadow, and it made him look more intense than normal. "Why do you care? Don't you have a date right now? You could have come right out and said it, you know. You're not that hard to read."

This again. "I don't see how who I choose to have a sandwich with is anyone's business. But making sure you don't pass out from exhaustion or hunger is *my* business right now if you aren't going to do it yourself. You're my partner and, believe it or not, I do care if you live or die, even if the feeling isn't mutual."

Rafael shot a glance upward at Jonah, and he wondered which one of Rafael's nerves he'd hit just then. Jonah was determined to ignore that little moment in the car, as it had obviously been a sign that the artificial tropical scent at the hotel had driven one or both of them just a little insane.

"You think I hate you." It didn't sound like a question as much as it sounded like a harsh realization. Jonah couldn't help but notice how long Rafael's eyelashes were as he looked down and closed his eyes in resignation.

Jonah sighed and took his hand off the door. "No. I don't think you hate me. I think I'm the newbie partner you didn't ask for and no matter how hard I try, I can't seem to hit that magical combo of being the experienced partner you need and the hardened personality you want. And I think you're terrified that if we don't solve this case soon all the public will remember of the case and this precinct is the stupid nickname that I didn't mean to give it and you *really* blame me for the mess we're in right now and nothing I do is going to get me in your good graces. I also think that the more I apologize, the more you realize just how many times I screw up. And I screw up a lot. And all I can do is say I'm sorry one more time and tell you that I'm trying."

Probably not the best time to drop a truth bomb of self-awareness on anyone, but Jonah was tired and frustrated, and hell, if things didn't go well on this case he would probably get transferred or worse, so there really wasn't much to lose, anyway. All of this was so familiar. It was Orlando all over again. An early screwup that was going to affect the trajectory of the rest of his career here if he stayed, but in this case a *lot* of early screwups that led to his partner hating him. And that was no way for a cop to work.

Rafael bit his lip and shook his head. "I'm… sorry you think—I'm sorry if I made you feel that way. Go to dinner, and we'll talk about this later, okay? Gotta get through this mess first."

"Raf—"

"Just go. A.J.'s waiting. He's walked by the window six times already. He's like a damn three-year-old." Rafael opened another case file and spread it out among the others. The conversation was over.

A.J. grinned when Jonah finally emerged from the conference room. Jonah faked a smile back and immediately felt bad for doing so. Mixing Rafael and A.J. seemed like a bad idea, and he didn't really know why. Jonah felt he should be able to tell his maybe sort of boyfriend he was feeling down and why, but getting everything out on Rafael had seemed easier.

"Ready to go?" A.J. reached out and grabbed Jonah gently on the arm and led him to the front entrance of the station. The good food truck was parked on the street, and even though it was sort of illegally parked too close to a fire hydrant and probably not properly licensed through the city, county, or state, it smelled like heaven, and Jonah was so hungry he couldn't bother to care about the blatant disregard for breaking the law in front of a police station. Several uniforms and plainclothes cops had already patronized the truck and were out enjoying the salty and fresh spring air. Obviously the combination of nice weather and good food made everyone else equally susceptible to overlooking the violations too.

With his ritual silent prayer to whatever saint protected against hepatitis and salmonella, Jonah ordered a grilled fish taco while A.J. got an empanada. He felt a little more at ease when he sneaked a peek inside and saw the grill guy wash his hands before and after putting his fish down on the grill. Rafael would really kill him if he was taken out by some kind of food-borne illness from a dinner he insisted he have when, really, a snack from the vending machine would have sufficed to help him go another few hours.

Garcia and Edgewood waved them over, and the four of them sat on the front steps eating and making small talk. The fish taco was actually kind of perfect—dripping with lime and roasted tomatillo with a bit of heat—and Jonah savored each bite, not wanting to go back into that stuffy conference room anytime soon.

"Too bad we couldn't get Rafael to join us. We could just stay out here all night and at least enjoy the fresh air while we sit around and get nothing accomplished," lamented Jonah, not meaning to say it out loud. The sun was starting to dip behind the tall buildings that surrounded the station, and there was salsa music accompanied by the off-key singing of the grill guy drifting from the food truck.

Edgewood nodded between bites. "Do you think he's still in there all alone?"

"When I left he seemed like he was content to stay in there. I told him he had to eat something or he was going to pass out or get sick or something, but even if he were hungry he'd starve before he took my advice." Jonah didn't want to talk about this, about the shame of his partner hating him, but when did he ever keep his mouth shut?

Garcia cocked her head to one side and squinted. "Why, *papi*? He's your partner."

"That's what I said, but I don't think he wants me to *be* his partner. He kind of hates me, in case you haven't picked up on that." Okay, it felt good to say that out loud. Didn't make the being hated part any less of a sting, though.

Garcia smiled a bit and shook her head. "That's not true, Jonah, and you know it."

"Perhaps you are thinking of the wrong Rafael. About yay high, green eyes, dark hair, Cuban, is literally always ragging on me?" Perhaps Rafael was like that cartoon frog that sang only for one person and went silent when anyone else was around.

"If he hated you, he would have pushed you for a transfer a long time ago. When he wants something, he usually fights until he gets it, and that goes beyond his arrest record," chimed in Edgewood.

Jonah shrugged. "He constantly pushed for me to transfer to Palm Beach and help rich old ladies cross the street a lot when I first got here."

Garcia blew a raspberry and grinned. "That sounds like Rafael. But, listen, Brad's right. If he wanted you gone, then why did I hear him turn the captain down when she suggested separating you two the other day?"

"Whoa, Luis wants me gone?" Man, he'd just settled in. Or so he thought. Too many transfers didn't look good on a record, and if this whole Tahiti Tweety mess was going to follow him as well, he might as well start looking for openings in podunk towns in the middle of the state now.

"Not gone, man. Just away from Rafael. She was concerned that you two weren't a good fit, personality-wise, and maybe you both needed different partners. Rafael flat-out refused to switch. Are those the actions of a man who wants you dealing with upper-crusty old blue hairs?" Garcia pursed her lips and raised an eyebrow. She looked like she was interrogating someone, and it was always unnerving to have that face turned on him by another cop. Jonah knew everyone was waiting for a reaction.

The problem was that Jonah didn't know *how* to react, so he let it hang and vowed to revisit it later when he had space to work it out. He took another bite of his taco and waited for the silence to get so uncomfortable that someone else would steer the conversation away from him and Rafael.

Garcia thankfully took the hint and started talking about basketball or something. A.J. slyly made a grab for Jonah's hand and started distractedly playing with his fingers as they talked odds and records. As nice as it felt, it was a subtle reminder of just how slowly things were happening between the two of them. A.J. was always touching him in almost respectful ways and Jonah was ready for a little… *disrespectful*. A.J. graduated to rubbing slow circles on a sensitive part of his wrist, clearly meaning to drive Jonah slowly crazy. Part of him wanted to grab A.J. and throw him down a back alley to show him how much more they could be doing.

The free hour waned quickly, and the tone turned from casual to resigned as they all packed up their trash and contemplated just how much time they had before Rafael would start the angry texts demanding to know where they were and when they would be coming back. Garcia and Edgewood took the last few minutes to check in with their respective family members and assure them that they would be home before the month was over. Probably. Maybe.

A.J. sneaked a kiss from Jonah before heading back inside. Jonah took a little initiative and deepened the kiss, squeezing A.J.'s hips as he pulled him closer. A.J. stumbled a bit, but whimpered into Jonah's mouth, and maybe there was some hope yet.

Jonah waited until the last minute to go back inside, trying to steal a moment to contemplate what Garcia had told him about Rafael's unwillingness to give him up as a partner. He couldn't parse that with how Rafael was constantly acting and reacting to Jonah's constant screwups.

And still, no matter how anyone felt about anyone else, Rafael was still too stubborn to take a break and get food. That Jonah knew for a fact.

It was definitely just generic generosity and human kindness that compelled Jonah to purchase a second order of the fantastic fish tacos and set them down in front of Rafael when he got back to the conference room.

A simple act of kindness out of a need for his partner to be on his game so they weren't there all night.

That was all.

Until Rafael looked from the food to Jonah with a look that shot straight to his core. A wave of a thousand different emotions broke over

Rafael's face, and Jonah couldn't pin down any one of them. Suddenly Jonah's tiny gesture became something more, something heavier that seemed to push all the air out of the room just like what had happened in the car the night before, and Rafael seemed to laser focus on Jonah, his eyes even greener than normal thanks to the red that was ringing them from his refusal to take a break.

Jonah awkwardly reached into his pocket to take out the handful of napkins he'd grabbed and place them gingerly on top of the Styrofoam container. "I wasn't sure if you liked—"

"Thanks," Rafael said, still not looking away from Jonah until he popped the top of the container and the smell of bright citrus and spicy fish hit him. Jonah swore that Rafael went cross-eyed a bit when he finally looked down at it. "As much as it pains me to say this, you were right. I'm starving. This from the truck outside?"

Jonah nodded and watched as Rafael tucked into the first taco. "Yeah, I wasn't sure if you liked fish tacos…." But Rafael moaned the moment he bit into it and sighed almost contentedly.

"They're my favorite. God, thank you. I don't deserve—"

"Shut up. You're my partner." Jonah grinned at Rafael and sat down on the opposite end of the table, feeling good about himself for once, even if he couldn't decipher those confusing little moments between them or what would compel Rafael to fight for him like he did.

# Chapter 18

ANOTHER LATE night stumbling into his apartment. Jonah should have been more used to it after three straight days, but he just didn't have the strength to get much more off than his shoes before falling into bed. He didn't even turn on the light, trusting that what few possessions he owned would have the good sense to stay out of his way. He wanted two things: that moment that ranked just below seeing the face of God when he took off his shoes and his hot, tired feet hit the cool tile in his bathroom, and to sleep for at least a hundred hours straight. He managed one of them, and it wasn't the big one he was hoping for.

It wasn't long, though, before a big problem presented itself in the most annoying, nagging way imaginable. Jonah's frustration and confusion and uncertainty about everything had manifested themselves into a wave of sexual frustration that was begging for immediate attention. Before, with Chris, he would work out his feelings by fucking his brains out, but that obviously wasn't an option anymore, and things hadn't progressed with A.J. enough to make that arrangement yet, and judging by the relative lack of heat when they kissed, he doubted they would ever get to the stage where doing anything with A.J. would be anything but sweet and respectful.

He unfastened his trousers and pushed them down as he lifted his hips so they slid over his ass. The sheets were cool against his skin and just made his need more urgent. A.J.'s full lips and dark skin materialized in Jonah's mind as he shoved a hand roughly down the front of his boxers. He was just so *tired* and wanted to get off and go to sleep already. The A.J. in his mind grinned mischievously up at him and quickly swallowed Jonah's cock down without hesitation. Jonah groaned as he fisted his cock and fantasized about A.J. bobbing up and down, swirling his tongue around his length while Jonah grabbed handfuls of his long, dark hair and controlled how fast and how deep.

It wasn't enough, though. Probably wouldn't ever be enough with A.J. Even the A.J. he was inventing for his fantasies was annoyingly polite and vanilla. He needed more to get off like he wanted. The stress and anxiety were taking their toll on Jonah, and he needed the release more than he needed anything else in the entire world. It just couldn't come fast enough.

His fantasy A.J. looked up at him with those almost pitch-black eyes and grinned before pulling off and moving to get on top of him, but a hand slid up Jonah's body to touch his lips, and it was paler, more defined. A.J. moved up so he could lie next to Jonah and kiss him, and it was nice, but the owner of the mystery arm had his hand on Jonah's chest, using it for traction as he lowered himself onto Jonah's very hard cock. A.J. framed Jonah's face with his hands so he couldn't turn away as they kissed. Jonah fought his own imagination to spare a glance down and, oh.

*Oh.*

Shit.

Riding Jonah slow and filthy and glaring at him like he wanted to murder him at the same time, was Rafael Santos, completely naked and jerking himself off as he moved up and down. His green eyes were heavy-lidded in ecstasy, and Jonah didn't even have time to try to think of literally anything else before he came all over himself, hard and fast, groaning so loudly he was sure the little old Haitian lady who lived next door and claimed to be deaf—even when she screamed at him to turn down the television any time he turned it on—could hear. He hadn't had an orgasm like that in months. Possibly years.

He waited until he came down fully from it before having a proper freak-out, though. Betrayed by his imagination or not, he wasn't going to let that get in the way of feeling good.

*Rafael.*

He wanted to contemplate more, but just as his mind had betrayed him, his body betrayed him even worse, and he passed out until his alarm clock went off, the early morning sunshine mocking him as it streamed through the cheap blinds the place came with. He was going to have to break down and get to IKEA soon to buy real curtains.

He hit in the general direction of the button until the annoying buzzing stopped, and when he felt the dried remains of his bout with insanity on his belly as he stretched, the entire night came rushing back at him.

Rafael.

He made it to his shower and started to wash off the evidence that he had ever fantasized about his partner, but by the time he poured shampoo into his hand, he couldn't deny it any longer.

Jonah had a Big Problem. It was such a Big Problem that he finally understood how Tamatoa Teiki could imply capitalized words, because hell yes, he was capitalizing it.

Jonah had A Thing For Rafael.

This wasn't Jonah forcing a fantasy Rafael to fill in for his fantasy A.J. because he could imagine Rafael being into it more than A.J. This wasn't some kind of fucked-up hero worship. This went beyond trying to impress Rafael to get in his good graces. This was more than some ego boost whenever Rafael complimented him. Rafael was intelligent, authoritative, focused, driven, ambitious, and, hell, there was no use resisting, he was gorgeous. Even more gorgeous with that stubble he'd been sporting since the Teiki case began. Damn. He was deep in it.

Jonah stood in his shower with his hair lathered up and the hot water quickly fading away while his revelation ran around his mind. He had no idea how to handle this Big Problem or how to even get through the first day after admitting he had this problem, but time wasn't going to stop for his crisis, even if the hot water had no problem doing so.

How could he do this to himself? What possible motivation could he have for sabotaging himself in that way? His heart and his dick had conspired against him, and it was almost as if they wanted him to fail miserably in Miami....

Another realization hit him so fast he almost forgot to rinse off the suds cascading down his body. He narrowly avoided slipping on the wet floor as he raced to throw on some clothes. His mind was racing at light speed, and he couldn't get to work fast enough. He didn't even feel like he needed coffee, which would be miracle enough in itself, but not as much as if his hunch was dead-on.

# Chapter 19

RAFAEL WAS already in the conference room. Jonah doubted he had ever left. Only a fresh change of clothes indicated that he'd even taken a break during the night. Jonah wanted to drown him in the good coffee and give him a hot shower. Preferably with Jonah lathering him up and—*Later, Jonah. Oh my God. This is not the time.* Life was going to be difficult from there on out; he just knew it. This wasn't like every sci-fi movie or TV show he'd ever watched where giving a Thing a name took away its power. In the real world, it just fueled it. He almost wanted to talk to Edgewood about that. He would know more about that kind of stuff.

Rafael looked up from his notes, startled at seeing Jonah at such an early hour, but there was no time to let him catch a breath.

"It's Teiki," Jonah announced proudly. "The person who stole Teiki's stuff is Teiki. There was never a break-in. That's why the security footage is useless. That's why his own staff all sound like they're morons. They're having to lie to cover it up. I'd bet two weeks' salary that forensics is going to come up empty-handed too. Teiki staged the whole thing." Jonah crossed his arms and cocked his head to the side with a little raise of his eyebrow while he waited for Rafael's response in a ballsy show of confidence considering how much of that theory was, in fact, just theory.

Rafael squinted up at him like maybe he believed he was hallucinating. "*Lo siento?*" Rafael slipping into Spanish was never a good sign. The man clearly needed sleep.

"Raf, think about it. Teiki never wanted to be in Miami in the first place. The board and his father pushed him to put a hub here. He complained of a raw deal from the start. He knew that most people who wanted to leave Miami for another beach destination were already set on spending less at a cheaper destination like a cruise to the Bahamas or Puerto Rico and those are mostly retirees on a budget. And the ultrarich already have their own private jets or boats. He's a better businessman than anyone gives him credit for, I think. He didn't stand to make as much money as he would have grabbing up-and-coming new money and wannabe starlets dying for fame in another market. But the city pushed for it because of the potential for getting everyone south of Orlando willing to drive here to fly out on a luxury airline owned by a celebrity, and his father and the board pushed for it because of the money the city was willing to put into accommodating their whims. But it's not working out to Teiki's advantage, is it? He's having to offer serious discounts to get anyone on board. It's only attracting the upper middle class. The city is making out pretty well, though, and the board probably isn't thinking beyond the kickbacks from the city." All that Internet research hadn't gone to waste, even if he never wanted to see another search engine or newspaper article ever again.

Rafael clasped his hands together and pursed his lips. He was hanging on to every word, and it was almost scary how focused he was despite looking slightly crazed from exhaustion. "Keep talking."

Jonah blinked. He never actually expected Rafael to let him finish. He took a deep breath. "Okay, so Teiki either wants out of Miami, or he wants to renegotiate the deal with the city to get more money to stay. Either way, he needs something that makes Miami look bad and makes Teiki publicly hate it. I'd bet on wanting to leave so he could refocus all that investment in another city with better profit potential, like somewhere with fewer ultrarich people and more, like, mildly disgustingly rich people who are still concerned with appearances and probably can't afford their own planes. And Teiki has enough clout with the media to really do some harm to Miami's rep if the city doesn't roll over. So, Teiki stages a burglary. He has a legit reason to be pissed off and go on a rant that could harm Miami's reputation, and he's justified questioning whether or not he wants to do business here. We're never going to find the missing stuff or finger a suspect because the stuff is perfectly safe. Probably chilling out in Boca or something."

Rafael's eyes went wide like he couldn't believe he was actually considering the idea. "And how did you come to this conclusion, may I ask?"

Jonah waved a hand dismissively. "I guess you could say I know a little something about setting myself up to fail." He purposely avoided meeting Rafael's gaze.

Rafael let out a huge yawn and a loud cracking in his jaw accompanied it. He grabbed a file from the bottom of the pile and pored over it, chewing on his bottom lip and occasionally murmuring in Spanish. Jonah didn't know exactly what he was doing or why or if he should help or leave before Rafael yelled at him for such a whacked-out theory, so he stood there, frozen until he got an indication either way.

After the longest minute of Jonah's life, Rafael blew out a breath and buried his face in his hands, rubbing at his temples. "I can't believe it." He closed his eyes tightly. "It's so obvious now. I don't know what to say, kid. I think you're right."

That was twice in so many days that Rafael had admitted Jonah was right. The Big Problem was going to need more capital letters soon.

Rafael finally locked eyes with Jonah's. "So, Detective Landers. You take the lead. What do we do now?"

Jonah blinked a few times. "We... we lean on his employees... anyone working at the hotel who should have seen evidence of the birds but didn't because he never actually had them on the property. Any guests who should have heard them squawking on the verandah but didn't. Find out if any of Teiki's people were spotted off property and where they might have gone."

Rafael beamed like a proud father. "Good start, kid. Get Garcia and Edgewood in here and let's get started. We got a lot of work to do."

Jonah allowed himself a self-indulgent grin before walking out to call in the rest of the squad. He hoped his hunch panned out because everything felt amazing, and he didn't want anything ruining it. This might finally be the break he had needed. In more ways than one.

Secretly, Jonah wished he could be party to another one of Rafael's interrogations that weren't really interrogations, but this was Jonah's case now and Rafael had given him lead and he wasn't about to waste that to let his dick do the thinking for him. Garcia and Edgewood had their method down pat, and it was a lot of dirty (but legal) tricks and fast-talking to confuse the suspect, but Jonah thought it was a good idea to take it old-school. Good cop/bad cop was always a good lead-in. It was an old technique, but a useful one, especially when they had wrangled one of Teiki's assistants, Noa, into the interview room under the guise of "just needing some information."

Noa looked every bit the type of assistant one would expect from a Polynesian billionaire with a reality TV show. He was dressed in a garish but probably super-expensive button-down silk shirt and white trousers, with dark sunglasses atop his shaved head. Jonah had led him to think he needed to give a description and a timeline of some hotel employees' comings and goings, but soon found himself squirming at Rafael's thinly veiled threat-slash-promises of what happens when someone lies to him. Rafael had a way about him that belied his stature, and Jonah found himself a little terrified of him when he got like that, but maybe also a little—okay, a lot—turned on too.

Rafael worked his magic, yelling and looking insane while Noa sputtered and backtracked until Rafael threw up his hands and stormed out of the room, the unspoken tag out so Jonah could swoop in and show a little fake compassion for the guy.

He had this in the bag. He knew it from the moment he straddled the chair opposite Noa. The guy was going to sing like… well, like one of Tamatoa Teiki's supposedly missing birds.

And sing he did. A sympathetic smile here, a pat on the shoulder there. "Teiki just pushes and pushes for what he wants, and he never gives back, does he? Must be rough to work for a spoiled brat who won't listen to reason." Maybe just a hint of what Teiki was in for if they found him filing a false report and wasting so much manpower. And the lawsuits. Oh, the lawsuits. He might not have enough to pay for that nice fat salary to which Noa was accustomed. Those $400 ESCADA silk shirts (Garcia had supplied Jonah with the details on his wardrobe like she was a walking issue of *Vogue*), the $200 sunglasses, could all be replaced by clothes on sale at Target.

And if Teiki got cornered and blamed the whole mess on Noa and they had even a shred of proof that Noa knew where the birds were? Oh, man. That was a Bad Thing. Jonah was getting good at capitalizing letters now.

Jonah and Rafael had a signed confession within two hours, complete with the location of the birds and Teiki's other "stolen goods," on the condition of immunity from the ADA. Garcia and Edgewood were on their way to a house owned by one of Teiki's C-list celebrity hangers-on in Key Biscayne to retrieve everything while the ink was still drying. He felt bad that Noa would definitely be out of a job once Teiki found out it was he who ratted him out (it was *immunity* and not *anonymity* they had promised, and the guy never bothered to lawyer up. Pity), but the way the reality show world worked, he'd probably have his own by fall. The current station bet was the title of it. Jonah put a twenty down on "*Noa Limits*," but Grace threw out "*Noa Regrets*" like it was an afterthought as she picked at her split ends, and he cursed himself for not thinking of that one first.

"Good work, Detective. You did it. You put everything together, and you completely nailed this case. I'm… I'm proud of you, kid. You're a fine detective, and I don't hate you, okay? When everything settles we'll talk, but for now, just know that I'm proud to stand here with you as my partner." And with that Rafael Santos extended a hand for Jonah to shake. Jonah stared at it for a few seconds before offering his own up. Rafael was warm, and Jonah had never noticed just how large his hands were. He smiled at Rafael to distract himself from a rapidly forming and potentially distracting thought.

Jonah opened his mouth to thank Rafael, to try to put into words what he wanted to say to him about the case, about working with him, about everything, but Rafael knew him too well by that point.

"Don't get cocky, kid." Rafael clapped Jonah's shoulder for a split second and walked away before he could get a word in protest.

Jonah couldn't stop grinning for the rest of the day.

The fallout was spectacular, and Jonah wished he could have seen more of it with his own eyes, but Rafael was adamant about keeping the squad out of the limelight, and for good reason seeing as a recognizable face was no good undercover. Captain Luis, though, seemed to delight in the press conferences to clear Miami's good name. Teiki himself had a lot of wound licking to do, especially when Noa's confession, one Teiki adamantly denied at first, was backed up by the discovery that someone had indeed tampered with the security footage, but not, to Teiki's horror, so badly A.J. couldn't recover it and reveal the indisputable truth. The board was expected to vote away most of his control of the airline and keep flights to and from Miami despite Teiki's unfortunately sound logic for not wanting to be there. His reality show was in no danger, though, as the nature of celebrity tended to err on the side of controversy. The lawsuits alone from the hotel would ensure many episodes of drama.

The assistant district attorney decided against prosecuting for filing a false police report as it was only a misdemeanor and suing him into the ground seemed like a much more attractive option. Especially as it made the ADA, who was looking to drop the *A* off that title in the next few years, look good. It was a win all around for the city and the tabloids.

As much as he should have considered it a personal win too, he didn't feel it until Rafael selflessly went out of his way to bring it to everyone's attention just who made the big break in the case. That earned Jonah backslaps, high fives, and a round of applause throughout the station. Even Luis congratulated him heartily and promised him a few extra vacation days for his effort, but none of that meant more than the private moment between Rafael and him right after they cracked the case.

# Chapter 20

THE MOUNTAINS of paperwork and interviews with the DA and briefings eventually settled down to a manageable molehill, Jonah could finally go home for more than an hour at a time. He wanted nothing more than to crawl into a pair of sweats and fall asleep in front of the television, not thinking of Rafael or tropical birds or A.J. or anything but what toppings to get on his pizza.

Of course A.J. chose to show up at his door about ten minutes after the pizza (pepperoni, garlic, jalapenos) came and three minutes before *Back to the Future III* (not his favorite of the trilogy, but it would do) started.

Jonah opened the door to see A.J. standing on the step with a six pack of local brew and promising grin. Ah, hell, he deserved a little fun after everything he'd been through, and maybe A.J. could take his mind off the stupid, completely wrong crush on Rafael.

They made it to Seamus McFly's terrible Irish accent before they were kissing each other. Kissing A.J. was nice. Just nice, though. If Grace, the romance writing receptionist, were writing their story, it wouldn't be a bodice-ripping bestseller.

*And so our dashing hero kissed the swashbuckling young police technician, and it was… nice. He placed his hand on A.J.'s chest, feeling the smooth skin under his fingertips and suddenly a thought pierced his brain… "Did I leave the iron on?"* Maybe he should read one of her books just to get some inspiration. Not that he thought A.J. was a Grim Reaper or that there was a chance Rafael might be a secret gothic vampire or a Frankenstein's monster made specifically for sexual pleasure and had interchangeable dick attachments. Jonah mentally shook his head and vowed never to read one of Grace's books.

But still, Jonah couldn't figure out what was missing. A.J. was hot and intelligent and a lot of fun. He was a great kisser on top of that, with soft full lips and roaming hands. There was nothing wrong with A.J. He was perfect.

On paper.

There was just no spark, and Jonah didn't know if time would create one, or if he needed to get over Rafael already to make it happen. He didn't want to throw away a good thing, though, and he was determined to see where it could go with A.J..... He would have to figure out how to put Rafael out of his mind. It shouldn't be so hard with A.J.'s kissing getting more and more urgent, right?

A.J. leaned back a bit to pull off his shirt, leaving his dark brown skin exposed in the faint glow of the lamp. He had a tattoo of a bow and arrow on his chest, and Jonah reached out absentmindedly to trace it with his finger.

A.J. shivered under the light touch. "Proud Seminole, remember? I learned bow hunting when I was a boy. Never shot anything more than targets, except for that one time I missed and got my instructor in the ass, but, yeah... *yay, traditions.*" He shook pretend pom-poms while he mocked cheered.

"It's beautiful." It was also small talk. Jonah lifted his own shirt over his head, and even though his skin was a ghostly white compared to A.J.'s, it still netted him an appreciative whistle.

Jonah let himself get lost in A.J.'s kisses for a long time. He explored the feeling of A.J.'s long hair tangled in his fingers and the way the goose bumps rose on his skin when he let it fall across A.J.'s back. It was becoming... a little better than nice.

A.J. was getting more and more handsy, settling on Jonah's ass and playfully squeezing it. Jonah groaned a little into A.J.'s mouth and thrust his hips down harder into his grip. A.J. let go with a little smack and readjusted himself so he could straddle Jonah's lap and get a better angle on touching as much skin as possible.

Rafael ground down on Jonah—wait, no. Damn it. *A.J.* ground down on Jonah.

He was not going to fantasize about Rafael. That was off-limits, and his brain needed to obey.

A.J. ground down on Jonah, rolling his hips down so their clothed dicks came into delicious contact. A.J. moaned and sighed against Jonah's neck so his breath heated Jonah's skin.

Jonah slid his hands down A.J.'s chest and settled them on his hips, pulling him closer as he pushed his own hips upward. The feeling was amazing, and it didn't take long before A.J. was pushing at his sweats to get them down to his thighs so his cock sprang free. A.J. made a small, appreciative noise as his eyes trailed downward. He untangled his legs from either side of Jonah and stood to remove his own pants. A.J.'s bottom half—with an amazingly tight ass and strong thighs that made Jonah have some seriously inappropriate thoughts—was just as nice to look at as his top half, and Jonah wondered if the man had a flaw anywhere.

Jonah closed his eyes as A.J. settled himself back on Jonah's lap, palming both their dicks lazily as Jonah's whole body started to finally relax from the hard couple of weeks. He let his head fall back against the back of the sofa so A.J. could take it as fast or slow as he wanted.

A.J. rocked his hips as he touched Jonah, and soon Jonah was gone, lost in a fantasy he couldn't control when it popped into his brain. Rafael was throwing him up against a rough-hewn wall in the station where everyone could see them and see how Rafael really felt about him. Rafael pinned Jonah there with his body weight and pushed his erection into him as he kissed him violently, not caring that he was biting a little too hard or gripping him a little too tightly. Rafael yanked Jonah's shirt up out of the waistband of his trousers and shoved a hand into his boxers, feeling how hard he was for Rafael.

"Oh, you like this, don't you? You want me to fuck you right here in front of everyone? In front of Garcia and Edgewood? In front of *A.J.*?" Rafael spat out the name, and it made Jonah moan.

"Yes... yes, Rafael! Right here so everyone can see us! Please!" Jonah didn't know where this fantasy was coming from or where it was going, and it was rude to think of someone else when A.J. was jerking him off in earnest, but God, he just wanted to get off and deal with everything else later.

Fantasy Rafael roughly opened Jonah's button and zipper and unceremoniously sank to his knees until Jonah could imagine his hot breath right there on his aching dick. No one could ever accuse Jonah of dreaming small, and Rafael took Jonah in whole, like his mouth was made for Jonah's cock. There was no hesitation before Rafael started bobbing up and down, and Jonah watched as he disappeared in Rafael's perfect, dirty mouth again and again. The whole station was watching Rafael on his knees giving head to Jonah, giving him so much pleasure instead of all the grief like in the past.

He watched as Rafael unfastened his own pants and started jerking himself off, moaning in pleasure, and the sensation around

Jonah's dick sent sparks shooting up his spine. Jonah settled his hands on the back of Rafael's head, and he stilled Rafael so he could take over, thrusting into Rafael's mouth gently, fucking his face until he couldn't hold out any longer. The orgasm was spectacular and all he could think about was Rafael's hot mouth on him as everyone saw how they looked together.

Fantasy Rafael took in every drop of him while Jonah came in the hand of the very real A.J., who cried out and followed soon after on Jonah's stomach. Naturally—of course—it was a breathtaking sight that should have fueled at least a month of jerk-off fantasies, but instead Jonah felt himself admiring it like a painting at a museum.

A.J. collapsed on top of him, and Jonah tried to assuage some of his guilt by running his fingers through A.J.'s hair and up and down his back, pointedly focusing on it being A.J. he was touching and not Rafael.

He invited A.J. to stay out of politeness. It was excruciatingly late, and Jonah was too tired to kick him out. A.J. slept splayed out over Jonah, and it was a comforting weight that lulled him into a surprisingly peaceful slumber. He'd deal with Rafael later.

MORNING RUSHED at them sooner than Jonah would have liked, even if Luis had given everyone on the case the morning off. They just had some final paperwork to do that would probably take the better part of an afternoon, and Jonah appreciated the opportunity to sleep in after the unexpectedly late night. He woke up, not quite remembering that A.J. was there until something warm next to him stretched and yawned.

"Morning." A.J. smiled sleepily and gave him a peck on the cheek.

Jonah felt like he needed to be polite and be a gracious host, even though he really just wanted the morning alone to process everything.

"There's probably some pizza left? Or I think I may have some tuna and mustard? I don't really keep—"

"Nope! I've invaded your space and ate your pizza. The least I can do is take care of breakfast. You go do whatever you do in the morning, and I'll be back in a bit." A.J. jumped out of bed excitedly and, as much as he wasn't crazy about sharing a bed with A.J., Jonah immediately missed the warmth of his skin next to his. Confusion was rapidly becoming too weak a word to describe his feeling on the whole mess he was in.

A.J. insisted on making Jonah pancakes and excitedly ran down to the grocery store to get the ingredients and a spare toothbrush.

Jonah was so used to food trucks and late-night diners those days that a home-cooked meal seemed less plausible than aliens landing in the parking lot. Jonah stepped out of the shower and the incredible smell of A.J. cooking a real goddamned breakfast in his kitchen made him feel just a bit domestic and a whole lot guiltier than he had felt the night before. A.J. was amazing. And Jonah did not deserve a bit of him if he was going to sit around and mope over his stupid crush on Rafael.

There was fresh coffee and a stack of syrup-soaked pancakes with bacon and eggs waiting for him. Jonah ran his fingers through his damp hair to try to make sense of his curls and made a big show of kissing A.J. on the cheek before he sat down.

"This is crazy. How did you whip up all of this? I don't think I even own a pan."

A.J. grinned. "Well, Saturday is pancake day, but I made a special exception for Thursday. Magical things happen on pancake day, you know. Eat up. Garcia is planning something for tonight to celebrate, I just know it. She's already texted me three times and is being very vague."

Jonah stretched and speared a pancake with his fork, dropping it onto a plate. Also a thing he didn't know he owned. "And I suppose that claiming exhaustion and politely declining isn't going to get anyone out of this?"

A.J. popped a piece of bacon in his mouth and shook his head. "Not a chance. I learned that lesson a long time ago."

Breakfast was delicious, and they cleaned up the kitchen together, A.J. pausing now and then to steal a kiss or a touch. Jonah tried to keep things to lazy groping, blaming exhaustion, but he was secretly hoping A.J. would suddenly find a need to go home before they had to be back at the station. Jonah had too much on his mind to entertain A.J.'s newfound libido. Luck was not on his side, however.

# Chapter 21

NOON ROLLED around, and Luis's generosity extended to only about 12:30, so Jonah threw on his best suit, and he and A.J. were out the door. Garcia was stumbling in at the same time they both pulled into the employee lot, wearing what looked suspiciously like a walk of shame variation of the tight party dress she had been wearing the night before as she left the station with the intent of pre-celebrating: cleavage covered by a tasteful cardigan and sky-high heels replaced with sensible pumps they all knew she stored in her trunk for occasions like those.

She grinned sheepishly and shrugged when she saw Jonah and A.J. eyeing her up and down. When A.J. looked like he was going to say something snarky to her, she raised her hand toward them and shook her head. "Don't even start, *hijos*."

A.J. threw up his hands in surrender and extended his arm for her to steady herself with as she walked across the gravel. A.J. had narrowly missed being in the same situation and only a spare shirt from the back of Jonah's closet had saved him.

They were all three laughing and joking when they walked in, and Jonah could feel Rafael's eyes on him as soon as they reached the bull pen. Sure enough Rafael was glaring at the trio from his desk, looking almost a little put out.

Jonah was itching to go to him and explain himself, to assure Rafael that whatever he thought Jonah and A.J. had done the night before, Jonah couldn't stop thinking of him. He wanted to tell Rafael how *angry* he was that Rafael took up so much space in his head now and he didn't know when it had started or what he wanted to do about it and that made him even more angry that he finally felt like he had gotten some control over his life and his career and then stupid gorgeous Rafael had come along and ruined it all. Again. And most of all he wanted Rafael to know that no matter how pissed off Jonah was at him, he was even angrier at himself for falling for the asshole who had almost broken his nose in Orlando. How did it even go from wanting to kill Rafael that night after he revealed he was a cop to *this*?

Jonah stiffened and separated from A.J. and Garcia with a light touch on both their arms to excuse himself.

"Oh, I forgot to tell you. We're all going out tonight and no saying no because we need to celebrate, okay? There are several people here who want to buy you a drink, *papi*." Garcia was hard to say no to. Damn it. "Oh, and get that partner of yours to come out too. He looks like he could use some fun."

Jonah balked at the idea of Rafael letting go more than once a year, especially now with so much at stake for Jonah. There was no harm in asking, though, just to show some interest and make Rafael feel wanted even if he was going to flat-out reject it and probably insult him for even asking….

"Yeah. Yes, of course I'll be there. Sounds like a good time."

Jonah raised an eyebrow and didn't know how to respond to Rafael's acceptance. Was that a yes? Maybe A.J. had spiked his coffee with something.

Rafael was staring like he thought Jonah was about to retract the offer, and he realized he needed to respond and not just stand there with his mouth hanging open like a fish.

He shook himself out of his thoughts. "Great! Awesome!" *Okay, dial it back a bit.* "I owe you a drink anyway."

Rafael cocked his head. "You do? I mean, not that I'll turn down a free drink, but…."

"Rafi, let's be honest here. I never would have been able to put all that together if I didn't have you for a partner. You've been busting my balls so hard since I got here, but you've also helped me be a better detective, all right? Let's not get weird about it. Just let me buy you a drink as thanks for not having me transferred to Palm Beach or to another partner, okay?"

Jonah watched Rafael's face on that last part. He wanted Rafael to know that he knew about the offer to transfer Jonah. Rafael nodded a bit, and the faintest hint of pink colored his cheeks. "Yeah, okay. But, Landers?"

"Yeah?"

"You would have put it together just fine without me. You're still green as hell and only slightly less annoying than you were in February, but you're smart and you would have figured it out anyway." Rafael raised an eyebrow and pursed his lips a moment before continuing. "Probably with a lot more talking about it first, but you would have gotten there."

Jonah smiled and now he was blushing too. "Just let me buy you that drink, would you?"

Rafael actually smiled back, and it was glorious even if it was just a tiny one. Jonah tried to burn the image into his brain.

"Come on, partner. We have some follow-up at the hotel we need to take care of." Rafael reached into his pocket and pulled out his keys, which he tossed at Jonah without warning.

Jonah caught them gracelessly and stared at them for an uncomfortably long couple of seconds. "Ummm…."

Rafael raised an eyebrow. "Do you want to drive or not?"

*Magical things happen on pancake day.*

Jonah practically ran out the door.


SIX O'CLOCK came, and Jonah was so ready to get out of the station. Garcia had found yet another place in a long line of places she swore had the best fill-in-the-blank anyone would ever have, and he would have cast some serious doubt on her constant parade of hot spots if she hadn't been right about every single one of them so far. That night "drinks and dancing" at a bar in Brickell, a neighborhood *just* out of their jurisdiction that was constantly voted as having one of the best nightlife scenes in the city, filled that blank, and she swore by the bartender's ability to make up a fantastic drink for any occasion.

Jonah wasn't much of a dancer, or actually a dancer at all, but if the drinks were as good as Garcia promised, they could probably persuade him otherwise. He was only a little distracted by the wholly implausible fantasy of dancing in front of Rafael, moving like he knew how to and catching Rafael staring at him possessively from a dark corner table, just waiting for the opportune moment to grab him and fuck him somewhere private. Or the equally wholly implausible fantasy of actually dancing with Rafael, bodies moving together, sweating as much from the heat and exertion as the temptation to, once again, grab each other and fuck somewhere private. Jonah gave himself credit for the creativity in the first part of his fantasies, but there was no denying they all ended the same way. The fantasy was so enticing he almost wanted to try to sneak in a dance lesson somewhere before it was time to go, but he knew realistically that only a time machine and several years of lessons would make his hips move the way he wanted them to. Alcohol would have to fill in as dance teacher if he wanted even a tiny chance of, if not looking good, at least *thinking* he looked good out there.

He rounded back to his desk, and Rafael was hunched over his own, writing furiously.

"Rafi, come on." If Jonah stopped to think about it, he would have considered it strange that Rafael had never once called him out on the nickname thing. "It's time to get out of here. Everything else can wait till tomorrow." Jonah threw his jacket on and tossed a few pieces of scrap paper in the trash to make it look like his desk wasn't a complete disaster.

Rafael looked up and squinted. "Can't. Something's come up."

Jonah groaned. "Something—what's come up?"

"The board of commissioners wants a detailed report of everything, and they want it by tomorrow morning. The DA is deciding how to handle this mess, and it's been made *very* clear that he wants to move as quickly as possible before Teiki can distance himself from this."

"Politics?"

"Big time. No press is bad press, right? If Teiki is going to get a boost from this, so can the city. And the DA is pushing for everything to coincide with season so they can boost tourism numbers." Rafael looked annoyed.

Jonah started to take off his jacket. This was not going the way he planned… or, actually, fantasized. "Well, if you're stuck, I'm stuck too. What can I do?"

Rafael sighed. "You can go out with everyone else. This is something I've got to do, and you don't need to stay."

"Don't be ridiculous. You're going to be here all night."

"Wouldn't be the first time. Look, this isn't a group project. As the senior officer, I have an obligation to jump when the higher-ups tell me to. But you don't have that responsibility. Go. If you don't, I'm going to have Choya in here looking at me like a kicked puppy until you do whatever he wants you to do. I'm sure you're going to have more fun with him than sitting here with me all night anyway, so go."

Jonah didn't move. "Raf—"

"Landers, go. I tell you what. I'll see if anyone's still around if I get done quicker than I thought and try to put in an appearance."

Jonah still didn't budge, opting instead to glare at Rafael to let him know he saw through that bullshit.

Rafael's shoulders dropped. "I can't get this done with you staring at me like that." He made a tremendous effort to look like he was suddenly engrossed in his work again.

Jonah sighed. He was only mildly interested in the whole idea of going out when he walked into work. He was actually excited when Rafael said he would go. Now he just wanted to go home and consider his choices in life. *I should get a dog. They aren't complicated.*

But he also knew that people wanted him to be there. A.J. wanted him to be there. The rest of his squad, people he could now call friends, wanted him to be there. And maybe if he tried really hard, that would be enough.

He reluctantly left Rafael sitting there at his desk and went home to change, waiting until A.J.'s fifth text to leave his apartment.

# Chapter 22

IT WAS night and still disgustingly hot and humid, showing no signs that it was going to let up until at least the next December. Even though A.J. finally managed to lead the horse, or in this case Jonah, to water, he couldn't manage to make him drink. Or, more accurately, dance with him, since drinking was all Jonah was doing. "Not in the mood" didn't even begin to cover how Jonah felt right then, even if A.J. did look good out on the tiny dance floor, showing off and making eyes at Jonah, basking in the attention he was getting from half the department as he shook those hips. Maybe if he had enough to drink, he would forget about Rafael and how unattainable he truly was and start to appreciate what was right in front of his face.

They were dancing to too loud music—something they and everyone else would soon forget once the stupid trend of adding a "Lady" or "Saint" to your stage name and an air siren rising in pitch to every modern dance song thankfully waned. Jonah could tell the singer a few things about reading faces, and he couldn't really understand comparing poker and love since he'd never really lost in one, but lost a lot in the other. For instance, he knew he was losing as he watched A.J., hair damp with sweat, with his back to Jonah as Detective Garcia hooked her arm around the back of his head and pulled it down so she could rest her own in the crook of his neck. Garcia wasn't a threat in any way, and he knew that, but watching A.J. soak up the attention highlighted just how different the two of them were, and he didn't know if that was a problem or if Jonah would go out of his way to make it one.

Meanwhile, Jonah was still sitting at the bar, feeling the pocked wood thump along with the stupid bass line, watching the liquid in his glass shake like in that scene in *Jurassic Park*. A few of the uniforms had jokingly asked the bartender to invent a Tahiti Tweety drink, and it should have been hilarious how the cheap, rum-laced fruit punch concoction was overshadowed by a flaming tiki torch garnish made of fruit that was so gaudy it threatened to topple the whole thing over. Any other night and Jonah would be three in already, but he ironically found himself ordering good whiskey, courtesy of a few generous coworkers.

It was Ladies' Night and the feeling should have been right, but men definitely dominated the late-night crowd in this part of Miami. There would be a lot of disappointed guys going home alone tonight. And even if Jonah left with A.J., he would probably be equally disappointed.

His anonymous bar mates were quickly drinking themselves into a late-week oblivion, having all given up hope about an hour before. One or two more drinks and they would have probably started going home with each other; especially Steve, the charming blond next to Jonah, who was somewhere between slobbering drunk and passed out and looked years beyond his maybe twenty-five. He'd just lost his job, Jonah guessed. Steve had been researching unemployment on his phone. He'd also been twirling his wedding ring and ignoring the calls from Sharon as he slammed his seventh straight-up tequila down next to the phone. The picture on the screen was of Sharon and a baby, and it was obvious that Steve was the only source of income since the birth.

Jonah sucked down the last of his whiskey sour and let the puckery sweet burn hit him all at once. That damned song was playing, the one with the great title that quickly made him realize that any song that includes the word "feat." in the artist line was a ploy to make people forget that it was just a bad song.

The night was not going the way he planned at all. The DJ/bartender thankfully switched the music to something more '80s, which rang in the eleven o'clock hour like a synthesizer and keytar cuckoo clock. Garcia had warned everyone that the place turned into one of those nostalgia joints in the later hours. Jonah was glad to be rid of the modern dance music, anyway.

Steve was on the phone then, trying to tell Sharon he was out with the boys. He couldn't seem to conjure up any names, though, and Jonah was sure that if Erasure weren't singing about walking hand in hand in hand, he'd be able to hear Sharon's side of the conversation. Judging from Steve's end, he didn't want to. Steve would have quite a few problems having the affair Sharon was accusing him of, and Jonah wanted to lean over and tell Steve he'd better rush home any way that was legal when he was this drunk and clear things up because if he lost Sharon, he was pretty much done in that department. Jonah stopped when he realized that he was way too involved in Steve's life. And it just made Jonah bitter to wonder if any relationship was really worth all that anyway.

He thought about ordering another whiskey, but the crowd had actually picked up since the Auto-Tuned music gave way to the synthesizers. A.J. could manage on his own quite well, it seemed. He wasn't much of a drinker, and Jonah knew from her own admission that the formidable Detective Garcia could only handle two and a half normal strength drinks before she needed a ride home and a shiny new refill of dignity, so she had made a hasty vow to stay dry as well. Jonah would bet money that someone would still have to give her a ride home, though, from the longing, wanton look she made toward a triple strong Tahiti Tweety as one of the department's sketch artists walked by with one.

Jonah knew the amber that was the late-night crowd would swallow him whole like a mosquito and trap him for scientists to find and use his DNA to clone a new race of Jonahs (not that that was a bad thing) if he did not leave right then. Besides, he was just sober enough to make it back home without arousing suspicion, because as much as most of the MDPD liked him, drunk driving was not something they would overlook.

Jonah slipped the bartender money for his drinks and afforded himself one last look at A.J. and Garcia. He wouldn't say it was ironic or fate that "Jessie's Girl" was playing, but it was a good note on which to end the night. The crowd had thickened so much he could barely see the top of Garcia's head. He caught A.J.'s eyes and made as if he approved of him staying on even though he knew A.J. could see through it. Jonah wondered how long Rafael was going to get to him and ruin any more would-be dates. He knew he shouldn't worry about A.J. and where they stood, but he also knew that the undercurrent of anxiety running through him had nothing to do with what A.J. was doing and everything to do with his own state of mind concerning Rafael.

He stood to leave but not without one low whisper to Steve, telling him to get home to his wife and get the bad news over with and he'll feel better about it in the morning—after the hangover receded, of course. He also threw down a napkin with the number to a cab company written on it, because sometimes he could do something right, even if Rafael wasn't around to see it.

Once Jonah was through the doors and beyond the smell of sweat, expensive cologne, and alcohol, he could breathe easier, and the fresh air let him feel his buzz a little more.

Ah well, he could always walk home and pick up his car in the morning. Twelve miles wasn't *that* far.

It was breezy, finally, and, like a proper night out, the gel holding his calculated mess of hair had dissolved with his sweat, but unlike a proper night out, he was going home alone.

He kicked at a rock and vowed to stay feeling sorry for himself for at least another two hours before getting over it. Maybe he should call Rafael and hash this whole thing out while he was feeling just about as low as he could get.

While he was still deciding if that was just the whiskey talking, his phone rang, and hey, it was Rafael.

"You can't fool me, Santos. I decided to call you first." But he was still talking to a ringing phone, and he really needed to answer it.

"Detective Santos! What is *up*?" Jonah assumed that the booze had made his phone so small, but he couldn't be sure at the moment, not when the sidewalk had started rolling like an earthquake, and Rafael was saying something about how drunk he sounded. Jonah was just about to crack that he resembled that remark when he realized that he actually *did* resemble that remark. When did he start talking to Rafael, anyway? But there was Rafael's voice on the other end, tinny, and definitely… he would say exasperated if he could, in fact, say exasperated right then.

Rafael was asking about Garcia, A.J., and a few other people, assuming Jonah was still with them and apparently no one else was answering their phones.

Jonah didn't have time for this. He reached in his pocket and felt around for something to distract him from the hurtful drunk thought that Rafael only called him as a last resort, but all he found was some loose change and a coupon he had gotten in the mail and forgotten to use the week before at the smoothie place that had just opened up near the grocery store. He should do laundry more.

He should have been listening to Rafael, because it sounded important.

He did catch "trafficking" and "undercover," and also, "the captain wants you all here now," but Jonah also realized it was the reason Rafael completely ditched them tonight. Rafael was still talking, and Jonah was sure he was supposed to say something at that point.

"Landers, have you seen them or not and are you sober enough to get to the station?" Jonah snapped out of the fog because at no point before that had Rafael mentioned actually needing Jonah to be a part of whatever he had been talking about.

"Sober as a church mouse, yes. We'll be there in twenty. Or more." Jonah thought really hard for a second. "No less than twenty minutes. I gotta go back and get them. They're inside dancing and I'm not. You stay there and I will be there, with them, in more than twenty minutes but less than an hour." Yes, that sounded sober and also professional. Jonah was going to have to think about adding whiskey to the list of things he wasn't going to drink again. It was going to go right above mezcal but way below vodka.

Jonah didn't relish the thought of going back into the club, nor did he particularly want to ride in the backseat of the A.J.'s car because he wasn't sure if A.J. would forget his chivalry and go hos before bros when it came to picking shotgun. He had the feeling Garcia got carsick anyway and would insist on the front seat for better air flow or some shit.

Jonah turned to walk back into the bar. Rafael's gruff insistence had made the decision for him. A small wave of relief washed over him as he bumped into A.J. and Garcia at the door. A.J. had unbuttoned a few of his top buttons in the heat of the crowd, and it only momentarily distracted Jonah from the sight of Garcia, who had clearly broken her vow of alcohol chastity, swaying side to side into people trying to pass by and singing "99 Luftballons"—in its original German, by the way. Which was *awesome*.

"Need a ride home, Jonah?" A.J. had the grace to look awkward and vulnerable and Jonah appreciated that.

"I thought maybe we could take me on a tour of the city, you know? The parking lot, the street, Taco Casa, the police station…." Case or not, he needed sustenance and something to absorb the alcohol, and there was a burrito calling his name. He explained the situation to A.J. and Garcia as best he could, which amounted to "Rafael is all grumpy and says we have to be back at the station because I think crime happened."

A.J. turned to Garcia. "Jenny, you need a ride too. How many Tahiti Tweetys did you have?"

Garcia giggled and replied with a singsong, "I had *two* and yes I *do*." She paused dramatically and held her hands up like she had more to say. "Hey! I'm a *poet* and I made a *rhyme*. Wait. No. Let me try that again—"

A.J. sighed and threw Garcia into the car before she could figure where she went wrong.

A.J. didn't seem too happy to be dragged back to the station at a ridiculous time of night and having to cart two buzzed detectives around, but he was the only one with the wits to drive at that point, and Jonah was sure that he was more intrigued because Jonah could not seem to tell him what exactly happened and why they were all needed, and Jonah certainly wasn't going to say it was because he was too busy being drunk and pissy and distracted when Rafael tried to relay all this information to him.

Garcia was sobering up a bit then. Not enough to find her phone, which Jonah knew was in the little zippered compartment in the middle pocket of her purse because he had seen her texting with the guy she had spent the previous night with and was being obvious about being pissed when he didn't show up.

He should have told her where it was between mouthfuls of burrito (he wasn't kidding about the Taco Casa), but he was still kind of mad that A.J. had seemed to have a good time with her and Jonah couldn't manage to have a good time with anyone and she would just have to manage on her own. Jonah swallowed thickly and washed the Pico de Gallo down with Dr Pepper. The caffeine was chasing away the last vestiges of self-pity, leaving room for more spicy beef and an unhealthy dose of anger (he was right about the carsickness, by the way).

# Chapter 23

RAFAEL, STILL all buttoned up in his suit and tie despite the heat, bothered to almost look sad that he was not part of the trio walking toward him when they got to the station. Jonah took that as a hint that there was actually a human in there somewhere and resolved to try harder to get him to break.

Jonah chucked the burrito wrappers in the trash as A.J. had insisted (*It's bad enough I have to drive you drunks here. I don't want my car smelling any worse*) and chewed thoughtfully on the end of the straw in his Dr Pepper, not quite wanting the caffeine to be gone yet because it seemed to be the only thing standing guard at the gate of his stomach and all the little whiskeys and cows were trying to escape.

Rafael held a file that was stamped CONFIDENTIAL, and that wouldn't have been so unusual in the litigious 21st century, but the stamps seemed to be coloring the once light brown cover of the manila file a deep, angry red. Jonah couldn't think of anyone on the MDPD *that* stamp-happy for a normal crime. He wished he had been a little more sober when Rafael was talking to him on the phone, and he didn't want to face an angry partner having to explain it all over again. He needed to think fast to come up with a plan. That was the story he would stick to as he ran to the nearest restroom to watch his night come back up and, hey, no more burritos after whiskey ever again.

Jonah leaned his head against the cool tile wall behind the toilet, not caring that it may only be slightly cleaner than the floor, and vowed to suggest bowling or a bounce house rental next time they had a closed case to celebrate instead of a night at the bar.

He had maybe five minutes to find out what the case was about before he absolutely had to get back to Rafael, and he was sober enough then to know that the toilet wasn't going to start giving up any answers.

Cold water barely took away the bitter acid in his mouth, but Officer Andrew Davidson, so conveniently around to hear Jonah's retching, had been trying to quit smoking before his baby was born, and he kept the drugstore around the corner afloat with gum purchases alone.

"Davidson, buddy!"

Davidson was all too happy to oblige the small request for information along with the gum, and even more so after Jonah offered to "take him out for a boys' night," which, to everyone but the future Mrs. Davidson, meant giving him an alibi when Jonah dropped him at his ex-girlfriend's.

Jonah made a mental note to buy something pink for the baby now and a book about staying away from guys like Andy later before rejoining everyone in the conference room with the staggeringly small amount of information about the case. He had a name, at least, and Google had helped with some background on him.

"Landers. So nice of you to join us again." Sarcasm hanging in the air was better than Jonah's barf breath, so he let Rafael's remark go and sat in an empty chair at the table.

Rafael turned the whiteboard over where there were photos taped to it with information written underneath each one. He picked up a long pointer and smacked it so loudly against one that it echoed in Jonah's head.

"John Badcock."

"The jai alai magnate? Owns the biggest stadium in the state? Worth a few hundred million?" *Thank you, Andy*, though it looked like Jonah was about to get a full briefing anyway. At least the gum was the good kind that kept its flavor for a while.

Rafael actually looked impressed at the quick answer. Few people had heard of the sport outside of South Florida, and Badcock liked to keep a low profile. "One and the same, Landers. Got a tip on him running a prostitution ring that looks like it's going to check out. Word is he's blackmailing several high-ranking city and state officials, maybe a few politicians, couple of foreign diplomats… anyway, the same informant also made accusations of sex trafficking from Eastern Europe, and I'm not about to let this case go to the feds, so we're moving in on his mansion tomorrow night before this gets to them. Vice is taking care of the supplier. They've actually been in there for months, but with this new information, they're upping their timetable and should have control over it by tomorrow night. They'll have full access to get someone in there as merchandise. Choya, you're running surveillance and tech. He gets his blackmail from cameras he has there at his mansion when he throws his little shindigs. Find the source, find the evidence."

A.J. nodded and stood to leave. "Got it, boss." Suddenly being tasked with the new case seemed to sway A.J.'s attitude, and he almost bounced out of the room.

"Garcia, Landers, you're here gathering evidence. I want names, ranks, amounts, everything you can muster up on his vics. I'm going in as an interested party."

Garcia cleared her throat loudly. "And I'm supposed to let you get this collar all by yourself? No way. I'm going in too."

Rafael turned quickly toward Garcia and held up a finger to stop her. "Oh. Did I forget to mention it's a male prostitution ring, Garcia? You're not exactly anyone's type there."

"I'll go." Jonah chimed in before Rafael could move on. This was his chance to redeem himself for Orlando once and for all. Cracking a case was one thing, but a successful undercover mission was another, especially considering with whom he'd be going UC. And it was a potentially huge takedown of a very powerful man. This could make his career.

Rafael looked like he could barely contain his laughter. "You, kid? I don't think so. I'm not letting you go in UC on something like this. You have no idea what you'd be getting yourself into."

Jonah blew out a breath. "I'm an adult, Rafael, and I'm also a detective. I can make that decision on my own."

Rafael was getting angry. "No, you can't. You're not going. I don't need you in there. You're staying here and running point for me on the whos, whats, wheres, and how muches. End of story."

Luis, who had been silent through the exchange, looked up from her phone and suddenly stood and walked toward Rafael. "Can I see you a moment, Santos?"

Rafael threw up his hands and reluctantly followed Luis to her office, leaving Garcia and a handful of other detectives and officers watching Jonah with morbid curiosity.

There was only about a minute before Rafael's enraged voice rang out through the entire station.

"With *him*? Are you *shitting* me? He can't handle that! You *know* he's not ready for that!"

His was the only voice coming from Luis's office that anyone could make out clearly, but it was obvious Luis was trying to talk some kind of sense into him. However, it seemed Rafael was having none of it.

The back and forth went on for a few more minutes, mostly in Spanish as their tempers flared higher, with everyone within earshot exchanging awkward glances, until Luis's voice finally boomed over Rafael's complaining and told him to sit down and shut up.

A moment later her door was flung open and there was a split second of cacophony where everyone tried to look like they had been going about their business the whole time but failed miserably.

Not that Luis noticed. "Landers! In my office. Now!"

The door slammed shut again and suddenly all eyes were back on Jonah. Standing up and walking the fifteen feet felt more like a walk of shame with all those eyes on him. He honestly had no idea what was going to happen once he was inside; even though he was in a police station, he couldn't rule out being murdered at this point.

He found Rafael sitting in the chair opposite Luis, and she motioned for Jonah to sit down next to him. Rafael rolled his head toward Jonah and sucked his teeth at the sight of him.

"It seems now that Vice doesn't have a man to spare. Or at least a man who could pass for our purposes." Rafael blinked a few times like he was gathering himself to say something he didn't want to. "I have also been informed that, unlike Edgewood, you are a good physical fit for what Vice needs tomorrow night." It was like he was being forced to read, through gritted teeth, from a script.

Luis slammed her palms down on her desk in annoyance. "What Detective Santos is trying to say is that Vice is stretched pretty thin already. But, Landers, this isn't a cakewalk assignment. You've got to be absolutely comfortable with what will be happening at Badcock's. You'd be going in as merchandise—"

"Meat," Rafael said. "You'll be meat. Every senator, every county commissioner, every old crusty billionaire is going to paw at you like you're their personal pet. Until I 'buy' you. It's degrading and dehumanizing, and you're not ready for it. One look at you and they're going to have their hands in places you probably haven't even discovered yet."

"Detective Santos," warned Luis. Rafael would make a terrible advertiser if he ever quit law enforcement. But was that also some kind of weird admission that Jonah was not completely unpleasant to look at?

Rafael sighed. "Look, kid, all I'm saying is that there is a very good chance you'll be put into a situation that you can't handle, and I can't help you out if we get in the weeds. You're going to have pervy men all over you, including me. I'm going to have to pretend to buy you for the evening, and we are expected to go into a 'private' room and, well, basically generate some blackmail material for Badcock to use. Now, I'm not worried about that last part because once we're inside, Choya's team will be working on finding the source of the camera feeds, but you're going to have to put up with some crazy shit before that happens. Once we have a source, backup will move in. We'll get the evidence and start arresting every fucker in there. We get a millionaire blackmailer, a bunch of politicians, dignitaries, rich Palm Beach real estate moguls, and a sex-trafficking ring in one go, and I finally get to leave shit like that goddamned Tahiti Tweety nonsense behind. And I don't want you fucking this up. Or worse, I don't want this fucking *you* up."

Jonah's eyebrow shot up. Was this a sign that Rafael actually cared? Regardless, Jonah was a grown ass man. "I'll be fine. I'm not some kid off the street here."

"But you're not experienced."

"I'm experienced enough." Why was he still trying to hold Jonah back, especially now?

"You got no idea, kid. No idea. Captain, isn't there anyone else?" The hardened detective sounded more like a twelve-year-old getting a bum deal on a group project in school, and Jonah wanted to punch the whine right out of him.

"Santos, *mira*, I will not tell you again. Do you want me to read you the e-mail?" She clicked her mouse a few times and squinted at the screen. "'We have two pretty boys who could fit the bill, and they're both spoken for through next week.' You want to move on this now before the feds catch wind? You're taking our pretty boy—no offense, Detective Landers—and getting the job done. He understands what this might involve, and he consents. That's all I need. Now stop wasting my time and yours. Landers, Vice will set you up with everything you need in the morning. Be over there by 8:30 a.m. Seeing as it's almost two now, I'd say everyone needs to go home and get some sleep."

She stood and pointed an accusing finger at Rafael. "That means you, Santos. There's no point bitching and moaning about Landers's performance tomorrow if it's you screwing it up because you haven't slept."

Luis gathered her things and walked toward the door, an obvious and thinly veiled order for them both to vacate her office before she did. Or else.

Rafael and Jonah walked silently down the hall away from Luis and everyone still waiting for them in the conference room. It took about three seconds after they turned the corner before Rafael was in Jonah's space, throwing him roughly against the wall.

"You think you got this, but you don't know what you just signed up for. Mark my words: this time tomorrow you're going to regret not listening to me." Jonah looked up at Rafael, wide-eyed and, okay, maybe just a little scared of him. Rafael was going to give himself whiplash if he didn't stop going back and forth on Jonah like this.

Scared or not, Jonah couldn't show it. "After everything you said about how far I've come since Orlando and you still pull this on me? Do you think I'm any good or not? I can't keep up with you, Rafael. One minute you're telling me I'm doing a good job, and the next you're preventing me from doing it. I'm not the brand newbie I was in Orlando. And you can't exactly fault me 100 percent on that, and you know it. I'm ready for this. I'm not scared to get my hands dirty, and I don't know how else I can prove to you that I can do this without actually doing it."

Rafael breathed deeply and inched closer to Jonah's face, but he must have felt Jonah's body tighten up like it was preparing for something and loosened his grip on Jonah slowly before letting him go completely and walking away without another word.

He made it to the parking lot before realizing that his car was still at the bar and Rafael's crazy tight timeline prevented A.J. from leaving for at least three more hours while he and the rest of the tech team rushed to put together everything they needed to get into the security system and monitor Rafael and Jonah while they did their job inside.

Davidson came through a second time by offering him a ride to his car as he went out on patrol—after a breathalyzer test, though, and a reassurance that Rafael wasn't as bad as he seemed and A.J. was as much of an expert as he boasted about being. Maybe Andy would be all right, after all. Jonah wished he could say the same about himself.

# Chapter 24

WHEN 8:30 a.m. rolled around, Jonah had more Advil than hours of sleep, but he'd evened the score a bit with two shots of Café Cubano. He'd tossed and turned, getting a little pissier with each hour as he ran through Rafael's list of doubts about Jonah's ability to get the job done. This was his big chance to show the department he could do this job and everything it required and do it very well, and he wasn't about to let the idea of being ogled and groped by powerful, rich, and probably hideous old men stop him. Or the thought of Rafael doing those things to him....

"You got anything tighter?"

"Hmmm?" The short, perky blonde in charge of getting him into character, Sabrina, blew out her cheeks at his complete lack of attention span.

"Do you have anything tighter? You know, pants? Shirt? Something that doesn't scream cop? Something a little flashier? Trashier?" She pursed her bright pink lips in annoyance.

Jonah shook his head, and she blew out an annoyed breath. "Fine. We've got some stuff here you might fit into."

There was a small room off to the left, and her heels clicked on the tile as she went to rummage through it, giving instructions to Jonah on how to act and how not to act as she did. She, like Rafael, warned him of roaming hands and worse, and Jonah had to wonder if he looked so delicate that a few ass grabs would do so much damage to him.

"You ever go UC with Santos before?" She was eyeing a pair of skintight black leather pants she had brought out.

"Once. Well, sort of." Sometimes his face still hurt from the punch, and even though Jonah didn't think there was any logical way it could happen again on this case, he instinctively reached up to protect his face.

"He can be... a little too professional sometimes. Don't let him get to you while he's in character. He's only thinking of the job. If we were to give out awards for these things, he'd win best actor." Sabrina's eyes lit up when she spied a dark button-up shirt that looked two sizes too small for Jonah's already fit frame.

"You ever....?" Jonah reluctantly lifted his shirt over his head to try on the one that Sabrina had thrust at him.

She smiled. "Oh, yeah. Rafael and I have been Mr. and Mrs. more times than I would like. I don't like to kiss and tell, but he's a damn fine cop and if anything happens during a case, he always apologizes for it. Once had to be my abusive husband. Called me all kinds of names and shoved me around. Didn't hurt. He knows how to fake it, but I still got flowers every week for two months after that. He's not as mean as he makes himself out to be. But that's between you and me, got it?"

Jonah chuckled at the thought of Rafael filling out those little cards that get stuck in bouquets. *"Sorry I called you a bitch and pretended to beat you up. Sincerely, Rafael Santos."*

"I won't tell a soul." He didn't know how a shirt that tight fit him, but Sabrina gave him a nod of approval and shoved the pants at him with an evil grin. She had the good graces to turn away so he could try them on.

Clad in the tight shirt and boxers, Jonah bent over to put the first leg in.

"Boxers off, Detective." Sabrina was giggling and Jonah instinctively stood up and put the pants in front of his crotch.

"What—are you looking—how did you...?"

"Have you ever worn leather pants before, Detective?" He could almost hear her disapproving eyebrow go up.

"I—no. I mean—" *Way to look professional. Can't even put on pants correctly.*

Sabrina giggled harder but still didn't turn around. "Boxers off, Detective Landers."

Jonah sighed and took off his boxers. Getting into the pants was surprisingly easier than the shirt, though. Sabrina had a real eye for sizing, it seemed, even if he did feel ridiculous.

"Okay, how do I look?" Sabrina turned around, and Jonah held out his arms and did a graceless turn so she could see him from all angles. There was no way he didn't look as ridiculous as he felt.

Instead, Sabrina had gone wide-eyed and was nodding emphatically. "Wow. I mean… wow. Not going to lie here. If I were a gross old senator, I'd be all over you." That was surprising. Even though Sabrina was far from his type, the flattery was nice.

"It's just missing one last thing." She ran to a side table and started rummaging through a box.

"Oh, yeah? What is that?" But Sabrina had already made her way back and pushed him down into a chair.

"Close your eyes." Jonah was a little scared but also curious, so he closed his eyes. A moment later Sabrina was doing something to his eyelids.

"Are you putting makeup on me?" Great. That was just what he needed to complete this embarrassment.

"Shut up and trust me." She took another few seconds and then, instructing him upon pain of death not to open his eyes until she started to work on the bottoms, she pulled him to standing and walked him a few steps away.

"Open."

He did and barely recognized himself in the mirror in front of him.

"Wow." He could hardly deny that he looked good. Sabrina tousled his hair a bit and unbuttoned a few buttons on the shirt.

"Right? Okay, take these for tonight. I won't be here to redo all this." She pointed at his head and made a circle to indicate hair and makeup. "So you're going to have to remember how this looks now and try to recreate it."

"Yeah," Jonah breathed. Which was far more than he thought he would be able to do in the tight pants.

"Rafael is going to flip the fuck out. I don't think *I* ever looked this good on one of our cases." She handed him the eyeliner. "Good luck and all tonight. We've been working that supplier for months now. Crazy how this is all working out for everyone. Rafael is a good man and a great detective, and he deserves this."

"Thanks. I needed that. Everyone thinks I'm going to screw this case up." Sabrina chuckled and headed for the door so Jonah could undress in peace this time.

She opened the door and shot a final glance toward Jonah. "That's not what they're thinking you're going to screw up, Detective Landers."

Jonah started to shimmy out of the pants but paused abruptly when he realized what she had said.

"What? What does that even—Sabrina?" he called after her, but she was gone, and he had one foot out and one foot still in the pants. He tried bouncing on his free foot to the doorway, but even if he made it without smashing his face into the floor, he was still too hungover to go running after her anyway. He had a feeling he wouldn't get many answers from her even if he did catch up.

He had his costume. He had his character. He had another round of warnings. There was nothing left to do but wait until the evening, which, he felt, was best done from the comfort of his bed. He barely got his sweatpants off before he set his alarm, fell into bed, and slept the rest of the day away. Dreams of Rafael in Jonah's space—stealing him away from a crowd of men who were pawing at him, kissing him in front of them like he owned Jonah—dominated his sleep, and they didn't let up until Jonah's alarm went off.

Of course Rafael was already at the station well before anyone else involved in the case even thought about being there. He was dressed in a very expensive-looking gray three-piece suit that looked way out of the department's budget, his jacket folded carefully over his chair and his sleeves pushed up as he worked. The way it fit him told Jonah it was one of Rafael's own, and he made a mental note to find out who the tailor was and secretly thank him.

"Landers. Get dressed and get back in here. We have to go over the plan until you know it better than your secret diary detailing all the times I've been mean to you." *Nice. Starting with the insults already.* Maybe he was only a nice guy to Sabrina.

Jonah grabbed his clothes from his locker and tried to make himself look as good as Sabrina had earlier. How ladies did the eyeliner thing every day was beyond him, but he thought he managed to do it okay given that he knew he had maybe ten minutes before Rafael banged down the door and dragged him out to get things started.

He hadn't felt self-conscious when it was just him and Sabrina that morning, but walking out of the locker room and into the hall where every cop in the precinct could see him was something he didn't think he was adequately prepared for. Someone actually whistled, and he didn't know if it was a cop or a perp. He also didn't know which one he wanted it to be the least. Luckily the walk was short to the conference room Rafael had set up for them.

As much as he wasn't prepared for every uniform and perp to watch him try to walk normally in the leather pants, he was even less ready for Rafael's reaction to him as he tried to enter the room as quietly as possible to avoid too much attention.

Rafael's eyes went wide, and he looked him up and down a few times. He stumbled a bit over his words, and it seemed as if he had to force himself to remember what he had been saying. It wasn't an entirely unwelcome reaction.

A.J. was not as subtle, sliding up to Jonah with an appreciative whistle and Jonah's first official roaming hand of the evening. "Do you want me to come over after all this is over? Vice won't miss these clothes until Monday."

Rafael locked eyes with Jonah and gave him a weird look Jonah couldn't decipher.

"Choya, sit down and leave Landers alone." Or maybe it wasn't hard to decipher. Rafael looked almost… possessive. A.J. seemed to get the hint and sat back down with his tail between his legs.

Jonah swore that Rafael actually smirked at A.J. He would need to reflect on that later.

"Now, if we could get down to business, we have a very tight window, and the plan has to run like clockwork or we are all in deep, deep shit."

"You mean, like if some cop from, oh, I don't know, let's say *Orlando* is on deep cover assignment for the state and has already infiltrated in secret? That kind of deep shit?" Jonah would 100 percent blame that sarcastic outburst on nervousness later on, but he couldn't help but think how similar this assignment was to that fateful night so long ago in Orlando.

Rafael merely glared at Jonah and sucked his teeth before regaining his composure, but at least he knew that Jonah hadn't forgotten everything that happened.

They went over and over the plan until there was nothing else in Jonah's brain but timelines, names, faces, and how to avoid being bought by forty-year-old real estate agents from Palm Beach ("Craig Betz: married, couple of kids, lots of shady deals. Likes blond twentysomethings and will pay top dollar. Don't act dumb in front of him. Even though he has an airhead trophy wife, he prefers brain over brawn any day. Got it, kid?"). There was no way this plan could go wrong.

"What if it does go wrong, Raf?"

"Don't break character for anything, kid. This time it could mean more than a punch to the face."

# Chapter 25

IT HAD been twenty-three minutes since a combination of Badcock's security team, horny rich guests, and apparently-more-state-of-the-art-than-the-CIA computer network shot the plan to hell, but there was still a chance to escape unscathed if they played it cool and didn't break cover. The tiny high-tech devices A.J. had given them to place surreptitiously in any room with a camera in it were doing their job sending whatever info A.J. needed to try to trace the signals back to him, and both Jonah and Rafael were playing their parts as high-priced rent boy and high-paying buyer without fail.

There were always variables and unpredictabilities in any situation, though. Last time it was Rafael (or Jonah, depending on who was telling the story). This time no one could have guessed how popular Jonah would be with the men inside once he made his way into the great room of Badcock's mansion, and even fewer could have predicted just how good Badcock's security system was once A.J. got in there and started rooting around.

The mansion itself was modeled in the old Gothic style (Jonah could see Grace setting one of her novels here. He'd broken down and read one out of curiosity, and it was the tragic love triangle between a man, a woman, and the male ghost of the woman's former lover, and they all lived in a mansion not unlike Badcock's. The ghost ended up with the guy in the end, and they somehow managed to have some surprisingly hot sex despite the obvious difficulties they had overcoming one half of them having a pesky noncorporeal-form problem. It wasn't half-bad, actually) and stuck out like a sore thumb next to the modern, natural-light-filled monstrosities flanking it, the large dark rooms looking more at home in centuries past even if the technology guarding it was light years ahead.

It took quick thinking on both Rafael and Jonah's part to avoid Jonah being "bought" by several men while they waited for A.J. to hold up his end. The problem now was that A.J. was taking far longer than Rafael and Jonah had ideas on how to avoid ending up in the room they were supposed to go into to have sex, watched by cameras and the people Badcock had hired to make sure those cameras picked up everything they needed to from all the right angles.

Rafael led Jonah by the belt loops, pausing at every new security cam to push him against the wood and stone wall and, under the guise of a passionate embrace, relay more orders to him and A.J. waiting in a van not three miles from the site, listening in through their well-hidden two-ways. Jonah could feel Rafael's breath, hot and Scotch-tinged, winding down the shell of his ear and down his sweat-soaked neck, and it was becoming more difficult not to react to the show Rafael was giving Badcock's security team. Rafael's calculating hands grasped Jonah's shoulders tightly, and Jonah was sure the eyeliner he'd meticulously reapplied hours earlier to make him look every bit the irresistible rent boy was smudged.

A.J. had been trying frantically to trace the private feeds Badcock had set up to their source, which was the best bet for finding the proof they needed, but until they had that source, until A.J. could track it down, they had to play it out, no matter how A.J. felt about having to listen to them go at it, even if it *was* pretend. Or even, in Jonah's case, if it wasn't all pretend.

Rafael tried to protect Jonah, to stall going into the bedroom where they were expected to do much more than what they were doing out in the hallway, but Badcock was very good, as one would expect when hiding state secrets, and A.J. couldn't lock on to any definite sources. Of course Badcock had had help setting the place up—the best technology blackmail payouts could afford. And they could afford a lot, judging by the clientele in the room and also A.J.'s occasional swearing coming through their two-ways.

Rafael ran a hand down the side of Jonah's impossibly tight leather pants, and Jonah's eyes rolled up into the back of his head.

"If we break now, we're dead. This is more than I should ask of you, kid. I tried to warn you. Why didn't you just listen to me?" Rafael somehow managed to sound annoyed even as he whispered.

Jonah nodded weakly into the crook of Rafael's neck, praying that, by some miracle, A.J. would come through before they hit the room. God, he smelled good. Like woods and the ocean and a warm summer's day, and Jonah wanted to commit the scent to memory forever.

Rafael cupped Jonah's face and almost imperceptibly breathed a tiny, "I'm sorry, Landers," and kissed him. Jonah froze, even as he knew anyone watching could pick up on his body language. It wasn't the kind of kiss he'd fantasized about, but it was Rafael's lips on his, and his brain was having trouble processing it. Pushed up so close to Rafael, Jonah should be able to pick up how awkward it must have been for Rafael to be kissing a man… to be kissing *Jonah*… but there was nothing that indicated to him that this was a terrible ordeal for Rafael.

Rafael moved quickly away from his mouth and across his jaw line to his ear. "Play your role. I bought you, remember? You're mine for the evening. Now act like it, damn it." It was some small comfort to hear some of the real Rafael come out.

Jonah loosened his fists and lifted his head to expose more neck, trying to look like the wanton young man he was supposed to be. He tentatively raised a hand to grab at a fistful of Rafael's hair, his unbuttoned cuffs dangling at his wrists. Rafael's breath hitched and as he let it out, Jonah could hear the tiniest "that's more like it."

Rafael pulled back, and it would take something far less than an untrained civilian not to see the look of pure lust on Rafael's face. Jonah had never noticed just how green his eyes were. Jonah blinked, and Rafael was back on him again, this time not waiting for Jonah to catch up. Rafael's hand snaked around to caress the back of Jonah's neck, and he made a noise he absolutely didn't mean to. Jonah's eyes snapped open to protest, to explain, to try to make sense of it, but Rafael seemed to take it as an encouragement and exploited the moment Jonah's world was knocked off-kilter to deepen the kiss.

From the moment he felt Rafael's tongue, Jonah couldn't help but wonder how much of this was acting and how much of this was meant to give Rafael something to lord over him later when all this was over. But Rafael seemed a little too comfortable shoving his tongue down Jonah's throat, like this wasn't his first time kissing a guy, and, after letting a small moan escape, Rafael jerked slightly against him. This was Rafael, though, and a wave of confusion washed over Jonah because, of course, Rafael was acting and right then they were both caught up in this web they'd had to spin to get them where they needed to be to bust this case open. It was about the case, Jonah kept thinking, even though Rafael was playing dirty with Jonah. Whatever petty revenge game this was, it was working. There was no way Rafael couldn't tell this was affecting Jonah.

"What are you—" But Rafael cut him off with a bite to his jaw and that just wasn't fair.

"Shut up. Please. God. This is not the time, kid."

Jonah let his head fall against the heavy wood paneling behind him, rattling a painting next to his head of someone who looked like a 17th century lord, just as footsteps came around the corner. Badcock's security detail. Armed to the teeth. Every moment they were in the hallway and in range of the many cameras was a moment closer to being discovered for who they really were. And Badcock was already on edge and suspicious, judging from the glares he'd given Rafael over his glass of 100-year-old Scotch. Jonah would be eternally grateful that Badcock was not the type of man who wanted to sample the merchandise before letting it go to a buyer. Money might be able to buy a lot of things, but it didn't seem to be enough to fix Badcock's face, worn and lined too much even for his sixty years.

Rafael pulled away from Jonah in mock annoyance. "Do you mind? We're a little busy here, and your ugly mug isn't doing anything for my dick."

For emphasis Rafael snaked his hands around to Jonah's ass and squeezed so Jonah's crotch pushed into Rafael's hip. Jonah let out a sharp breath at the sensation.

The taller of Badcock's men turned his shifty gaze toward them and sighed out a halfhearted, "Take it to the room. We're a respectable club here," before motioning to the others to keep walking.

Rafael buried his face in Jonah's neck and kissed along the underside of his jaw until the footsteps finally faded.

They needed to get to the room and quietly plan their next move so they could get away from everyone who expected them to have sex, and Rafael could go back to being plain old Rafael Santos, the law-abiding detective who couldn't stand Jonah, and not the man who was currently swiping his tongue across his collarbone. Which was also not fair.

Rafael broke the contact and pulled Jonah down to him by the neck. "Next time you'll listen to me, yeah? I can't stall forever out here."

"Do what you have to. What's the plan?" He hadn't meant to sound so out of breath when he said that, though. Jonah prayed that Rafael had some decorum in him so the teasing that would surely come after this stayed between them and didn't make it to the whole station. And somewhere in that thought he remembered that A.J. was still listening to every word they said.

Rafael glared at Jonah for a split second but took his hand to lead him on. He laced their fingers together, and Jonah stared at it, not quite knowing how to feel about something so simple when he was still trying to process everything else that was happening. Rafael sighed, seized another opportunity, and took the other hand, lifting them both up over Jonah's head.

Rafael backed him once again against the wall for another kiss before he angrily hissed in Jonah's ear, "I don't have a plan. It was never supposed to get this far. Now get with it. Don't fuck this up, Landers, I swear to God."

It was only kind of sad that an angry Rafael was comforting only because it was the only thing familiar about the whole ordeal.

Jonah shook his head and bucked his hips up into Rafael's. "I won't. Just let me know what you need me to do." Why didn't he listen to Rafael's warnings, again?

"Just promise me you won't ever volunteer for a case so far over your damned head ever again after tonight."

Jonah closed his eyes. *Never gonna have the upper hand with him, am I?* Jonah wasn't an equal partner in Rafael's mind. Not like this, anyway. Rafael wasn't thinking about how they could work this together because he was too busy thinking he had to protect Jonah from all of this. How Jonah couldn't cut it. Jonah could hear Peter's voice running under Rafael's in his head: "You're not ready, newbie."

He was left with two choices: let Rafael keep on like this—let him have his way and continue to see Jonah as a small-town detective who couldn't keep up in the big city—or finally show Rafael what Jonah Landers was made of and beat him at his own game. It was a dangerous game of chicken, even more so in this situation, but they'd both gone too far now, and if Jonah had learned anything from the last few months in Miami, it was that he had a definite danger boner.

Jonah surged forward and kissed Rafael. He stopped holding back, attacking Rafael's lips with his own and pushing as far into Rafael's space as he could manage in his position. It was more natural this time. Even in the midst of the danger, even though they were supposed to be just acting, the sigh that escaped from Rafael sure sounded real to him, and then nothing made sense.

He let Rafael take it as far as he was willing to go, tongues exploring each other's mouths like they both wanted it, and they stood there for a moment lost in it. Jonah felt the moment Rafael snapped out of his daze, and the soft groan that escaped his lips made Jonah smile.

They reached the room Badcock had set aside for them. *Ordered us into*, Jonah thought. Unless A.J. managed to trace the source and manipulate the feed quickly, the next step was going to be sex with Rafael Santos.

And Jonah was not so sure that was a bad thing.

One last distraction, one last stall. Rafael pushed Jonah against the door, frantically unbuttoning his shirt, like he couldn't wait until they were inside. Rafael buried his face in Jonah's chest, cheek nuzzling into his chest hair. Jonah reached down and cradled Rafael's face, hiding his mouth so he could relay more orders without being picked up on the security cams.

Rafael's voice rumbled against Jonah's skin. "Choya." Rafael's lips and tongue skimmed over a nipple, and Jonah sucked in a breath. "Tell me you have something."

Rafael bit, just a little. Jonah's hips shoved forward just as his eyes rolled back. "A source, anything. Please!" He dug his nails into Jonah's skin, and Jonah's entire body trembled.

"Rafael, God, Rafael, I'm sorry. Nothing yet. This guy is… really good. His firewalls have firewalls, and I've never seen code like this." A.J. sounded as frustrated as Jonah felt, but most likely for different reasons. And it could not be comfortable for A.J. to listen to this all go down.

Jonah made a small sound, and Rafael blinked like it had distracted him. Rafael wordlessly pushed a finger into Jonah's mouth so he could hear A.J. better, but then groaned like he was thinking twice about that decision when Jonah's tongue started circling it slowly and deliberately for anyone who might be watching.

"Choya, I swear to God. Tell me you can do this." Jonah couldn't get a read on Rafael beyond his frustration with both A.J. and him. He had no idea if this was really affecting him like it was Jonah. He would bet a paycheck that Rafael could fake an erection if he needed to, just for the sake of staying in character.

"Oh, oh yeah, Rafael. I can do this. It might be another ten minutes, but I can do this. No code has beaten me yet. You just, eh, do what you have to. I'll keep working on my end. You keep working on your ends—" Rafael could hear the cringe. "Eh, God. You know what I mean."

Jonah heard the comm switch off, but he wasn't too far gone to know that A.J. was still listening to everything that was going on as they acted out their charade. Jonah didn't know what this would mean for him and A.J., but there was a growing part of him that didn't care right then.

They were still pressed up against the door, Rafael holding Jonah in place with his entire body. Jonah was breathing fast and shallow, and he knew it was going through the two-way, interspersed with breathy, constant apologies from Rafael.

They managed to get the door open and go inside the sparsely furnished but somehow still grand room. It had what it needed, though: a bed, a few chairs, a dark wooden table, furniture for all kinds of different sexual positions. Jonah could actually feel the trepidation in Rafael's body language as they entered and Rafael spotted the well-hidden cameras within three seconds.

Rafael started the string of apologies again. Jonah knew that being a cop and accepting this assignment meant he had to be ready for anything—*anything*—and this was just another thing they had to do to solve the crime and put away the bad guy, but Rafael was breathing it, like a litany, "I'm sorry, Jonah. I'm so sorry," over and over again until Jonah stopped him with a kiss.

For a moment it was all breath and moan and finally, low and confident, "Rafael, it's okay." Because it had to be. Because maybe it always was. And maybe this would be the final nail in the coffin for Jonah's future with A.J. and that had to be okay too.

Jonah brought Rafael close for another kiss, groaning a little as Rafael's tongue slid its way in. Jonah's hands flew to the back of Rafael's head, grabbing at handfuls of hair. There was no logical reason for tongue. Yet there it was. Not that Jonah was complaining.

Rafael snaked his hands around Jonah's and pinned them over his head, leaning more and more into Jonah's space. He coiled Jonah's wrists together so he could free one hand.

They couldn't delay it any longer. Badcock had been suspicious from the start. No doubt he or one of his highly paid security guards was keeping a watchful eye on the proceedings from the place A.J. was trying desperately to find.

Rafael worked his way down with his free hand, gliding over hot skin until he reached the top of Jonah's trousers. They were skintight, even tighter then with the obvious bulge in them—a bulge which, up until right then, Jonah had harbored some insane delusion he could hide.

Rafael's hand skimmed downward, and he at least had the good graces to look up at Jonah with wide eyes that might have been shock or at least some kind of understanding, but the look quickly faded into something more sinister and dark.

"Do you like that, boy?"

Jonah nodded. That voice wasn't helping. At all. *So fucking sexy.*

Rafael wasted no time and pushed harder into Jonah's erection, almost as if he wasn't quite sure if he actually felt what he thought he did, especially since Jonah was going commando under them, and there was nothing between the leather and his dick. Jonah knew his face was flushed, and there would be no explaining things away later. Not to Rafael. Not to A.J., who was still able to hear everything. And certainly not to himself.

Rafael kissed him again, but it was slower and deeper than before. Jonah struggled against the hand holding his wrists to touch Rafael back, but Rafael didn't let go.

"Stop." Rafael murmured it against Jonah's neck, and Jonah couldn't stop himself from shivering.

"Stop what?" At least he thought that's what came out of his mouth. Jonah's brain wasn't firing on all cylinders.

"Stop fighting me." Rafael gripped Jonah's wrists harder.

"Why?" Jonah curled his fingers into tight fists. He just wanted to *touch* him already.

"Because we've already gone further than what you signed up for on this assignment. You can hate me all you want later for this, but I don't want you hating yourself after this is over, partner." For a detective who thought so highly of himself and his detective abilities, Rafael was frustratingly slow on the uptake now, even as he finally admitted that Jonah was somewhat of an equal.

Jonah needed to touch like he needed air, but he had to follow Rafael's lead, so his hands stayed put. He canted his hips forward, however, and flexed his legs so they could slide Rafael's apart. He wasn't quite ready to say out loud what his body was practically screaming, though, and he didn't know if he was staying quiet for his own benefit or to spare A.J. any more discomfort. He could make all the excuses in the world for how he was acting out the scene, but as soon as he spoke the truth, everything would change. As if naming The Thing hadn't given it enough power, saying it out loud would make it unstoppable. Probably also something Edgewood and his sci-fi knowledge would know.

For the first time, Rafael looked like he came damned close to breaking as Jonah pushed his hips forward, desperately trying to make contact. Rafael grasped at Jonah's shoulder, the back of his neck, his hair, anything to pull him closer, and Jonah felt lost, reacting on pure sensation and adrenaline, and that was what it must have been when, a second later, Jonah forced himself free and shoved a hand between them. He couldn't concentrate without knowing if this was affecting Rafael in at least some small way.

What Jonah found as he pressed his palm against Rafael's trousers was a noticeable erection strained against the fabric. Rafael jerked against him and let out a small, pained noise.

Jonah had every confidence that A.J. would come through and find the signal so they could get the job done and be forced into pretending none of it ever happened, even if Jonah would never forget the feeling of Rafael's bulge in his hand. *I believe in A.J... I believe in A.J... I believe. I do. I really, really do.*

They were stuck there until A.J. actually came through with it, though, and if Rafael was into his character, following his lead meant Jonah was too. Jonah squeezed Rafael's dick through his trousers and looked up at Rafael through heavy eyelids.

"You don't have to do this, Landers." It was barely a whisper, shaky and cracking, and finally a sign of some chink in Rafael's armor, but Jonah didn't stop, and Rafael didn't stop him, not even when Jonah brought Rafael's free hand back to his mouth and starting sucking on those long fingers again, never once breaking eye contact with him.

"A-about, eh, two minutes, uh, guys... should have...." A.J. sounded breathless through the tiny earpiece.

Jonah explored the sensation some more. He tried to memorize the taste, the smell, the feel of Rafael. He committed the small groans and sighs to memory so he'd never forget. Jonah had no idea what he was doing or if either of them were even acting anymore, but until they had the next move, it was all they could do to avoid actually having sex.

He grabbed Rafael's cock through the fabric, bolder this time than the tentative cupping he'd tried before, outlining it with his fingers until Rafael whimpered and tightened his grip on Jonah's shoulders.

Frantically, Rafael pulled Jonah close. "I paid for my fantasy. Not yours. I still own you, boy." *Don't do something you're going to regret. Don't do something you can't take back.* Rafael didn't have to say a word for Jonah to understand what he really meant. This far into things, and they were still fighting each other like they both thought they knew better than the other.

Jonah closed his eyes. "So what do you want? To fuck me? Fuck my mouth? I'm all yours. Just tell me what you want and I'll do it."

And there was the truth. Out loud and hanging in the air for everyone to hear. Cameras or no, case or no, he'd let Rafael fuck him right here, and he couldn't blame staying in character for how he was reacting to this whole situation.

Rafael bit his lip for a second before blowing out a shaky breath. "Oh, would you, *kid*? Just let me throw you down and do what I want to you?"

*Kid. He can see right through me, can't he?*

"It's what I'm here for, isn't it?" Everything was breaking down, and God he wished he'd listened to Rafael about staying away from this.

Rafael breathed harder. He was breaking, and it was reckless and irresponsible and dangerous for Jonah to continue, but he didn't want to stop. There was going to be hell to pay later, but every thrust into his hand, every breathy "yes," every time he squeezed Rafael just a little bit harder, and it was easier to believe that Rafael always wanted this just as much as Jonah did.

"Ehh… guys… uuhhh…. W-we have a source." A.J.'s voice coming through their earpieces made them both jolt. "Uhh… it's… there's a bunker. Thirty yards north of the… eh… west entrance. Hidden. Trees… not on the specs. Sending in backup now. ETA a minute and a half." It had to be torture for A.J. to listen to them, but not as much as Jonah felt right then. He didn't want to stop.

Jonah breathed hard and braced himself against the wall as he gathered himself, but there was little time for contemplation. Raging erection or not, they had a case and a bad guy to bust.

Rafael sighed and straightened his clothes and in an instant it was like nothing had ever happened. He glanced back at Jonah for a weird second and ran out the door, leaving Jonah to force his body to struggle to catch up with his brain and follow.

# Chapter 26

EVERYTHING HAPPENED so quickly after that. It always did once the objective made itself clear in operations like these. When he would think back on it later, most of it was a blur. Badcock didn't go quietly, but no one expected him to anyway. There had to be hundreds of hours of footage on walls of hard drives, enough that every detective in the station would have to watch more than his or her fair share of what basically amounted to amateur gay porn to see just how far this case was going to go. But that was a task that would have to wait until the dust settled. The holding cells were full of men from the party and all of them were screaming for their lawyers and to be put in a private cell. Sorting that out would take the better part of the rest of the night, and between evidence, witness statements, confessions, and Badcock not cooperating with even the smallest request, Jonah didn't plan on seeing his bed until sometime the next week. He didn't even have time to change out of his clothes that were an increasing reminder of what he and Rafael had done.

And he couldn't even think about facing Rafael after what happened, which made it extremely awkward when Luis called the two of them into her office at about 4:00 a.m. Even more so when he walked in to see A.J. sitting in the corner holding a hard drive and looking… a little hurt.

Luis circled around behind her desk and motioned for Jonah to shut the door behind him. There was nowhere else to sit except right next to a sullen Rafael. There was no way this was going to go well.

Luis sighed before she started to speak, and it was heavy and resigned and in no way an indication that Jonah was wrong about the direction of this meeting.

"I'm going to ask one question. Just one. And your answer will determine my course of action. Got it?"

They nodded in unison without looking at each other directly. Jonah didn't know Luis too well yet, but he would bet that neither Rafael nor A.J. had even seen her this deadly serious about anything in their time.

Luis sucked her teeth and looked skyward for a moment, like she was gathering strength. "Did you do what you had to do to crack this case safely for the people involved, including yourselves, and efficiently for the department and the taxpayers of Miami?"

Jonah cocked his head to the side in confusion and embarrassment at the thought of their captain watching the two of them go at it like horny teenagers, but Rafael spoke before Jonah could open his mouth and probably ruin everything.

"Absolutely." There was no hesitation in Rafael's voice.

Luis threw her hands up and shrugged, her demeanor decidedly different in a split second. "Then that's all I will ever want to know about what happened. Choya, can you destroy just that file off the hard drive and leave whatever else is on there intact like it was never tampered with?"

"Yes, Captain, but isn't that—"

"You never saw it. I don't know about it. Badcock won't know what was on the hard drive because we got it before anyone could see it, so no one will ever know. Are we clear, Detectives?"

No one spoke for a good long while. Jonah must be more exhausted than he thought, because there was no way a police captain had just demanded that one of her employees destroy evidence.

"What about anyone in there who saw it?" Rafael sounded uncertain for the first time since Jonah had met him. It was a fair question. Tampering with evidence was one thing, even if it was considerably easy. Shutting down a witness was another and not something Jonah was willing to do even if it *were* easier for him in the long run.

Luis sighed and pursed her lips. "Well, Santos. That's the crazy thing. There was no one in the room at the time we raided it. Despite reports to the contrary, there was no one watching on the other side. We got lucky." She looked the both of them up and down. "You two got lucky, I guess."

Jonah had a feeling he would enjoy the double entendre more in a much different situation.

Luis clasped her hands together, letting her chin rest on her pointed index fingers. "If we enter this drive intact into evidence, there will be what I hear is a very juicy sex tape starring two of my detectives. A sex tape, by the way, that you two will have to testify about in public if it makes its way out of this room. And if you think that ridiculous nickname for Teiki's case was bad, you won't know what hit you if this gets out. We have more than enough evidence to convict Badcock and everyone else involved, but if you want this entered into public record, then by all means, throw it up on PornTube, because that's basically what will happen when it all comes out in court, and I will not have a huge bust overshadowed by a sex scandal. And I'm sure Internal Affairs would have something to say about what Choya tells me is on this thing, so go ahead and say good-bye to your undercover ops after that."

*Oh, God, A.J. saw it all.* Jonah couldn't hide the blush that heated his skin. At least Luis claimed she hadn't seen what was on the hard drive. He could probably look her in the face again someday. If the mess with Teiki weren't enough, watching two of her detectives go at it like horny teenagers would probably make her pack it up and head for some small town where there were no '80s pop stars, raucous drag queen dance troupes, or missing tropical birds.

"Oh, and speaking of," chimed in Rafael with a touch of incredulity in his voice. "What the *hell*, Choya? None of this would have happened if you had done your damned job! How much longer could you have possibly taken? Until I was actually having sex with him?"

A.J. blinked hard and turned to Rafael. Jonah had seen Rafael angry plenty of times, but A.J. was pretty even-keeled, and Jonah was actually curious how he would react.

"Oh, okay. No problem. I'll tell you what, Rafael. You go ahead and go to MIT so you can do even half of what I do and then get back to me." A.J. cocked his head to the side and crossed his arms. He wasn't even a tiny bit intimidated by Rafael. "You have *no* idea how difficult it was to break that code and get in there. Someone less experienced than I would have taken three times as long, and you know it. You think it was a picnic having to listen to you two go at it like that? And then to have to see it? Believe me, I was working as fast as I possibly could. And then some."

"Santos! Choya! Enough! It's almost dawn, I'm exhausted, you're exhausted, and I'm not going to get into the fuck ups on both sides of this op right now. I'm sure all three of you can at least agree with me that it's better if this never sees the light of day." Luis did not sound happy about any of her options.

This was not what Jonah had signed up for coming to Miami. For the first time since he thought about leaving Orlando, investigating who stole a herd of cows in Lakeland sounded appealing.

Jonah looked down at his shoes and sighed. "Understood."

Rafael and A.J. followed soon after with equally uncertain agreements. Jonah selfishly hoped they felt as wrong about this as he did, but Luis was right. No one involved in the case or Internal Affairs would be okay with what they did. Hell, Internal Affairs would probably have an axe to grind over everything that happened after Rafael had "paid" for Jonah. Getting as physical as they did was a huge violation of protocol and everyone knew it, but, much like their first botched undercover mission, there was a breakdown somewhere along the line and this time, sadly, it was A.J. not being quick enough getting past the security system.

*"Even a routine bust can go so, so wrong."* Peter's words the night of Jonah's first undercover op in Orlando came roaring back to him. It was so long ago that Rafael had been the part that had gone so wrong, and now he was standing there next to Jonah as his equal—both in the job and in responsibility for the mess they'd made relying on everyone else working the case to get their jobs done. It was a goddamned miracle they hadn't had to go further than they did.

"Choya. Get on it. I need to talk to these two for a minute." There was no emotion left in her voice.

Jonah still couldn't look at A.J. as he ushered himself out. There was going to be such a mess to clean up. A.J. wasn't stupid—far from it. Jonah could try to talk A.J. into dismissing what he heard in the mansion, but even without seeing the video he knew that there was no way to explain away just how heated things got between him and Rafael. Or maybe he just didn't want to explain that away. Maybe he didn't want to lie to A.J. and tell him it was just the job, that he was just acting. Even with Rafael maybe just *mostly* playing his part, it was still hotter than anything he'd experienced with A.J. And Rafael was going to be another mess to deal with. Seeing what had happened between them was one thing, but actually being a part of it and feeling Jonah's body react to everything Rafael was doing was another. Jonah couldn't lie his way out of it.

The door clicked back into place, and Luis clasped her hands together and brought her index fingers to her lips in thought. "I don't have to see it to get an idea of what happened in there. Is this going to be a problem for you two?"

Rafael could go either way on that, but Jonah wasn't about to let him use this as an opportunity to get rid of him after all they'd been through, so this time Jonah piped in before Rafael could speak.

"We did our jobs the best way we could under the circumstances. We are professionals, and we made a good bust tonight." Jonah hoped he sounded as casual as he wanted to sound even as every cell in his body was screaming at him to tell the truth, that it *would* be a problem because he was in love with Rafael and he would never get the taste of him out of his mouth or the smell of him off his skin.

Luis paused and stared Jonah down for a few long seconds, perhaps to see if he would break. Finally she nodded and broke her gaze with a quirk of her eyebrow.

"That's what I want to hear, Landers." Jonah had lied again. How did this end up so badly?

"Santos?"

Jonah afforded himself a glance at Rafael just to get a read on his mood. He was stone-faced and refused to look back at Jonah. "Absolutely not a problem, Captain. We had a job and we did it. We're not letting small, *inconsequential*, *meaningless* details get in the way."

Jonah wondered how out of it Luis must have been to miss that subtle insult, but it didn't get past Jonah, that was for sure. Rafael had just let Jonah know that it hadn't meant a thing to him, despite the heat Jonah had felt between them. Despite the very noticeable erection Rafael had pushed into him. Rafael must be as good at going undercover as everyone said he was, because he had certainly made his own partner believe that there might be something more there.

Luis rubbed at her forehead with the palm of her hand as she yawned and motioned with her free hand that it was time for the two of them to leave her office. Jonah was too tired to wonder how this would affect his working relationship with Luis on top of his worries concerning A.J. and Rafael.

They made it as far as the entrance to a rarely used evidence storeroom, and Rafael grabbed Jonah by the collar and shoved him in it, slamming the door shut behind them.

"I warned you! Didn't I warn you? Do you not remember me distinctly telling you that you weren't ready for this?" Rafael was in Jonah's personal space again, but this time there was no mistaking whether or not Rafael was acting.

Three months before, Jonah would have never dared roll his eyes at Rafael when he was this worked up, but Jonah was sick of this game.

"Wow, great job, Landers. Thanks for helping me catch the bad guy and all that." Jonah hoped Rafael wasn't too blind with misplaced rage to miss the sarcasm dripping off the remark. He pushed at the sleeves of the tight shirt in a futile effort to jab Rafael into giving him a little space.

Rafael ran a hand through his dark hair and ignored Jonah's unspoken request. "What, you think this is funny? Let's just remember whose boyfriend it was that got us into trouble. It could have ended so badly if I hadn't—"

"If *you* hadn't what, Rafael? If I recall correctly we were in there together, and we both played our parts and did our jobs. I'm not broken or on the floor in the fetal position because of what happened, and I'm pretty damn sure I held up *quite* nicely in there on my own. We got the guy and we're both alive. I think you just wanted this to be Orlando all over again so you could find a reason not to work with me anymore. Make Luis see with her own eyes what happens when we go undercover together."

Jonah didn't know how he could feel so relieved to get that fear out in the open yet so sick to his stomach with anxiety over putting it out there. He was certain Rafael would either finally request a new partner or make Jonah's life even more of a living hell to force him to put in for a transfer like he suggested that first day, and neither option was good in Jonah's mind.

And another thing…. "He's not my boyfriend." Even if Jonah had actually wanted him to be, he was pretty sure that train had sailed the moment A.J. had watched the video. And the strange sickness of relief washed over him some more. Maybe he needed some therapy since he wasn't making any progress on a drinking habit and the landlord said no pets so getting a dog was out.

Rafael opened his mouth to speak but closed it just as quickly and looked away for a few seconds. He chewed on his bottom lip and sighed, and it was enough of a distraction for Jonah to think that those lips had just been on him… his lips, his neck, his chest… maybe it would be for the best if they didn't work together. Dealing with a partner who hated him was one thing. Dealing with a partner he had feelings for was another, and he should have done something the moment he realized they were there.

But Jonah couldn't change the past.

He braced himself for Rafael's retort. There was really no need for him to hold back now that Jonah had said it out loud.

"You're right. I'm sorry. Again. I'm sorry. You did… amazingly well in there tonight. Better than I could have hoped for considering what I had to—"

Jonah had been ready to snap at Rafael, but had to hold his tongue to stop himself from reacting to the response he thought he was getting. He cocked his head to one side in confusion.

"Wait, what?" Because he definitely didn't hear what Rafael had said correctly.

Rafael blew out a breath and looked Jonah right in the eyes. It was unnerving to be under the scrutiny of one of his intense stares and still not know what to expect next after all this time.

Of all the things he didn't expect, though, Rafael walking out without saying another word wasn't one of them.

Jonah took a few moments to gather himself in the restroom before rejoining the squad in the bullpen to continue questioning the seemingly endless parade of men in high places and the angry, unappreciative, and much younger men who had been brainwashed into thinking they didn't need rescuing.

Rafael didn't so much as look at Jonah when he made his way back. It was probably for the best.

Luis finally forced them all to go home and not come back until at least two days later. Jonah was 100 percent sure he was not going to be able to sleep for a very long time, but he did appreciate the chance to get out of tight clothes and get a hot shower that might at least take the edge off. He stumbled into his apartment at a quarter to eight and fell short of both of his goals as he passed out, in all his clothes, until sometime late that afternoon.

# Chapter 27

JONAH WOKE up starving and a little confused but mostly overwhelmed. His feelings on A.J. were clear. How he planned to deal with them was not. His feelings on Rafael were as murky as the Everglades after a storm. And he didn't even know how to *start* dealing with those.

First things first, though. The sweat of a hard night's sleep had molded the leather pants to his body and getting them off was probably one of the more unpleasant memories he would associate with the whole operation, and obviously, that was saying something. The shirt smelled of a fading mix of all the expensive colognes he'd picked up as he pretended to work the room. He hoped the department had a good dry cleaner for both. At least it wasn't blood from his busted face this time.

Despite the shitty water pressure, his shower was a gift from heaven, even if he couldn't scrub away the memories of Rafael touching him in such an intimate way. He wondered how someone in Vice would handle the aftermath of undercover detectives gone wild and came to the conclusion that jerking off in the shower was probably not their first choice. He came to that conclusion as his hand instinctively slid downward to his aching dick and further concluded that he didn't care what Vice would do as he started stroking himself to thoughts of just how far he had been willing to go if A.J. had completely failed to do his job.

When the hot water finally ran out, Jonah managed to pull on some loose sweats and a hoodie before collapsing on the sofa with a large glass of water and leftovers of something he found in his fridge.

His decision on what to eat for dinner, much like his decision to eat it alone, was simply his only option, and he couldn't help but notice the parallel between the future of his social calendar and the inside of his refrigerator: empty.

If he were being honest right then, he would have admitted dating A.J., a guy he wasn't sure he could see himself with in the long run but could grow to have feelings for maybe possibly one day, was better than toast with mustard and watching *Law and Order: SVU* alone any day.

Slumping down in his oversized chair, the one he had bought from IKEA with his first paycheck in Miami (it had taken only four hours to put it together, even if there were quite a few parts left over), his toast in one hand and the remote in the other, he briefly considered throwing on some real clothes and going for a drink before burying that thought underneath all the times that had been a terrible idea.

Olivia Benson was on and getting personally involved with a case, but a knock on Jonah's door distracted him before he could try to guess who had committed the crime.

His too-long sweats swished on the carpet as he made his way to the front door, and before he could spy on his unannounced guest through the peephole, A.J.'s booming voice accompanied another knock.

"Jonah! I know you're in there! I can hear your self-loathing all the way from out here!"

With a sigh Jonah opened the door. Not because he was going to ask for forgiveness, but because A.J. wouldn't go away until he had his say, and he might as well get that part of the "Jonah Landers really fucked up" tour over with.

"I brought pizza." Like he was doing Jonah a favor he definitely didn't deserve.

"A.J." With the heavy sigh Jonah had come to reserve for all matters of his own screwed-up love life, he realized he couldn't ignore the smell of whatever was topping the pizza. "I don't think it's a goo—"

"Your growling stomach tells me otherwise. And I think we need to talk." And there it was. Jonah opened the door wider and waved A.J. in.

Jonah didn't offer him a drink or even an indication that he should sit on the sofa, but then again, he had never actually offered an invitation to come over and A.J. had done that without hesitation, so Jonah figured he'd do what he wanted anyway.

And what A.J. wanted, it seemed, was to engross himself in *Law and Order* and eat a slice and not say a word. After five minutes of waiting for the other shoe to drop, Jonah joined him.

It was sometime after the second slice—Olivia Benson was arguing with the new sassy ADA—that A.J. finally cleared his throat and shifted on the sofa to face Jonah.

"I'm not going to lie, okay? We're both smarter than that." A.J. swallowed hard and shrugged. "I watched it. I had to."

Jonah chewed on his bottom lip. He couldn't even look A.J. in the face. "I'm sorry. I was just doing what I—"

A.J. held up a hand to stop Jonah. "No, please. Let me finish. I obviously heard everything that went down in there, and as hard as it was to listen to that, it was nothing compared to watching you two together like that."

Jonah rubbed his face. "Jesus, I'm so—"

"Stop. Not finished. Listen, you're gorgeous. And you have a seriously amazing pair of lips that I could do all kind of things to for *hours*. But those lips aren't meant for me, are they? God, I wish you could have seen what I saw on there—you two together like that. I like you a lot, Jonah. I really do. But after watching you and Rafael together—"

"A.J., that was an act. We were acting. It was part of the op. You've run tech for a hundred of these." Lies. Lies. Lies. He had told himself it was a bad idea to even try that unbelievable rationale and he hadn't listened. Jonah knew where this conversation was leading.

A.J. smiled wistfully. "You're right. I *have* run a hundred of these ops. And I've never seen two UCs more into each other than you and Rafael. That wasn't acting, and it's kind of an insult to try to get me to believe otherwise."

Jonah couldn't think of a response that would make anything better. Even if Rafael *had* been putting on an Oscar-worthy performance, Jonah hadn't, and there was nothing he could say to the accusation.

A.J. held up both hands in a sort of surrender. "Look, I didn't come here to fight. I know when I've lost, okay? I just figured I would get a jump on things before it got too weird. I wish I had found out about the two of you in some other way, obviously, but I also can't pretend that you and I are going to work with that elephant always in the room."

"God, I'm such an asshole. You must think I'm a terrible person, A.J." Jonah hung his head in his hands. Why was A.J. so nice? He'd effectively dumped Jonah for being into someone else, and it was the nicest dumping he'd ever been a part of.

"I think you're in love, Jonah. Just not with me. And that's okay because this was never supposed to be anything serious. Am I wrong?"

Jonah looked up. "Wha—yeah, wasn't planning on it being serious, I guess."

A.J. shook his head. "No, Jonah. I meant am I wrong about you being in love with Rafael."

Jonah shifted uncomfortably. "It doesn't matter what I feel, A.J. He hates me. He's hated me since the day we met, and I couldn't change that if I tried."

"I can't believe I came over here to break up with you, and now here I am helping you get with the guy who broke us up. You need to open your eyes, Jonah, because Rafael Santos has been shit crazy in love with you for a long time. Probably since before you and I got together. He never treated me like he's been treating me before you got here, and I have never seen him pull anyone's pigtails like he does yours. I thought it was harmless until I watched him react to you and what he was doing to you last night. I almost wish I hadn't destroyed it so you could see for yourself."

Jonah felt a fresh surge of guilt run through him. "I'm sorry, A.J. I'm sorry for all of this. I like you. A lot. You're so attractive and intelligent and fun and a really great guy. But you're right. I do have feelings for Rafael. God help me." *Could he be right about Rafael having feelings for me?*

A.J. stood up and dusted the crumbs off his jeans. "Then there's really nothing more to say, is there? I don't want to drag this out all night. We're both really tired, and we still have so much to do when we get back. But, Jonah…."

Jonah stood to face A.J. and finally felt a little of the tension start to ease in his head. "Yeah?"

A.J. extended a hand, and Jonah reached out to shake it. "Jonah, it's been fun. I hope that you figure this out with Rafael, though, one way or the other. I just don't think any guy can compete with him, so you owe it to yourself more than anyone."

It was a cordial good-bye, and A.J. even left the pizza. Jonah didn't know how to process what had just happened. He had known for a while that he and A.J. weren't going to work out in the long run and he couldn't justify being *too* disappointed, but getting dumped by even a casual fling meant he was now alone.

And soon he *would* have to face Rafael and whatever happened between them and what all that could possibly mean for them. They could not ignore that no matter what had happened, or almost happened, in that mansion, they were still partners.

And he had the whole weekend to wallow in it by himself.

# Chapter 28

MONDAY CAME, and he actually managed to get even less sleep with nothing to do. His mind was a chaotic swirl of Rafael and A.J. and the mansion and the future of his job, and no solution had presented itself in the two-day break. Rafael steadfastly refused to look Jonah in the face, even going so far as to cut him off with a curt "I don't want to talk about it" when Jonah tried.

Throwing himself into his work seemed like the best idea, and it was easier now that A.J. wasn't distracting him. Where A.J. would frequently stop by the bull pen to say "hi" before, he was noticeably absent since the breakup. Jonah didn't feel it was anyone's business, and he didn't want Rafael thinking it was anything that happened in the mansion that led to it, so naturally it started spreading like wildfire within the first week.

"Oh, sweetie. I'm so sorry about you and A.J." Garcia had rushed him as soon as she heard and hugged him tightly right in front of Rafael. "Are you okay?"

Jonah stood there awkwardly as she mother-henned him, looking him over to make sure he didn't look pale or hungry or whatever she thought he was going through. "Garcia, I'm fine! A.J. and I weren't even that serious, and it was a totally friendly breakup. We're just taking some time away from each other before we attempt to carry on as friends, okay?" That was a lie. They hadn't actually discussed the idea of a friendship, but Garcia needed coddling.

"But what happened? You two looked so cute together! You must think I'm a terrible matchmaker." She hugged him again, even tighter this time. *Oh my God, Garcia, get the hint.* Now he had to reassure Garcia, and he really just wanted to stop talking about it. Especially in front of Rafael.

"It just… didn't work out, all right? It wasn't any one thing. It was coming for a while. He was fun and cute and everything, but there was no… chemistry. It's totally fine. You helped me get over the hump with my ex in Orlando by introducing us. Your reputation is intact... can you let me up so I can breathe now?"

She loosened her grip and gave him one last once-over before walking away with a wistful and melodramatic look on her face.

Jonah looked toward Rafael just to get the smirk he was expecting over with, but Rafael looked a bit distressed.

"Sorry... about you and A.J. This is the kind of thing I was worried about, messing you up. Messing things with A.J. up. Sometimes it's hard not to bring that stuff home with you."

Jonah tried to stay emotionally distant. "Rafael, there's nothing to feel bad about. This had nothing to do with what happened. I wasn't lying to throw Garcia off. It was something that was coming before last week."

"I'm sure it wasn't helped by A.J. watching... you know. And what I had to do to you...."

"Whoa, let's get this straight *right now*. If even one atom of my being were uncomfortable or couldn't handle what happened in there, I would be requesting a transfer. And you know Luis would grant it. Your concern for my well-being is strangely comforting, but Raf, I'm not so delicate here." Jonah could have sworn that was relief washing over Rafael's face. Did he really think...? "Hold up, do you feel like you... do *you* feel uncomfortable with what happened? Do you feel guilty about having to touch me like that?"

"I don't know what I feel, okay? I've never had an op go down like that in all my years. I've never been so...." Rafael trailed off and Jonah swore he was looking at his lips again. "Especially not with someone I have to see every day after what I did."

"Do you think I don't bear *some* responsibility for what happened in there? I wasn't exactly dead weight, if you recall." Flashes of kissing Rafael, of touching him, ran through his mind. He tried to shake them away before his body betrayed him and gave away exactly what he was thinking about, but he knew it was already too late. *In for a penny, in for a pound.* "Did you...did you enjoy it? Any of it? I mean, it certainly... unless I was reading it *really* wrong...." *Do you feel the same about me? Do you want me like I want you?* He just couldn't make his mouth form the words.

Rafael pinched the bridge of his nose between his fingers. "We shouldn't talk about this. Not right now."

"Then when, Rafael? I think we *have* to talk about this—about what we… if you're going to keep ignoring this I might as well request that transfer. You've got to let me take some responsibility. Or what good am I to you as a partner?"

"I—I should go." The color had drained from Rafael's face. It wasn't like him at all to walk away from an uncomfortable situation, and it was pissing Jonah off.

"Raf—Rafael, no. Let's talk about this." Jonah reached out for Rafael, but he twisted away and maybe that was all the answer he needed for the millions of questions he had concerning his place with Rafael.

He started absentmindedly researching transfer opportunities that afternoon. It was long overdue. He didn't want to pick up and move again for the second time in a year thanks to his botched love life, but Miami was a big enough city that transferring to a different precinct would be enough to ensure that there would be no contact between him and Rafael.

The day ended… and then the week. New cases still poured in and thankfully they were the kind of routine that stayed routine and required minimum contact with Rafael. Jonah didn't try to bring up that night again.

He put on a good show for the rest of the station, though, as did Rafael. At least no one would know the reason why he wanted to leave this time.

He made an effort to get out the next weekend, but he felt like he was lying to himself. Food had no taste, the sun had no warmth, and the brilliant colors of Miami faded into grays. How could one man do this to him? More importantly, how could Jonah let himself feel this way? This wasn't like him at all.

Another Monday came, and he dragged himself into work, coffee in hand, hair a mess, and he didn't bother to shave. He plopped himself down at his desk and clicked open his e-mail.

There were hits on the job board. Good hits. Jobs he was qualified for in North Miami, Hialeah, Coral Gables. All he needed to do was click "apply."

Jonah took a deep breath and clicked on the first posting.

"Detective, a word?" The voice startled him from his typing.

Rafael.

He was strangely cavalier after all the time that had passed, and Jonah almost wanted to ignore the request that was definitely a demand.

Jonah shrugged and sucked down the last of his coffee. "Fine. What's up?"

Rafael glanced around the bull pen and set that crazy intense gaze back on Jonah before leaning in closely and lowering his voice. "Not here. Walk and talk?"

Jonah shrugged again because Rafael wasn't going to give up until he said whatever he needed to say to Jonah, and obviously it was bad enough to warrant a little privacy. "What the hell. Let's get this over with."

Jonah stood and could at least appreciate the opportunity to stretch a bit. He tossed the coffee cup in the recycling bin and followed Rafael out to the main hallway.

For a walk and talk, there was an awful lot of walking and no talking, and Jonah couldn't even begin to fathom what it was all about until they passed the evidence storeroom and once again Jonah found himself being pushed into it.

Jonah stared at Rafael because he figured *someone* needed to say something, and since it was Rafael who had initiated the weird clandestine meeting, he probably had something on his mind.

"I don't want to talk about it," Rafael finally offered after a tense minute of silence.

Or maybe he didn't have something on his mind? Why drag Jonah in here if he didn't want to—

Rafael grabbed Jonah by the collar to pull him close and kissed him violently, interrupting whatever thought Jonah was trying to finish. It knocked Jonah off balance and sent him stumbling backward a bit. He didn't mean to break the kiss, but gravity took over and Jonah reached out to the wall behind him to steady himself.

That alone was embarrassing enough, but the fact that he was *panting* from just a kiss made him want to crawl away and put in for a transfer to somewhere in Wisconsin. But he couldn't deny that there was the spark that had been missing with A.J.

Rafael was wild-eyed then, a possessive hunger in his eyes that Jonah had caught glimpses of that night in the mansion but had chalked up to playing the part.

"I had to know… had to know if what happened at Badcock's wasn't…. Tell me I'm not imagining things here. Or tell me I am imagining things! But I have to know, Jonah. I can't eat, I can't sleep, hell, I can't even think straight when I'm around you, and it started way before the mansion. You're overenthusiastic, kind of annoying, a smartass, and sometimes I think that you aren't a person as much as a hurricane made of caffeinated puppies, but I can't tear my thoughts away from you. So, I need to know. Right now. I can't take much more of this, so, Jonah, do me and my career a favor and either lock the fucking door or get the fuck out."

Jonah's eyes went wide at this uncharacteristic and strangely flattering confession. It was a lot to take in in one sitting, so of course Jonah had to blurt out the most surprising part of it all without thinking first.

"You… called me Jonah." Jonah couldn't move while he tried to figure things out. He gave up that idea about three seconds later and reached for Rafael's belt loops, hooking his fingers around them and pulling him close. "You never call me Jonah." But, thinking back on that, it wasn't true. Rafael had slipped and called him Jonah at Badcock's, in the heat of everything. He should have realized then what was happening.

Rafael breathed out a shaky breath. "This going to be a problem?" He wasn't talking about his choice in names.

Jonah shook his head. "Not from where I'm standing."

Rafael was so close Jonah could feel the heat from his burning skin through both of their clothes. "If we're doing this I probably should stop call—"

Jonah cut him off with a kiss, this one less violent but just as dangerous. Rafael pushed a little into Jonah and thankfully this time the wall was there to hold them both up. It didn't surprise Jonah that both of them were already incredibly hard, and he resigned himself to the fact that walking out of the storeroom door without taking care of that would be a disaster and would probably undo every centimeter of progress they'd made with each other.

Not that he could stop now if he wanted to. Not with Rafael pawing at him like a horny teenager, kissing down to his chin, his jaw, his neck, all the places Rafael had only touched on in the mansion and never really got to see just how crazy it drove Jonah when someone paid attention to them.

Rafael made it to the spot where Jonah's neck and shoulder met, and when Jonah couldn't help how his hips thrust against Rafael, he knew it was all over. There was never really any going back before that, but moaning into Rafael's mouth as he grabbed Jonah's ass had sealed the deal. Whatever there was before, whatever happened in the mansion, whatever had happened two years ago in Orlando, Rafael and Jonah were here now and there was no one around to act for, no one to keep cover for. It was just the two of them, alone, forcing themselves to confront their feelings for each other.

Jonah didn't want to count the minutes since they had left, since they'd slipped into the old evidence storeroom, praying no one noticed them. It was crazy and stupid and risky for them even to entertain the *thought* of sneaking in there together and right then, both still so angry and exhausted and impatient that either one of them was equally likely to break and accidentally reveal to passersby that there was more than contraband and illegal weapons behind the door.

And Rafael bit his lip, like he was frustrated—with himself or maybe with Jonah—like he couldn't get enough or couldn't take enough of what he wanted, and Jonah knew he needed to somehow let Rafael know that it was okay to be greedy without breaking the spell. Jonah wanted Rafael to take and take and, fuck, he wanted to give it to him. He wanted it—wanted Rafael—and Rafael was *still* treating him like he would break.

Jonah couldn't shake the memory of the last time he had found himself like this, so fresh off the case and wondering how everything was going to play out, but everything was different now. Jonah was different. And to leave now, to suddenly become self-conscious and start dissecting what it meant to willingly do this with Rafael instead of trusting his gut and going with it, wasn't even an option to consider.

And Jonah was sure Rafael would feel the same, so if Rafael wouldn't take the initiative out of whatever guilt or uncertainty was running through his mind, Jonah was determined to do it for him.

He closed his eyes and sank slowly to the floor until his knees banged against the cold concrete floor.

"What are you—" But Jonah didn't want Rafael to finish that. The time for second-guessing had long passed.

Jonah looked up at Rafael with his eyes wide open. "What I wanted to do that night in the mansion. What I've wanted to do for a long time. Are you going to stop me?"

Rafael whimpered but shook his head and reached down to touch the back of Jonah's head. It was all the consent he needed. Jonah pressed his open mouth against the silky fabric covering Rafael's erection. Rafael had been so vicious, cutting Jonah down every way he could, laying into him at every turn, and now it was Jonah's turn to be as equally vicious with his own mouth.

Growly little noises slipped out from Rafael, and Jonah would replay them later in his mind, but he knew a distraction when he saw one and unzipped Rafael's trousers to free his cock. He wanted more time to admire what he saw, but, like second-guessing, the time to take it slowly was also long gone.

Jonah didn't bother to warn Rafael before he took him in his mouth as far as he would go, and Rafael rewarded him with a choked-off moan and long fingers that gripped his hair tightly. Rafael was hard and hot in his mouth, and Jonah's lips stretched at the corners as he let more and more of him in. He hadn't expected to end up on his knees in an evidence storeroom of a busy police station he worked at while he blew his partner, but then again, nothing had gone according to plan since he got to Miami, and maybe that was for the best.

Rafael's hands were a comforting weight on the back of his head, and that Rafael hadn't stopped touching him in any way he could since Jonah had started was a promising sign that there wouldn't be much fallout afterward.

Jonah quickly found a rhythm that Rafael seemed to like and relaxed into it, letting sensation and the sounds Rafael was trying hard to pretend he wasn't making tell him how to proceed. It wasn't long before Jonah felt Rafael's body tense and he came with a hoarse moan, pushing into Jonah's mouth, finally greedy and making it about what he wanted and how he wanted it from Jonah.

Jonah licked Rafael clean and rose up to tongue fuck his mouth a little. His lips were already so sore and swollen and part of him wanted Rafael to notice that just as much as he wanted Rafael to taste himself in Jonah's mouth.

Jonah was still trying to impress him, even now.

It was that line of thinking that had always gotten him in trouble in the past, and it was no different now. Jonah grabbed Rafael's hand and shoved it down into his own trousers.

"You can't leave just yet. Not leaving me like this, okay?" Jonah almost instantly regretted sounding so needy. He had just swallowed Rafael whole and given him an orgasm so hard he'd nearly bitten off the arm of someone's stolen fur coat so he would stay quiet, and now Rafael was panting and kissing Jonah and stroking his cock, and Jonah was still going to worry that he was being weird or clingy?

Rafael's hand was damp with sweat, but not slick, so he coated his fingers in Jonah's precome, swallowing Jonah's groans at what his fingertips were doing to the head of his cock. He slid his palm down Jonah's shaft and curled his fingers tightly around it, and Jonah gripped Rafael's wrist possessively.

If Rafael seemed embarrassed at the tiny noise he had made before, Jonah was downright ashamed at the starved sounds he made then— sounds like he hadn't come in months, like if he didn't come that second from just a kiss and a few strokes, he might die.

He *was* right there and Rafael knew it, had to know it from the way Jonah moved against him and from how hard he was in his hands.

"God, Rafael! I'm gonna—"

Jonah grabbed Rafael's shoulders, holding on when it finally hit him. His eyes screwed shut and his head arched back, exposing more of his neck that Rafael seemed eager to suck on so it drew an even harder orgasm from him.

Jonah didn't care that there was going to be a mark there. Maybe he wanted everyone to see it and wonder. The idea of a secret, of something more between him and Rafael that wasn't tainted by all the eyes that had been on them that night in the mansion making him feel dirty and exposed, was a powerful feeling, even if he would have to explain away the bruises just like he'd been explaining away the dark circles under his eyes every morning since this whole thing went down.

Rafael dragged his teeth over Jonah's raw flesh and drew another cry from him, pleased and sore and slightly pained, and Jonah had a feeling that maybe he'd have to wear high-necked collars for a while if this was the way it was going to be with Rafael from then on. His mind briefly flashed on Rafael exploring him with his mouth, his tongue, those long fingers, at his own pace, relying on the volume of Jonah's moans while Jonah's hands were tied and his mouth gagged so he couldn't tell Rafael to go faster or harder or guide him to the right spots. It was, perhaps, a twisted thought so early on in this bizarre reconciliation, but

Jonah loved it and planned to think further on it when he had the chance to be alone with it.

He was starting to calm down then, his pulse fluttering as Rafael finally slowed his kisses as he untangled himself from Jonah.

There was a mess on his shirt but his jacket should cover that. No one had to know.

It had been eleven—no, thirteen—minutes since they made the escape, and someone was going to need one of them. Rafael planted a last kiss on Jonah, and he hoped it was a promise of something more later.

Jonah bit Rafael's lip, squeezing his ass, threading his fingers in a matting of sweaty hair; he was not yet done with Rafael, and Rafael needed to understand that.

"I should be able to have that final report done by eleven. I will probably be home by a quarter till midnight." Small talk, but obviously not when Rafael murmured it against Jonah's neck. The invitation hung heavy in the air.

A sound caught in the back of Jonah's throat when Rafael sucked at his Adam's apple.

He hung his head low from exhaustion or relief or some combination of both, hair flopping onto Rafael. Those long fingers squeezed Jonah's shoulders, and he pushed Rafael away slightly to look into glassy green eyes, unfocused and heavy-lidded.

Jonah sensed it, saw it quirk in Rafael's ever-stoic face, and he smiled. Rafael had finally lost control of the situation. The next move was Jonah's to make, and that terrified Rafael. Jonah held all the power. He could say yes or he could walk away before things got too crazy.

Jonah took Rafael's hand and intertwined their fingers. He guided Rafael's hand to his lips and kissed a knuckle.

"Midnight?" Not that Jonah was taking advantage of his newfound position in charge or anything.

"Y-yeah. Midnight." Detective Rafael Santos was stammering. Amazing. Jonah just smiled and adjusted Rafael's tie, smoothing it down to the end before walking out.

# Chapter 29

JONAH FELT good about himself for exactly .03 seconds after sneaking out of the storeroom; then Garcia waltzed around the corner with a case file.

"Landers! Just who I was looking for! Where have you been?" If Jonah was still flushed or his lips too pink or was buttoned wrong, Garcia didn't show any signs of noticing it, thank God.

Garcia didn't give Jonah time to answer the question before shoving the case file at him and excitedly going over the new details. If anything, her enthusiasm for the tiniest piece of evidence made for a good distraction as Rafael quickly emerged from the storeroom.

Jonah pointedly ignored Rafael as he walked by. As far as anyone else was concerned—as far as anyone else *needed* to be concerned at this point—Rafael and Jonah were still not getting along. But that didn't mean Jonah couldn't gain a little more of the upper hand.

"Garcia, we can't *blow it* if we decide to follow this lead. It's shaky at best, and if we blow it, it'll *bite us in the ass*. Do you agree?" Jonah didn't look up, but he couldn't miss the sound of Rafael's stumbling footsteps behind him. Weirdly sexual truce or not, Jonah wasn't about to let up on being a little shit. He was pretty sure that Rafael would expect nothing less anyway.

Garcia responded with something Jonah was sure made perfect sense, but he couldn't concentrate on her words long enough to make it out. He was probably going to kick his own ass for the distraction, but he vowed to keep this up as long as he could to force Rafael to think of him all day.

"…Edgewood and I will go check it out and let you know."

Jonah shook his head to clear it. "Yeah, yeah, that sounds good. Let me know what you find." Torturing Rafael was going to be just as hard on himself. He ran his fingers through his hair and went back to pretending to ignore Rafael as best as he could.

# Chapter 30

IT WAS not an easy evening after that, of course. Jonah wavered between subtle flirting, taking every opportunity to work in some kind of sexual reference or posture all while making it look completely innocent, and wanting to jump Rafael's bones right there in front of everyone.

And when midnight finally did come, Jonah knew he was going to be in for it after cock-teasing his partner half the damned day.

Ten thirty rolled around, and most of the regular day shift had long since left. Jonah needed leave too, before the threat of overtime sent Luis into a tizzy. He couldn't complain too much, though. It gave him just enough time to swing by his apartment to freshen up a bit and have a few mini panic attacks on the way. This was both the best idea and the worst ever, but there really was no going back after the mansion.

Part of him wanted to dress a little nicer than the plain white button-down and black waistcoat he'd decided looked great just that morning, but he also wanted as few distractions and obstacles as possible. In the end he ditched the waistcoat and untucked his shirt so it didn't look like he had tried *too* hard.

The only indication Rafael gave that they were still on for that night was a short text with his address in it. It was in Buena Vista, in North Central Miami, east of Liberty City and south of Little Haiti. It was a neat mix of older homes reflecting the styles of the past like craftsman and art deco and newer homes inspired by the neighboring Design District.

Jonah didn't really have the chance to appreciate Rafael's house, but it was a typical Miami bungalow home with stone railings surrounding a small front porch at the top of the steps. It was much nicer than the old clapboard siding house Rafael had grown up in Little Havana. Someone—Jonah doubted it was Rafael; maybe he had a landscaper—had taken great care to give the front yard that tropical desert look so popular in the unpredictable weather of South Florida. Come drought or flood, plant for both occasions and at least one half will survive, they say. Birds of Paradise and hibiscus mingled with yucca and agave in the front beds. So much nicer than the carelessly planted and never-trimmed palms at Jonah's apartment building, though, and was he really that anxious that he was suddenly interested in the landscaping?

It was 11:57 p.m. and no, he couldn't wait the extra three minutes. A moth buzzed around the porch light while he waited for Rafael to answer the door, and Jonah was glad it was still early enough in the South Florida spring for the humidity to hover only around 75 percent so he wasn't *completely* soaking his shirt in sweat in the few minutes he had to spend outside.

Rafael answered the door in the same clothes he had been wearing before, but with the benefit of a Scotch in his hand. He hadn't even removed his shoes. He either had just gotten home or was asserting a little authority over Jonah. Either way Jonah was getting those clothes off him soon. Rafael quietly motioned for Jonah to come inside and closed the door behind them.

Jonah couldn't help but take in the surroundings to see how Rafael lived. It was tastefully decorated, with a lot of dark wood and warm light, and it put Jonah instantly at ease.

Rafael took a long sip of the Scotch and set it down on a nearby table, oblivious to the way Jonah had just stared at his throat when he tilted his head back.

"You're early." Rafael sounded almost flippant, but Jonah saw through the act.

Jonah shrugged. "I'm right on time." This was how it was going to go down, and Jonah could play the game.

Rafael blinked slowly and smirked like Jonah had seen him do so many times before, but this was a new game and one Jonah could win, and Rafael looked like he wanted a good challenger.

"There's one thing I have to do before I—before we—it'll take just a couple of minutes. Pour yourself a drink if you want. I'll just be in my office." Jonah had no doubt that whatever it was could wait until the morning, and Rafael was just trying to regain the upper hand.

"Yeah, that's fine." Jonah pushed up his sleeves and turned to walk over to the built-in bar while Rafael disappeared around the corner. Once he disappeared, Jonah quickly took off his shoes and unbuttoned his shirt all the way so it exposed his long, pale torso.

Jonah padded on the thick carpet quietly until he found the converted second bedroom Rafael was using as a home office. He really did seem to be doing some kind of last-minute work at his desk, but Jonah's patience had officially run out.

He leaned against the door frame looking as filthy as he could imagine himself being.

"Can I talk to you, Detective Santos?" Jonah's mouth turned up at one side, and he knew he wasn't fooling anyone in the room, but he was making it so easy for Rafael to play along.

Rafael exhaled a breath he sounded like he had been holding since Jonah left him in the storeroom, but only briefly looked up at him.

"Of course, Landers. Come in and take a seat. I'll be finished in a minute." He, like on any other busy day, looked back down at his paperwork, putting pen to paper and blatantly ignoring the obvious rustle of Jonah's shirt coming off and hitting the floor.

Jonah was just wearing his trousers then. "Rafael, this really can't wait."

"I said just a minute, Landers." Jonah smiled because Rafael's voice had definitely cracked then. For the first time in a long time, things felt right. This was playing for fun, for seduction, and after the mansion, this was something they both knew they needed to play out to erase the damage they had done there. It was almost cathartic.

Jonah walked toward the dark mahogany desk (of course Rafael would want the best and most expensive desk he could manage) and around the other side to where Rafael was sitting. He swung a long leg between Rafael and the desk and used it to push the chair back so he could straddle Rafael and grind his hips into him.

"It's very important, Rafael."

Rafael used his feet to push his chair back in as far as Jonah's back would let him. He had Jonah boxed in. Controlled.

"I hope it's important enough to interrupt me like this, Detective Landers." But his hands were on Jonah's hips. "I have a meeting at midnight."

Jonah tried to grind again, but the desk edge in his back and Rafael's hands holding him firmly were making it difficult. He whimpered slightly, needing the friction, but Rafael obviously wasn't going to give it to him that easily. Not without a fight. It was on.

"I was hoping…." Jonah reached down to cover Rafael's hands, still at Jonah's hips. "Can you clear your schedule for a while?"

Jonah tried to move Rafael's hands down toward his lap, but Rafael decided to run them over Jonah's smooth stomach instead.

"Detective Landers. Sometimes I think you forget the chain of command here." Jonah arched back when Rafael's hands slipped over his chest. It pushed bare skin more toward Rafael, and Jonah felt heat through Rafael's clothes.

Jonah looked down at Rafael with his sweaty hair falling into his eye, and he shivered slightly in the air-conditioning.

"Then why don't you tie me up with it and make me remember." It was not a question.

Rafael's eyes went wide, and Jonah couldn't resist kissing Rafael then, sucking on his lower lip, and taking Rafael's face into his hands before pushing himself away.

Now the next move was Rafael's, and Jonah dropped his hands and waited. He just hoped he'd shown Rafael that he was more than capable of keeping up with him. Had there not been a case and several armed guards and a maybe would-be boyfriend watching and listening that night, Jonah would have let Rafael fuck him without hesitation.

Rafael pushed his chair back and gently guided Jonah to the floor so he could kneel in front of him. "You were such a little cocktease today. Were you enjoying yourself?"

Jonah bit his lip and smiled. "Yeah." He knew he looked vulnerable from that angle, and Rafael looked down at him like he was going to make sure he stayed that way.

"Do you want me to lose the jacket, Landers?" Rafael was almost nonchalant.

Jonah nodded, but Rafael caught his chin and gently turned him so he could look Jonah in the eye. "What was that, Landers?"

"Yes. Please."

"Much better, Detective Landers." Rafael took off his jacket and placed it on the desk in front of him.

The penny dropped and all of a sudden the lines were drawn. Losing control before, in the mansion, on a case, meant one or both of them could get hurt, and Jonah had *still* fought Rafael for some semblance of control at the mansion to show that he could handle it.

Jonah knew Rafael was at his happiest when he was in charge of himself and the situation. Jonah had already shown all too many times that he was willing to fight Rafael in every single one of those situations, but to make whatever this was work, it was time to stop fighting Rafael and trust his partner.

"How about the tie? Should I take it off?" Rafael had his fingers at the knot, and Jonah was so hard he could barely stand too much more, but this wasn't just foreplay happening.

This was a negotiation.

"Yes, please."

"Yes. I think it's a good idea too. You need to learn some patience, Landers. This will help." He untied the tie and motioned for Jonah to stand up. Rafael gripped Jonah's hips again and turned him around.

He pulled Jonah's arms back, gentle but with a purpose. The silk looped easily around Jonah's wrists, and Rafael tied an expert knot to secure them. Rafael's fingers grazed Jonah's ass a few times while he worked, and Jonah tried hard not to make the noise that came out of his mouth. Rafael blew out a shaky breath and turned Jonah to face him again.

"Back on your knees, Landers." Now Jonah couldn't try anything unless Rafael approved it first. He leaned forward to kiss Jonah.

"You fight me and fight me every day. Are you going to stop fighting me and learn to trust me?"

Jonah nodded, and it was easier to submit to Rafael than he thought it would be. "Yes, I will." He never broke eye contact with Rafael.

Rafael unbuckled his belt, unbuttoned and unzipped his trousers, and pushed them down to his thighs to reveal just how hard a tied-up and willing Jonah could make him. Jonah sucked in a breath and bit his lip.

He started to move toward Rafael's exposed cock, but Rafael guided him in with one hand to the back of his head gently, giving Jonah some say if things went too far, and the other holding himself to give Jonah easy access. Jonah eagerly pushed forward, and the moment Jonah's lips touched him, Rafael gasped, and Jonah could feel his muscles work to stop himself from arching up and choking Jonah. He closed his eyes to focus himself entirely on Rafael and his reactions.

He wanted to make Rafael come, but he also wanted to see how far Rafael was willing to take this. And he wasn't willing to submit completely to Rafael when he could still be a little shit and make obscene noises around Rafael's dick to force some kind of decision out of him a little quicker.

His plan worked, and a few seconds later, Rafael pulled Jonah off and looked down at him. Jonah knew his lips were spit-slicked and pink, and his eyes were glazed over.

"You don't get off that easily, Landers. Do you want to make up for what you did to me all day? Do you want me to forgive you for teasing me all day like you did?" Rafael was smirking down at him.

"God, yes." But it took a few seconds for the words to come out properly. Jonah was well past the point of no return, but Rafael was nowhere near finished with him.

"Good." Rafael breathed it out, running a hand down Jonah's face. "I'm going to untie your hands now. Can I trust you too? Will you do as I say this time?"

"Yes." Jonah's breathing was shallow and unsteady. There was a fine sheen on Rafael's skin that Jonah wanted to lick off, but this was Rafael's game, and Jonah really wanted to see how it all ended up.

Rafael helped Jonah to his feet, taking every opportunity for skin on skin. He still had his trousers around his legs so, like a king on his throne, he didn't bother to stand. He turned Jonah so he could free Jonah's hands, pausing only to lean forward and suck lightly on his long fingers.

"Mmmmmm, Rafael." Slowly, so slowly Jonah was dying, Rafael untied him. Like the fast learner he was, Jonah stayed still until Rafael could tell him what to do next.

Rafael didn't speak, though. He pulled his trousers back up and stood behind Jonah. He reached around Jonah's hips and, with as much contact as he could, worked Jonah's zipper and button and pushed down his trousers and boxers.

Now Rafael was mostly clothed, and Jonah was naked. The inequality of it all should have been jarring and uncomfortable, but Jonah squirmed out of anticipation instead.

Rafael raked his eyes up and down Jonah's body and, in a heartbeat, the look on Rafael's face changed to something feral and wild, and the game seemed to be forgotten as Rafael shoved Jonah hard against the edge of the desk and kissed him violently, fingers pushing into his skin so hard he would definitely have bruises. Jonah desperately grabbed at fabric, trying to get Rafael's clothes off any way he could.

Jonah just about managed Rafael's shirt without too much incident and started to work on his bottoms, failing at his undershirt and boxers when Rafael momentarily lost control, but Jonah was prepared for the emotional whiplash this time and let Rafael do as he needed.

Rafael groaned. "God, I want to fuck you so badly! I thought I could—thought I needed to take it slowly with you, especially after… but I can't stop thinking about you since—"

"God, Rafael," Jonah breathed in awe. "You're… ah… I…." And there was the endgame. Rafael wanted to fuck him as badly as he wanted to get fucked by Rafael.

Rafael pushed Jonah down to sit on his desk and spread his thighs so Rafael could step between them, bringing their dicks together. Rafael pushed his cock through the slit of his boxers and stroked them both so Jonah felt the contrast between Rafael's calloused hands and the velvety softness of his cock.

Rafael used some of the wetness coming from both of them to make it feel even better as he sucked and bit his way down Jonah's neck over to his shoulder, leaving marks like he wanted him to remember this every time he saw them for the next few days.

Jonah cried out sharply as he squeezed Rafael's shoulders and threw his head back. Rafael clamped his hand over Jonah's mouth and took the other one away from their dicks to yank Jonah closer.

"You drive me fucking crazy, kid. Every day. Sometimes I want to punch you in the face again, but I come home, and I can't stop thinking of you—and this. Even before the case. Watching you and Choya together drove me insane. I'm not going to stand here and lie and tell you I didn't enjoy every minute that he had to listen to us in there. And then to feel how much you were enjoying what was going on in there? Feel how stupidly responsive you are to even a kiss? I tried to convince myself it was just good acting, but you weren't playing when you said you were all mine in there."

Jonah shook his head and pulled Rafael's hand away from his face. "No. I wasn't playing."

Rafael threw his head to the side. "God, kid! What are you even doing?"

But Jonah cupped Rafael's face and turned it back so they could look at each other.

"Rafael." Jonah pulled Rafael's hand back down to his still hard cock. "Does it *feel* like I don't know what I'm getting into here?"

Jonah stood upright for a split second to get better footing, and Rafael used the moment to tongue Jonah's shoulder and neck.

"Rafael, please. I can't go much longer." How much more convincing did Rafael need?

"You want this?" Rafael pushed his cock against Jonah. "You want me to take you to my bed?"

Jonah nodded furiously. "Please, Rafael!" Jonah pushed Rafael away to try to make a play for his bedroom, but Rafael was one step ahead of him, pulling him along down the short hallway.

Rafael's bedroom was dark and sparsely furnished, and it was several degrees cooler than the rest of the house, but Jonah had to be honest with himself: it had a bed, and that was all he cared about. Rafael had other ideas, though, pushing him up against the door as it closed and putting them in a position not entirely unlike at Badcock's. "I couldn't stop thinking about how far it could have gone that night. How far I could have taken it with you. All the way, even? I thought about it after it was all over. I felt terrible because I thought what I had to do was too far, too intimate for an op, but, *fuck*, it was so hot too, no matter how much I beat myself up over it afterward. I didn't want to believe that you were telling me how you really felt in there."

"You play it so close to the vest, Rafael. I thought there was no way you were into… *this*…. I mean, you know, me. You and me. Like this." *Shut up, please.* "But you seemed so, um, into it at Badcock's? Like the idea of being with a man didn't freak you out, and I wanted to believe that was more than acting, you know?" *Oh my God, shut up. For the love of God. You're embarrassing yourself.*

Rafael sighed. "I've never really… never sat down to put a label on it. All these kids today want to put themselves in these tiny boxes, but I've always just… if I wanted something, someone, I didn't feel like dissecting it when I could be, you know, out there making it happen. I had the freedom to do that. My parents didn't, and they went through a lot to come here to give my brothers and me the freedom to be who we wanted, so I never wanted to restrict myself to those tiny boxes. And it just wasn't a big thing to be whatever you wanted down here."

Jonah breathed out sharply. "So you're—"

Rafael cut him off with an impatient throat clearing. "Wasting time, yes. I thought there was something we both wanted to do right now…."

Jonah got the hint and nodded. "Absolutely."

Rafael pulled Jonah along to the bed and playfully pushed him down on it. Of course it was soft and giving. It almost made sense for grumpy, stubborn Rafael to have a bed softer than a cloud and sheets that were probably eight million thread count and made of some super rare, super soft cotton found only in a twenty-square-foot patch in the Andes or something.

He sat next to him, and Jonah closed his eyes, kissing Rafael, holding nothing back. Rafael didn't waste any time responding to him, pulling him into his lap like he weighed nothing, holding him closely while they explored each other.

He slid his undershirt off over his head, and Jonah admired all the new skin he could claim.

"Is this okay?" Rafael looked almost self-conscious about exposing so much of himself.

"Absolutely." Jonah slid his hand across Rafael's chest and for a moment there was nothing but heat and skin.

Jonah ground down on Rafael, and they were both so hard. Rafael groaned into Jonah's mouth at the extra friction to buck up against and lifted them both together so he could lay Jonah down on his bed and get on top.

"Anything you're not comfortable with…."

"You'll know, I promise." Jonah ran his fingers down Rafael's back to punctuate, making Rafael shake a little.

"I just don't—" Rafael still looked so guilty despite Jonah practically shouting off the rooftops that he wanted Rafael to just fuck him already.

"Rafael, shut up. I want this. I want you. I'll stop you if that changes."

Rafael leaned in for a quick kiss. "Just know that you're in control of what we do, okay?" How badly had what happened in the mansion shaken Rafael?

Jonah reached between them and pawed at Rafael's boxers, the last layer between them. Rafael smiled and gently moved Jonah aside so he could push them down and off completely. Jonah wanted to get a better look at a naked Rafael, but he didn't want to lose the skin-to-skin contact he was thoroughly enjoying, either. He hoped this wasn't a one-time thing and there would be plenty of time to admire Rafael from every angle.

"What can I do, Jonah? Just ask and I'll give you whatever you need." It was an intoxicating turnabout to have Rafael present himself in such a vulnerable way.

"I want…." Jesus. He wanted everything. He wanted to erase every bad memory of everything that had happened, from the first night they met, every petty fight, every big fight, every guilty feeling they had about everything that happened. He just wanted every part of Rafael and he wanted Rafael to take every part of him.

"Anything, Jonah. I want to give you anything you want." Jonah had never seen Rafael so eager before. About anything.

The possibilities were dizzying, but one particular fantasy he'd had a lot came roaring to the forefront. "Your mouth on me."

"Oh God, yes." Rafael settled into a good position where Jonah could watch him, and he took him in his mouth slowly, sliding down onto it an inch at a time until he could go no farther in. Jonah thought he might actually die from the feeling.

Jonah made a noise that made Rafael look up at him curiously, but Jonah reached down and grabbed a fistful of hair and closed his eyes, a silent consent to never stop that.

Rafael found a rhythm that threatened to drive Jonah out of his mind, and he didn't think it could get any better until Rafael took the spit-slicked fingers he had been holding the base of his dick with and moved them down, pushing Jonah's thighs open a little as he went.

Jonah knew what was coming, but wasn't quite prepared for the feeling as Rafael slowly pushed a finger in. He bucked his hips up hard and Rafael pulled off in a hurry, looking alarmed.

"Shit, is that not—"

"No, God! Keep going! It's just… it's been a while." A long while. He grinned at Rafael to let him know everything was fine and playfully pushed Rafael's head back down. Rafael didn't protest.

Rafael found his rhythm again and tried once more with his finger. This time Jonah relaxed into it, and soon Rafael could ease more into him and there was nothing merely nice about it. It was incredible.

Jonah moaned and let his head fall back on the pillow, trusting Rafael to make it so good. "More."

Rafael seemed only too happy to oblige. He added a second finger next to the first and started a similar rhythm to his mouth, and Jonah had a hard time breathing and processing all the sensations.

He fisted Rafael's hair and felt his lips stretch around his cock. He wasn't going to be able to last long at all. The orgasm was building, heat curling down in the pit of his stomach that made his skin flush and sweat.

When Rafael added a third finger, his body short-circuited, and he couldn't stop from crying out Rafael's name. It was a much needed release of everything that was still bottled up inside him. Rafael held him with his free hand throughout the entire orgasm, touching him everywhere he could in an almost comforting way as Jonah spilled in his mouth and Rafael swallowed him down.

Before the aftershocks were over, Jonah yanked Rafael up with strength he shouldn't have and kissed him hard, tasting himself on Rafael's lips before he had the chance to swallow it all, and Rafael moaned into his mouth like it was the most erotic thing he had ever witnessed.

Jonah was still breathing pretty hard and sweating, and Rafael's skin felt so good against him like that, but he wanted more. He wanted to give Rafael more. He wanted to give and give to Rafael.

"Fuck me, Rafael."

Rafael blinked. "Are you sure, Jonah?"

"Fuck, Rafael. This is mine to give. It's just you and me, and no one's watching. I'm not putting on an act for anyone's benefit. As much as you feel terrible for what happened in there, I need you to know how much I wanted it to be real. I don't care how unprofessional that sounds either. You didn't do anything in there that I hadn't been fantasizing about for weeks before it. You didn't do anything to me that went too far for me personally, okay? I'm not here because I developed feelings for you after that. They were already there. I didn't think there was a chance in hell, though.

"A.J. is a great guy. A really great guy. He's smart and funny and easy to get along with. But he's not you. I wasn't lying to Garcia when I told her there was no chemistry there, but part of that is because I couldn't stop thinking of you. Every time he kissed me. Every time he touched me… man, all I wanted was it to be you instead."

Rafael was strangely silent after Jonah's confession, and Jonah thought maybe the spell was broken, that he'd gone too far.

"Been a while…. You said it had been a while since—you didn't sleep with him? All that time?"

Jonah blushed a little and shook his head. "I'm not…." He cringed. "Yeesh, I must look like a teenaged girl saving myself for the right person."

Rafael's eyes went wide. "You mean you've never….?"

Jonah realized what he said a moment too late. "Oh, no. I don't mean, not ever! Just, not recently. Not since Orlando." He grinned. "Don't worry. You're not deflowering me."

Rafael breathed a sigh of relief and actually managed to look humbled by Jonah's confession. "God, yes, I'll fuck you."

Rafael lowered his head to start again, but a sudden, unstoppable thought hit Jonah.

"Wait! Have... have *you* ever before?" Rafael *seemed* like he knew what he was doing, and Jonah knew he needed to shut the hell up, but his nerves had taken over, and there was no stopping them.

Rafael looked up at Jonah like he was a moron for even asking. It was reminiscent of the way things used to be between them, the way it was in the beginning, but at the same time not at all.

"Sorry! Sorry. I'm, well, I'm me and the more I worry about screwing things up the more I start to screw things up."

Rafael shook his head and sighed. "I know, kid. We'll have to work on that. Later. Right now, though...." Rafael settled back between Jonah's thighs, kissing along his hipbones. "Nightstand drawer. Pass it to me."

Jonah was confused for a second at the sudden demand but reached in and pulled a bottle of lube and a condom hidden in there. Jonah chuckled. "Did you *plan*—"

A raised eyebrow shut him up fast.

Rafael slicked up his fingers properly, and it was much easier for Jonah to relax around them. He thrust in and out slowly, stretching Jonah until he was ready to take Rafael. He removed his fingers just as slowly while Jonah whined at the loss of the sensation, even as he knew he was about to get more.

Rafael pushed Jonah's legs up and apart and lowered himself down for a hot kiss. "If it's been a while it still might hurt a little. If it's too much—"

"Do it, Rafael. Please." The slight risk of pain couldn't compare to the pain he'd felt the past few weeks of not knowing where they stood.

Rafael took himself in his hand, slicking himself up, and guided himself to Jonah, pushing in as slowly as he could. Jonah trembled and grabbed at whatever he could of Rafael's and, yeah, it hurt a little, but it was so good too, and every push brought Rafael closer to him. The pain ebbed away, replaced by a divine fullness. The look on Rafael's face told Jonah it was good for him too.

Jonah put his hands on Rafael's hips, feeling bold enough to dictate how fast and how deep, and it made Rafael growl and grow pliant in his hands, which was fucking amazing because Jonah really needed Rafael to just *move* already, and if he was too scared of hurting Jonah or whatever else could have been running through his head, Jonah taking control right then might go a long way to reassure him that everything was still fine.

Jonah pushed, pulled, *controlled*, and he could feel himself grow hard again. It was not going to take much for him to come again watching Rafael obey like that. He kept one hand on Rafael and shoved the other between them to take his own erection and stroke in rhythm with Rafael's thrusts.

"God, yes, Jonah. So good… do you trust me to take over?" And Jonah did. He trusted his partner. In so many ways.

Jonah nodded, and Rafael repositioned himself a bit so he could get a better angle inside Jonah. They moved together, and Rafael jerked Jonah's cock for him so he could have the freedom to touch Rafael again.

Rafael's breath hitched, and Jonah could see every muscle in his body tense at once. It was going to be beautiful. Rafael threw his head back and cried out an inhuman growl as he came inside Jonah, and it was terrifying and gorgeous and, in an instant, Jonah was ruined; he never wanted to see anyone else besides Rafael come ever again.

The sight of him coming, the knowledge that Jonah did that to him, sent Jonah over the edge again as Rafael collapsed on top of him.

They lay wrapped in each other's arms until not even the air-conditioning could make the sticky, sweaty heat between them bearable. Jonah stretched awkwardly and felt the familiar pangs of what would be a bit of good soreness the next day.

"I should—uh…." He didn't want to go home. Not when he wasn't sure what to make of everything that had just happened, but he didn't want to overstay his welcome and piss off Rafael before things really had a chance to get going.

"Stay," Rafael murmured sleepily. "Unless you have something you've—"

"Nope. Nothing." He tucked himself back in. That settled that, then.

After a quick clean up, they stayed in each other's arms until they both fell asleep.

# Chapter 31

A LAWNMOWER woke them early the next morning—the domestic sounds of a suburban Saturday morning. It startled Jonah, who had forgotten where he was momentarily, but Rafael just seemed annoyed by the loud whirring of the motor.

*Rafael.*

Jonah was naked and snuggled up to an also naked Rafael, who was on fire under the thick blanket they were sharing. Jonah was dreaming. He had to be. But he was sore in all the right places, and it certainly *felt* like he had had sex, but in what reality would Rafael Santos let him into his bed?

Rafael groaned and buried his head into the crook of Jonah's neck. His breath was just as hot as the rest of his body, and it was then Jonah decided this was the best fever dream he'd ever had. He had been sniffling earlier the day before. He had somehow developed full blown flu or something even more terrible and was probably dying on his couch back in his apartment. It was the only explanation.

Rafael pressed the front of his body up against Jonah's side, and it was more than obvious that he had a raging case of morning wood. If Jonah were truly dying, he was going out in style. He nudged Rafael off and turned so he faced him, reaching between them to gently stroke Rafael's erection.

"Are you always this handsy in the morning or is this a special occasion?" Rafael hadn't even opened his eyes yet and he was already grumpy. But now it was just cute.

"I'm trying to decide if this is happening, or if I'm just imagining it while I'm dying of Ebola or the plague in my apartment." *Sexy.*

"You know, I don't even want to know. I don't even... just don't stop what you're doing. You can ramble on all day, but just don't stop."

Jonah chuckled and stroked a little faster until Rafael moaned and whimpered with every slide.

"I'm an old man. You're gonna kill me like this, I just know it." But it didn't stop Rafael from rolling over to his back and arching his hips upward.

Jonah grinned. "You're forty." He licked a long trail down Rafael's neck to his chest, stopping to pay attention to a dark nipple that was begging to be bitten. "Besides, if you die right now, I can't finish this."

Rafael shifted under him and stretched out like a cat before clasping his hands behind his head so he could look down and watch Jonah work his way down to Rafael's cock.

"Well, if you insist, I guess." Rafael's valiant attempt to sound put out by the whole ordeal just made Jonah bite him on the hip bone.

"Hey!" Rafael thrust his hips up, but Jonah had already prepared for it and pushed them back down.

"I see neither good sex nor sleep can shake the grumpiness out of you." Jonah spread Rafael's thighs and settled between them.

"There's about a five-minute window in the mornings after I finish my first coffee. It's terrible. Sometimes I sing."

"Remind me to have my phone handy for that." Jonah lowered his head and proceeded to make a beautiful mess of a still sleepy Rafael until he was slightly less grumpy. He hadn't gotten to the point of actual *singing*, but the noises he made as he spilled down Jonah's throat were like music to his ears anyway.

Jonah refused any reciprocation but only because Rafael looked so relaxed for the first time ever that he didn't feel right about him doing anything beyond lazy kissing and groping. Besides, if Jonah's hunch was correct, his days of lonely jerk-offs in the shower to kill his frustration might be coming to an end.

Rafael was slow going after that, moving at the speed of a drunk tortoise toward the shower, and Jonah figured at that speed he had enough time to sneak out to Ramon's and pick up breakfast—and the largest *cafecito*, or Cuban coffee, he thought Rafael's heart could take before exploding—before Rafael was even finished washing his hair.

It was between the breakfast and lunch crowds, and as little wait as he had to get his order, the selection was about as small. There was, ironically, only one *pastelito de guayaba*, or guava pastry, left. Jonah smiled wistfully to himself and ordered it—and a plain cheese pastry for himself.

Jonah heard the water shut off about three minutes after he sneaked back in. He laid out the pastry and the coffee on the small table Rafael had set up in the dining room, which had clearly seen more late nights of paperwork than good food.

Rafael came stumbling out of the bathroom wearing nothing but boxers and grinned sheepishly at the sight of Jonah sitting at the table with breakfast.

"I told you I'd make that guava pastry up to you. A little later than I expected, though." Jonah wanted this to be the beginning of something and not just a crazy one-night release of tension they would regret later.

Rafael sat down and scooted his chair closer to Jonah, peering at Jonah's breakfast. "No guava for you?"

Jonah snorted. "In a crazy twist to the story, there was only one left."

Rafael nodded briefly and took a long sip of his coffee before picking up his own pastry in both hands.

And broke it in half.

Guava and pastry crumbs fell to the table as Rafael placed a half on Jonah's plate and Jonah looked from the pastry to Rafael a few times in shock.

"Well, if we're righting wrongs here...." Rafael looked at Jonah, and he was eerily intense and unreadable. "Orlando. That's on me. Always has been. I had no business getting pissed off the way I did that night because your captain was right. It was a stupid coincidence that led to us popping the same club that night, and I should have checked in when I moved in on it, but I was so deep in there I just couldn't come up long enough to do it. I was angry about the potential of losing everything I had worked for, and I took it out on your squad and especially you, Jonah. I'm so sorry about that."

Waking up in Rafael's bed, *sharing his food*, and now an apology? The possibility of it all being a dream wasn't off the table yet.

"Jonah, I feel terrible about it. Every day." Rafael screwed up his face in thought for a second. "Well, every day since I realized you weren't *all* bad, that is." His tone was playful.

Jonah wanted to react to that, but he also didn't want to stop this new and fascinating side of Rafael Santos. He settled for pursing his lips in a mock sour way.

Rafael smiled and leaned in for a kiss. "Couldn't resist. Anyway, I feel like shit about it, like I may have sabotaged your career a bit that night. I don't even know why you're here now...."

"Rafi, any screwing of my own career that night was my fault. I tried to break cover, and that is on me. I know that now and I paid for it, but I overcame it, and I think I've learned a lot since then about staying in character. As for the other stuff, well, I'm here now and that's further than I ever thought I would make it. That's all that matters in the end, right? Even if that night never happened, I would have stalled out in Orlando just the same, I think. *You* might not ever be welcome in The City Beautiful professionally, but Captain Malone takes care of his people, and he made sure that we came out of that looking as good as we could."

Jonah expected Rafael to get upset by the ding on his reputation, but instead he sighed like a long-suffering weight had been lifted. "Thank you."

"For what?"

"Forgiving me. I mean, you wouldn't be here otherwise, right? I've been, Jesus, I've been a real dick to you. I've pushed you, thrown you into things, took a long time to trust you. I was jealous as hell of you and Choya. And you're here."

"And you've taught me, toughened me up, and trusted me in those situations you pushed me into, made me want to be a better cop, and made me into a better person. You challenge me in a way that no one else has. You don't coddle me. You may have ragged on me pretty hard in the beginning, but, at least now, you *respect* me. I think it just took me a while to figure out that's what all this was about."

Rafael pushed a stray curl out of Jonah's face. "I knew you had it all along, kid. I wouldn't have been such a dick if I didn't think you could be amazing with some pushing. Now eat that before I do. I'm only human here. A Cuban human at that. I can only resist so long."

Jonah picked up the pastry and took a bite, but something was still weighing on his mind. "Why did you try to push me away from the Badcock job, then? The truth. You had no idea that A.J. would take so long in there, so it wasn't in fear of what actually happened."

Rafael sighed and took another long sip. "Honestly? I think it's something that's going to keep coming up, and it's something we're going to need to address in the very near future. It was difficult to separate my feelings for you. The thought of Choya with his hands on you was bad enough, but all those well-groomed rich men pawing at you? And leering at you looking like that? And then having to stay in character and degrade you like they were doing, I hated it. You walked out in that outfit, and it was over. God, you looked so good I wanted to maul you right there in the station. I had been trying to chalk my feelings up to temporary insanity or mentor-like affection or *something* to explain them away, but I knew it was over that night. And then we kissed. I thought unless you had won an Oscar I wasn't aware of, you weren't faking what I felt between us.

"And there was *always* a chance things would go wrong. You know that. I had to plan for what would happen if they did, and honestly I was kind of afraid that if things went south, they would go south for us too. Luis knew that was a chance. That's why she asked about it that night, if it was going to be a problem. I've seen it happen before, and the fallout was messy."

"So, probably not something that would have happened with Edgewood in tight pants and eyeliner, then."

"Not a chance in hell." Rafael shook his head emphatically.

"So what do we do now? I mean, we're still partners. We can't exactly keep both of these relationships going." Better to know now.

Rafael chewed his lip in worrying thought. "For now we keep this low. No one needs to know anything. We take this one step at a time until we figure it out. But I'm not going to have the department dictate what we decide to do and how to go about doing it. Agreed?"

Jonah nodded his head. "Yeah. Okay. Agreed. But Rafi, you can't protect me from shit. Either I'm your partner or I'm not. *This*"—he pointed back and forth between the two of them—"can't affect our work until we settle things. Can we agree on that too?"

"It's been a long time since I had feelings for anyone, okay? I'm really rusty at this, and it's even more difficult with you being a cop and my partner. These things aren't supposed to happen this way."

Rafael was avoiding the question. "*Raf.*"

"Yes. Okay. I agree."

Jonah took Rafael's free hand in his own and felt the warmth from where he had been holding his coffee. "Good."

Rafael visibly relaxed. "Good. Now, are you going to finish that, or....?"

Battle lost. There was always tomorrow morning if Jonah really wanted guava.

Jonah spent the rest of the weekend at Rafael's save a short trip back to his apartment for his toothbrush and some clothes—not that he actually needed to wear any at all. They made love and showered and ate and made love some more until the alarm clock signaled Monday morning and a reluctant return to a reality where they were just police partners and nothing more.

With a promise that nothing at work would change or give away their secret, they parted with a kiss.

The promise lasted until approximately Friday.

# Chapter 32

JONAH AND Rafael had both been doing what Jonah thought was an *amazing* job of being the old versions of themselves, butting heads and Jonah being too loud and annoying where Rafael was quiet and annoyed. If anyone suspected anything, no one dared say it to their faces. They played it cool at the cheesy tiki bar Garcia decided on that week, Rafael drinking his usual whiskey at the bar with some of the older cops while Jonah ordered mai tais and danced the hula with Garcia and a few of the younger traffic cops. A.J. was there and Jonah even sent over drinks to him and his apparent date, a nice-looking guy Jonah didn't recognize. A.J. caught Jonah's eye and raised his glass in his direction with a smile. Jonah nodded at him and smiled back. It seemed there were no hard feelings there, and it was another weight off his shoulders as he went back to attempting the hula with a flower crown and lei now adorning him, thanks to Garcia.

It wasn't quite the sexy dancing seduction scene Jonah had had in mind the night Rafael bailed on them, but later that night, Jonah had barely enough time for one knock on Rafael's door before he was pulled inside violently, slammed up against the back of the door, and showered with hot kisses and roaming hands.

And then Friday happened.

It was a relatively small wound, once they dug the blade out. Even the doctor agreed with Jonah, who was trying his hardest to just leave the emergency room already, but even though it missed all the important stuff, the knife still dug in pretty deep, and it hurt like hell. There was no way to avoid it, either.

Gang fight, domestic dispute, robbery gone wrong—those were too normal for Miami. No, of course it had to be a suspected murderer. At a traveling circus. Some pretentious European arty circus shit, complete with bendy acrobats, gravity-defying gymnasts, jilted lovers, angry exes, and… a knife thrower who didn't want to get arrested in connection with said suspected murder.

A fucking good knife thrower at that. The small sharp blade had hit Jonah in the upper right shoulder—a godsend for the southpaw or he'd be out a lot longer than the doctor was reluctantly compromising on. But it still hurt like hell.

But still Rafael had gone—disproportionately, to outsiders—ballistic when he realized what had happened to Jonah. He'd tried to tell Rafael he was okay, but Rafael was on autopilot and chased the guy down with superhuman speed, throwing him to the ground and scaring even Jonah with the anger and rage he let out on the guy as he was cuffing him. It took Edgewood and three uniforms to pull Rafael away from the knife thrower, who, Jonah heard, would soon be wishing they let Rafael finish him off. Assault on police officer was a steep offense to add to murder, and they had enough evidence on him that pleading not guilty would be a joke even the judge would laugh out of the court.

The doctor was refusing to let Jonah go without at least a tetanus shot and a sling for his arm to wear over the weekend, and there was still the matter of the stuff they'd given him as they worked to dig out the blade. It was making Jonah just a little loopy, and the doctor was insisting on him staying until Jonah was sure the clock on the wall was displaying numbers and not, as he wildly proclaimed several times, the first twelve lines of Hamlet (Jonah didn't even remember Hamlet). Jonah stuck out his tongue and blew out a breath before he finally agreed. It was another hour or so before any of those compromises would be fulfilled, and he was itching to find out what was happening in his absence and to get to Rafael to see if he was okay.

He secretly hoped Rafael would be waiting for him in the lobby when he was all done, but he knew there was no way he was done with the paperwork or the fallout of freaking out on the suspect. Instead it was Garcia who stood at the nurse's station, looking annoyed and impatient, when Jonah ventured out to use the restroom.

Jonah didn't want a scene, and he knew Garcia would push the doctor out of the way to mother-hen him if she saw him, so he ducked a little and sneaked around to the bathroom at the far end of the triage unit.

It was annoyingly public, with three stalls and just as many sinks. Jonah guessed that only better-paying patients who stayed in a grossly overpriced room, paying $100 a pill for drugstore painkillers, would warrant something more private, but he had to go, and he couldn't be picky until the annoying doctor came back with his sling.

He caught a glimpse of himself in the mirror as he washed his hands. He looked tired and washed out, and he really wanted to get to Rafael already and make sure he was okay too. He gingerly lifted his arm to see how bad it was and was met with a sharp burst of pain. Sneaking a look at it in the mirror was even more of a mistake. It was definitely going to leave a nasty scar. His first police related scar, at that. He always thought he would be shot first, but a flying knife from a Polish circus performer might be just as good a bar story.

The door flew open without warning, and Garcia stormed in, oblivious to the fact that she was definitely in the men's room. She stomped toward Jonah with the kind of purpose and intensity reserved for perps and pushed him up against the sink, also seemingly oblivious to his pain.

"You wanna explain what happened back there? Don't play dumb, *mijo*. You and Rafi have been acting funny for a while now, since that UC op, actually, and he's not talking, so you better because I've never seen him get so crazy and I know you know why!"

Jonah blinked hard and blew out a breath. "Garcia, I—"

Garcia's eyes went wide and she gasped dramatically. A long string of Spanish interrupted him that ended with a very English, "You and Rafi are…. How long have you been sleeping together?"

"What? No! We're not—" What were they thinking, trying to fool a station full of cops?

"You are! Oh my *God*, you are! You two are totally sleeping together, and I can't believe I didn't see it sooner! What? Like right after you and A.J. broke it off, right?" She laughed and sounded so proud of herself for putting it all together.

"Garcia, please—"

"Oh, you're right! That's none of my business, is it? Sorry, sorry! I don't know what came over me. But it's true, right? You two are—"

"*Yes*! Now would you please not spread it around the station? We're trying to figure everything out, and I don't think Rafael watching me get stabbed helped any, okay?" Jonah had no idea what the events of the day meant for any aspect of his life at the moment.

Garcia immediately shut her mouth and made a show of pretending to lock her mouth with a key and toss it. Jonah figured it was a good sign that she had been able to spend more time with her kids lately since he hadn't seen that particular move since grade school. "You have my word. But Jonah, you and he gotta work this out soon. Putting aside how frowned upon this is, it's never a good idea to sleep with your partner."

Jonah sighed. "I know, Garcia. This just happened, okay? We weren't really thinking about anything beyond, you know…."

"Your own dicks," she supplied helpfully.

"Our *hearts*, Garcia. Geez."

Garcia gasped again and clutched her heart dramatically. She was in danger of sucking all the air out of the room. "Jonah Landers, are you two… could this be love?"

The door swung open again, and this time it was a middle-aged guy with a neck brace on, who stopped as soon as he saw Garcia and started to back out the door slowly.

"Oh my *God*, Garcia! I don't know! Would you please get out of the men's room and we'll talk about this later?" She was worse than his mother. At least the formidable Mrs. Landers would never force her way into the men's room.

Garcia looked put out but nodded and finally left Jonah to finish washing up and contemplate what had happened.

The doctor finally released Jonah a half hour later with a strict regimen that Jonah promptly left at the discharge desk and forgot about ten minutes later. For prying into his private life, he forced Garcia to stop and also pay for his lunch before convincing her to take him to the station instead of to his apartment, which he vaguely remembered the doctor telling him to go to instead of the station.

The bull pen was a circus, but literally because the entire cast and crew were crammed into it, giving their statements and demanding justice for their fallen friend, the ninety-six-pound aerial artist who held on to the ropes and swings using only her teeth.

Jonah managed to slip in almost unnoticed until the last second, when Edgewood, with all the grace and decorum of a dragon in a fireworks shop, announced his arrival from across the room. It was enough to distract Rafael from his questioning of a witness who looked like he could snap a coconut with his thigh muscles.

Jonah expected a scene, but Rafael swallowed hard with a funny look on his face. Jonah held up his sling and gave Rafael a thumbs-up, letting him know it was okay, that he was okay. Rafael turned visibly redder and turned back to his witness with a sour look on his face, and it was then Jonah knew it wasn't going to work out. Either they were partners in their off-hours or on duty. But not both.

# Chapter 33

JONAH STAMPED his feelings down deep when he ended up at Rafael's that night. He barely made it through the door before Rafael attacked him, but with desperate kisses, gentle touches, and intimate confessions of how scared Rafael had been when he saw the knife fly into his shoulder instead of the now usual passionate gropings.

Jonah let Rafael do whatever he needed to do to assure himself Jonah was okay before even trying to broach the heavy subject matter on his mind. Rafael was a cop. Jonah was a cop. Neither was willing to give that up, and it wasn't fair to ask either of them to do it.

Jonah spent another weekend at Rafael's, but the sex was separated by long conversations about the future and trying to come up with potential solutions. Jonah talked about how he had been looking at other precincts across the state right after Badcock's, and Rafael revealed that he could always pick up again with the state until another alternative looked better, but every idea ended with them separated, and that was no solution at all. By Sunday night nothing viable had presented itself, and neither of them knew how to proceed with the upcoming week.

A further complication, this one a potentially damning one, steamrolled them both in the form of a cryptic phone call from Captain Luis late Sunday, demanding that Jonah be in her office by 8:00 a.m. Jonah was pretty sure they'd been found out, and all the brainstorming was for nothing.

It was a sleepless night when they finally decided to go to bed, and Jonah dragged himself out the door at 7:15 a.m., not even remotely prepared for the massive nosedive his already spotty career was probably about to take.

Luis was dressed in a more Garcia-style pantsuit that made her look a lot like a Hollywood movie cop. She had been dressing that way more and more since the Teiki case, and it seemed that showing up on paparazzi sites had boosted her ego a bit. She sat behind her desk and motioned for Jonah to sit down across from her when he knocked on her door at exactly 8:00.

"Detective Landers. I'm not going to mince words here. My job here is to keep my detectives working efficiently and safely and solve every crime we can possibly solve. And I am *more* than aware that sometimes there are hiccups in that plan and that threatens everyone's work. Including mine. Now, I'm not going to pretend that I don't know something is going on between you and Detective Santos. I'm not even going to pretend that it doesn't involve you and him and whatever was on that hard drive that night."

Jonah raised a hand to try to get a word in edgewise, but Luis shut him down with one finger.

"I *am*, however, going to pretend that you aren't sitting here trying to interrupt me to deny it all because we're both smarter than that. In fact, I'm counting on you being smarter than that. Detective Landers, I'm torn right now between many, many things, but at the top of that list is the fact that you and Detective Santos are both amazing detectives, and it would be a detriment to this station to lose either of you. And just under that is the fact that I have known Rafael Santos for a very long time and not once have I ever seen him as happy as he has been this past week. But judging by his actions Friday, whatever you two have going on is definitely going to affect the both of you if you continue working so closely together. I've been mulling over this all weekend and I—"

"Transfer me. Don't punish Rafael for this. I just got here, and it won't look as—"

"De*tec*tive Landers, while I appreciate your willingness to self-sacrifice, if you'll let me finish." She rang up someone on her desk phone and simply told whoever it was to "come on in."

The door opened after about twenty seconds of Jonah sitting in silence wondering what was going on. Blonde hair appeared when the door opened, and it was attached to Sabrina, the lead detective from Vice who helped him get into character.

"Detective Landers! Nice to see you again." She sat down in the empty chair next to him, gaudy pink lips stretched into a wide grin.

"Sabrina! How are you doing?"

"Well, that's why I'm here, actually. We just lost two in Vice in the last month thanks to a promotion and an unexpected transfer. I'm just a bit shorthanded at the moment, and your name is at the top of a very short list for people who could fill the job."

Jonah cocked his head to the side. "I'm sorry?" Had he misheard that?

"We had our eye on you since Badcock. You did a great job in there by all accounts and you played your part wonderfully. We think you'd be a great asset to our team. It takes a different kind of detective to be Vice. You're young, you look young, and I hear you handled yourself like a pro in there that night, considering. Of course, it does mean a pay raise. A little one for now. And a new desk in a new part of the building. A view of different palm trees than you have now. And, oh, you'd have to have a new partner." Sabrina looked at him pointedly. "But it's a whole new opportunity. *Opens up a lot for you.* If you're willing to go for it."

Jonah stared at Sabrina for a long time before turning to Captain Luis. She nodded at him and raised her eyebrow. Rafael and Jonah were the worst kept secret in the station, it seemed, but it also seemed to have the station's approval. A transfer to Vice meant they were no longer working together. It meant the freedom to be together and not have to take it long distance. More importantly, a transfer to Vice meant a step up in his career. This was what he had left Orlando PD for. But something Sabrina said was sticking in his brain.

"Wait. By all accounts? How would you—"

She pursed her lips. "Detective Landers. I'm the lead detective on Vice. Badcock was a joint case. You think I didn't sit down with Choya and watch what had gone down? I had men in there too."

Jonah hung his head low in embarrassment.

"Now don't get all shy on me now. It's what made me put you at the top of the short list. That was a crazy case and not one of my squad could have handled it any better. In fact, I'm not sure they would have handled it that well. Besides, if I've seen you, you know, *like that*, and I'm still fighting for you? You have nothing to worry about. And let's face it, you helped me win fifty bucks. I had you and Rafael getting together before fall."

Jonah's head snapped up. That's what she had meant that day she had outfitted him for the op when she was cryptic about him screwing things up. How many people had noticed what was going on? And just how much money had he made his fellow cops in bets? And shouldn't he share in some of that if he were the subject of those bets?

Sabrina smiled. "What do you say? Give yourself some time to heal from this and come work on my team?"

A slow smile spread across his face. "Yes. Absolutely. I'll do it."

Jonah could barely contain his excitement when Rafael came in an hour later.

Of course there were rules. Jonah and Rafael could not work together if Vice needed Rafael for anything. And Luis strongly suggested they keep the more dangerous details of their cases to themselves until the danger had passed. Jonah found that there wasn't much he wouldn't agree to if it meant the chance to make this work with Rafael. He couldn't know the future, but in any case, no matter how things went with Rafael, Vice was a good career move and a nice bump in his paycheck. Maybe he could even buy the matching sofa to his oversized chair.

Jonah unsubscribed from the job board alerts that afternoon.

# Epilogue

THE MOON was rising on the Atlantic Ocean, and Jonah and Rafael were enjoying the sun's last warming rays before it sank behind them and gave way to the chill of the nicest day of the year: that one glorious day in February when they actually needed a jacket all day long.

It was Jonah's one year anniversary with MDPD, and instead of going to a wild blowout of Garcia's making, they decided to keep it small and intimate and relax on a beach up in Palm Beach County, where the neon lights and loud music of Miami were replaced by nothing more than the gentle waves of low tide.

Vice, in all respects, was absolutely the right move for Jonah. He was never happier—as a detective and as Rafael's boyfriend. Rafael eventually got a new partner, a transfer from New Jersey. Hilary was seasoned, sarcastic, and walked in taking no bullshit from anyone, including the second appearance of the year of the drag queen ballet troupe. She was a good match for Miami.

Jonah and Rafael let their relationship progress at a natural pace and didn't force anything just because Jonah had taken the giant leap of transferring to Vice for the opportunity to be with Rafael. They quickly found they didn't want to spend any time apart in their off-hours. It took only about a week of curling up on the sofa at night watching *Law and Order* reruns and *Noa Regrets* ironically (he was all too happy to lose that twenty bucks to Grace, even if she did threaten to make him and Rafael the main characters in her sweeping romance novel as a consolation. "Hmmm… boring, bland, newbie detective gets transferred to Miami and gets paired with a gruff, older detective. This has potential," she had murmured to herself, pretending not to hear Jonah's halfhearted protests. There was really no use. He'd read a few more of her books and recognized quite a few coworkers as inspiration) to figure it all out.

Jonah may have been talkative and energetic, and Rafael may have been quiet and focused, but they balanced each other out and made each other happy. And the sex wasn't bad either. Or, actually, it was amazing. Rafael and Jonah never talked about work and never brought it home.

It was just better that way. They both knew the dangers of the job and agreed to keep work at the station.

Jonah sank his toes into the cool sand and snuggled closer to Rafael for warmth under the flimsy blanket they'd brought. A few other brave souls were littering the shoreline, enough for a few businesses to be open despite the un-beach-like weather. The smell of something amazing wafted down the sand in their general direction. It tickled his nose and made its way to his stomach, which growled in protest.

"I'm starving. You want anything?" Jonah didn't want to leave the warmth under the blanket, but he didn't want to starve, either.

Rafael sniffed the air. "Whatever that is. And something strong to drink. I'm freezing."

Jonah grinned and kissed Rafael before throwing off his end of the blanket and braving the rapidly dropping temperature to run over to the beachside café from where the smell originated.

It turned out to be fresh local coquina soup and conch fritters, and Jonah ordered a double of both, figuring the garlicky soup would warm them up. He reached into his wallet for some cash and a small strip of paper fell out and landed on the counter.

*Someone from your past will be a big part of your future.*

Jonah read it a few times and remembered the night he got the fortune, so long ago watching Rafael interrogate a killer and thinking it was the most amazing thing he'd ever seen.

Someone from your past.... If he told himself three years ago that he would end up falling for the gruff, cocky man who had punched him in the face and given him a nasty black eye that took a month to fade, he would have laughed himself out of the room.

A big part of your future.... They'd been talking of moving in together. Jonah was always at Rafael's anyway, and Rafael had been pointing out that it was no good paying rent on an apartment he wasn't even sleeping at. Jonah had finally agreed after getting Rafael to accept the fact that if Jonah was moving in, so was his oversized chair that Rafael hated with a passion. It was a huge step, even if at that point it was just a formality.

Jonah smiled at the fortune, long forgotten in a sea of receipts and store loyalty cards, and shoved it behind his driver's license. Maybe he should have played the lottery with all twenty-threes like the back of the fortune said. But he had a feeling he'd already won.

Jonah made his way back to Rafael with the food and drinks and sat quietly with him until the temperature dropped below sixty and it was just too cold for the Floridians to bear.

Jonah and his favorite chair moved in the next day. Rafael made sergeant by the next summer.

When they married a year later (they hired the drag queen ballet troupe to perform at the reception, and it led to an early start to the year for their arrests—public intoxication and public indecency—but the performance itself was beautiful and tasteful) they made sure that there were enough guava pastries from Ramon's at the reception for everyone who wanted one.

# The Tahiti Tweety: A Guide

THE TAHITI Tweety is a real Tiki-inspired drink born out of desperation and college paychecks. It, like the future according to Doc Brown in *Back to the Future III*, is whatever you make it. But usually, unlike the future, you won't make it a good one. It gets its name from a hard to find and probably regional fruit punch called Tahiti Treat, which becomes Tweety Tweet or Tahiti Tweet the more booze you consume.

The rules of Tahiti Tweety are as follows.

1. Be drunk already. This helps. Drink the good stuff first so you can remember that instead of the Tahiti Tweety.
2. Use the cheapest, most neon colored fruit punch you can find.
3. Add rum. What kind of rum? Yes.
4. Pineapple is a must. You can use pineapple rum in tandem with pineapple juice for maximum effect.
5. It gets a little fuzzy after this. Get creative. It doesn't matter. You're already drunk. I believe in you.
6. The glass must be able to double as a goldfish bowl. This is not so much because you're going to want to drink a lot of it, but more because of rule 7.
7. You must garnish the Tahiti Tweety with a creation that could be mistaken for public art. It must be capable of toppling over a normal glass. It should have an element that's on fire. If you're really super drunk already you can probably skip the fire. Or get a friend who can handle their liquor better to do that part for you. Making a tiki torch out of lemon halves and mint sprigs on a skewer is always a good start. Tropical flowers? Yes. floating cherries? Go for it. Cocktail shrimp? Mini sliders? Packets of taco sauce on a skewer? It's your drink. You do you.

Happy drinking! Drink responsibly!

PIPER DOONE is the red-headed, left-handed, Scottish/First Nations child of hippies. She had the typical small-hippie-commune/big-city-dreams childhood and decided her big dream was to work for Disney, where she learned to live off 30 cents a week after rent, food, and tuition.

She then managed to stumble into a ten-year career in professional sports that lasted ten years too long. She now works a more reasonable job in professional sports marketing, which is far less dangerous than actually doing sports.

You can sometimes catch her with her cameras. She shoots digitally and on film and some of her cameras date back to the 1940s. She'd like to say she's a serious photographer with journalism awards and stuff, but she's been featured in exactly one gallery in New York and the photos were of a cow on her farm and a close-up of grapes, so, yeah, she's not going down in history there. Other times you can find her with her trusty bow and arrows. Being a Scottish ginger archer, she's heard every *Brave* joke you can imagine, thank you. On a really good day, you can find her with ridiculously tiny paintbrushes painting on stupidly tiny canvases. She's going to make it into an art gallery with one of her tiny paintings even if she has to "accidentally" hang a canvas in one when no one is looking.

She hates long walks on the beach, sunshine, and summertime, so obviously she lives with her husband, two kids, three hedgehogs, and a dog in sunny, beachy Miami now.

You can find her on Twitter or Facebook.

Ethan Robertson never asked to be the latest in a long line of werewolf hunters, but the war between his family and the werewolf Kinnairds has raged on for a millennium, and he is expected to fight like all the Robertsons before him. But then he meets Liam Kinnaird, a gorgeous, mysterious werewolf Ethan falls hard for. Despite the danger, they carry on a torrid affair until a terrible explosion destroys everything, including Liam and Ethan's memories of their time together.

Twenty years later, Ethan is embroiled in battle once again and catches a glimpse of Liam. It triggers intense, erotic dreams that Ethan thinks might not be dreams at all. But he's never been anything but enemies with Kinnairds. He's certainly never been in love with one. Or has he?

www.dreamspinnerpress.com

Josh Tucker lives a blessed life—great job, great family, perfect husband, and two wonderful children—but a mysterious man named Adam who haunts his dreams and soon his waking life threatens everything when he stirs doubt as to whether any of it is real. Adam makes Josh question the world he's taken for granted—as well as the origins of Adam himself.

Even if Adam's claims are true, Josh has nothing to live for beyond his fabricated life—except the possibility of a real man out there somewhere who can love him. Josh is left with an impossible choice: stay in his delusion where he's assured some happiness or take a great leap of faith for a chance to make a life with Adam.

www.dreamspinnerpress.com

www.ingramcontent.com/pod-product-compliance
Lightning Source LLC
Chambersburg PA
CBHW060059260626

47160CB00005B/1718